Thunder
in the Dust

Thunder in the Dust

ALAN LEMAY

Sagebrush
Large Print Westerns

Library of Congress Cataloging-in-Publication Data

Lemay, Alan, 1899-1964.
   Thunder in the dust / Alan LeMay.
     p.   cm.
   ISBN 1-57490-349-7 (alk. paper)
   1. Large type books. I. Title

PS3523.E513 T48 2001
813'.52—dc21   2001019043

Cataloguing in Publication Data is available from the British Library and the National Library of Australia.

Sagebrush Large Print Westerns are published in the United States and Canada by Thomas T. Beeler, Publisher, PO Box 659, Hampton Falls, New Hampshire 03844-0659. ISBN 1-57490-349-7

Published in the United Kingdom, Eire, and the Republic of South Africa by Isis Publishing Ltd, 7 Centremead, Osney Mead, Oxford OX2 0ES England. ISBN 0-7531-6446-9

Published in Australia and New Zealand by Bolinda Publishing Pty Ltd, 17 Mohr Street, Tullamarine, Victoria, Australia, 3043 ISBN 1-74030-303-2

Manufactured by Sheridan Books in Chelsea, Michigan.

Thunder in the Dust

CHAPTER 1

WHEN THE THREE BROWN-FACED RIDERS HAD FOUND Juan Amador, they consulted together, briefly, before taking word up to the boss of the Flying K. Those riders were not the pick of the border, nor of Baja; they were riffraff such as the Flying K had been able to get and had to like—a chop-headed Indian boy, a lank mestizo with a neck like a turkey, and a shifty-eyed vaquero who slept in his boots. And now for a moment they didn't know what to do. They never understood Tom Cloud, owner of the Flying K; they could hardly follow his quick broken Spanish, let alone figure out what to expect of him. And they hesitated to carry bad news to this tall, potentially violent man.

Presently, though, they rode back up the twisting cow trail to where Tom Cloud sat his horse on the crest of a hill, studying the throw of the broken land. They approached him slowly, each trying to maneuver his horse so that the others would be ahead. Then they sat silent for half a minute or so, each watching Tom Cloud covertly whenever he was looking at the others.

They were seeing a big, lean, loosely angular man perhaps thirty years old; big enough so that he made his tough mustang pony look like a dog, but so easy in the saddle that not even those three, all of whom had ridden before they could walk, could claim better horsemanship. But though he was darkly tanned, his grey eyes, squinted against the everlasting straight-rayed blast of the sun, must have seemed to them unnaturally light, as when a bay horse has the blue eyes

1

of a pinto. So far as they could see, he had no God and no amusements. They regarded him with a faint curiosity, a faint distrust.

Tom Cloud said, "Come on, come on—what is it?"

The Indian boy accidentally met Tom Cloud's eyes, and jerked his own away as if his lashes had touched steel. The down-country vaquero uneasily stepped to the ground and tightened his cinch.

"*El esta muerto*," the turkey-necked mestizo said at last.

There was a moment's silence. "How was he killed?" Tom Cloud asked in a flat voice.

"A knife in the throat. His gun is still in his hand. Here—we'll show you."

They kicked their horses around, more anxious to show the way than to talk about it; but the boss of the Flying K was no longer in any hurry. He followed them slowly, so they had to keep stopping to wait for him.

Tom Cloud was thinking about Juan Amador, who was dead. And he was seeing Juan again as he had looked when they had ridden out that morning—a tall, lank figure on a runty horse, his restless hands twirling and spinning his reata. Juan Amador had had a long, hawk-nosed face the color of weathered rawhide, slanted eyes that carried the gleam of cruel humor sometimes seen in the eyes of coyotes, and a grin like a split melon. But to Tom Cloud, Juan Amador had been a saving mainstay, like one top cutting horse in a corral full of lame and unwilling broncs. Cloud would not have asked for a greater dependability, nor a more daredevil courage, nor a better knowledge of cattle in any man. And now be was realizing definitely and clearly that Juan Amador would never ride for the

2

Flying K or anybody else again.

He spoke to his vaqueros. "Is the knife there?"

"No, señor."

"No other sign at all?"

"No, señor."

"Which one of you knows who got him?" Cloud demanded.

The three vaqueros exchanged blank glances. "*No se, señor.*"

"At least," said Cloud, in the quick, bad Spanish so hard for them to understand, "you must have known the men we went against."

"They were lost in the brush, *señor.*"

"Not one of you saw and knew a single man?"

His hard glance went from one to the other of them, forcing them to answer one by one. "No, *señor.*"

Tom Cloud's eyes were bitter, his mouth grim. He was inclined to believe them—principally because he was certain that they had been skulking throughout the whole skirmish. In any case he could not hold them for failing in what he had been unable to do himself.

Juan Amador had been the only one of them all whom Tom Cloud had ever been able to depend upon in the least. It was Juan Amador who, from a high lookout, had spotted four riders prowling below Canyon del Lobo, where no riders should be. It was Juan Amador who had guided his boss and the three rattle-headed vaqueros through the deep smother of the brush, directly to the party of men whom they sought. As they dropped down upon the mouth of Canyon del Lobo, to cut off what was obviously another raid upon their calves, it was Juan Amador who had told Cloud the names of three of the four thieves.

3

The Lower Californian brush below Canyon del Lobo had the dense, passive hostility of the primitive; often the eyes of the riders could not penetrate a dozen feet in any direction, The clawing entanglement rose tall enough to hide a mounted man, and through it the ponies plowed and crow-hopped their way with noisy labor. The Flying K men approached as quietly as they could, but presently they could hear the movement of horses deep in the cover as the men they sought moved away, scattering and losing themselves.

The long, hawk face of Juan Amador had tightened. "Now!" he said. "*Sigamen—y pronto!*" He jerked out his gun and spurred his horse crashing into the brush. Cloud and the others went floundering after him, spreading out fanwise in the hope of picking up the unseen enemy.

The next quarter of an hour had been a nightmare— the more so because it symbolized all the long bafflement and defeat that Cloud had met in Lower California. He could see nothing but the blind brush, hear nothing but the uproar of his own horse. Presently he had stumbled upon a little smokeless branding fire, and beside it lay a hog-tied calf—his own calf. But this place yielded him no clue; not so much as a heel print, for the unshod feet of those who made a business of stealing from the Flying K left no mark on the baked soil. He was following a distant crackling where some horse passed, and he drove ahead doggedly through a tangle that smothered him as if he rode with his head under a blanket. To run down men born to the brush was like running down a lizard in a haystack; well mounted as he was, he found himself as helpless as if he crawled belly to the ground.

4

Far off to the right he heard a gun speak twice, where someone made a brief contact. Then followed, as he held his horse motionless, a silence utter and complete, as if not so much as a cactus wren moved below Canyon del Lobo.

And the end of it was an old story; the kind of end that he, it seemed, must always reach in Lower California. After a long time, when there was no further sound, and no signal of any kind from Juan, he worked his way back to the place where they had entered the cover, and found that his three vaqueros were already there. Juan Amador, however, did not come; he was never going to come. Sending his vaqueros to find out what had happened, Cloud went aside, skirting the manzanita, and climbed a bare ridge in the vague hope of seeing some of his enemy leave the brush. It was here that the vaqueros had at last brought him word of what they had found.

They led out, proceeding single file, for what seemed a long way; and as the close press of the brush clawed at his canvas jacket again, he felt himself overwhelmed once more by the weird sense of bafflement which the brush typified. This was the way always. If he rode one part of the range his enemies stole from another; he could strike out at them as he chose—but they would not be there. There was nothing in this country a man could get his teeth into or come to grips with. An elusive ring of thieves snapped at the flanks of his brand as coyotes harry an entangled steer.

"*Señor*," said one of the vaqueros, "it is here."

They drew aside and held their horses, so that he might come forward between them. As he stepped down from his pony it snorted and reared back from the spot where the body of Juan Amador lay sprawled among the

5

dry, twisted roots of the brush. In the dead man's throat was the deep, clean stab of a well thrown knife, but the weapon, of course, was gone. Cloud picked up Juan's gun, and, twirling the cylinder, confirmed his guess that it had been twice fired before Juan died.

He could find no other clue. Bitterly he reflected that in his present situation a clue would have been useless to him if he had found it. What service were clues, when there was little use he could make of definite proof?

He already knew what men had been in this brush, for though he could not know by what intuition Juan Amador had been able to name men Cloud could not even see, he had Juan's statement. The names Perez, Gomez, and Castro were fixed in his head; and though each of these names was carried by more than one large family, he knew just about which men Juan had meant. About this killing hung no least mystery; the cow thieves involved here were known to Tom Cloud before now. For that matter, the thing might just as well have been done by any one of twenty others who were also cattle thieves, and all of them were potentially as guilty as the unknown man who had thrown the knife.

When he had crossed the border and taken his leases here in Baja California he had not realized that a country so close to his own could be in all ways so different from his own Arizona ranges. He found his big leases bordered by a people which he in no way understood—a breed of cattlemen who rode barefoot or in blunt cheap shoes, each owning a few score head and a corn patch behind a one or two-room adobe; dark-faced men with unreadable obsidian eyes. He could no more win their cooperation than he could conduct an investigation among them. And through this porous

6

bordering ring his cattle had presently begun filtering away.

Thus the death of Juan Amador came to Cloud not as a murder mystery, nor as the beginning of anything new. It was part of the same elusive malignance that had been draining his herds almost from the first day he had moved in here two years ago; a thing against which he had tried every defense in vain. Perhaps, he thought, it would be better for him to admit that he was at the end of his rope.

"He was a good man," Cloud said slowly.

The three looked at their gringo boss strangely, and shot sidelong glances at each other. This stranger for whom they worked had here lost a man whom he could not possibly afford to lose; yet he had not cursed, nor raised his hands to heaven, nor called upon God. They could not even see that his face had changed.

It was strange to Tom Cloud himself that he did not anger. The stillness of approaching sunset was on all that vast motionless land, and Cloud found himself locked into the quiet. He was looking somberly into what was ahead. He had no more liking than any man for brush-country warfare—and in this country he was alone, at a disadvantage among strange laws more strangely administered; for the other American cattlemen in Baja were far away, and had different but sufficient troubles of their own. The laws of immigration were such that he could not even bring his own Arizona cowboys here to work his stock.

Yet now as he looked down upon the body of Juan Amador, he knew that he would never let go while any part of his holdings remained; and he knew what it was he must do.

7

He stepped aboard his horse again.

"Teco—"he addressed the Indian boy—"you come with me. You others, you bring Juan in. Tie him on the quiet horse—you two can ride back double, on the colt. And damn your eyes, you put a blanket over him as you lead past the Boyce *casa*, you hear me?"

"And Juan's horse?" they asked.

"We'll track it down and get the saddle tomorrow. Don't forget to cut loose that hog-tied calf; better earmark him before you let him up."

He turned and worked his way out of the brush, the chop-headed Indian boy at his heels.

As he crossed the first ridge in the direction of his camp he pulled up his horse, and the Indian boy stopped also and waited, his round meaty face expressionless. For a moment Tom Cloud sat silent, with those light eyes of his drifting over the broken land as a cowman's eyes are always drifting. On all sides the broad dry valleys of his domain were hemmed in by desert mountains that were sometimes gaunt upthrusts of rock, sometimes as roundly smooth and brown as the breasts of Indian women. Here and there in the mile upon long mile of his grazing leases he could make out the far-scattered specks which were all that could be seen of eight thousand cattle running under his Flying K brand. Those cattle meant one of two things—either such fortune as he could hardly imagine one man achieving in a single life; or else—what seemed inevitable now—the loss of all he had gained in his saddle years.

Cloud's tired horse stirred, and his mind came back to his work.

"Teco."

"Si, señor."

"Go find this man they call El Fuerte. You know where he is?"

"Si, señor."

"Tell him I want him."

The rider hesitated, looking blankly startled. It was plain that he thought the message peremptory—so much so that it might even be dangerous to carry. But—"*Si, señor.*" He dropped his pony off the hill in a new direction.

Cloud spat into a maguey clump, and turned his horse toward home.

CHAPTER 2

TOM CLOUD'S WAY TOOK HIM NOW THROUGH threading cow trails which clung casually to the rock-strewn slopes of a range of hills; thus to a high valley, brush-choked, and wooded with the short, massively conical trunks of sugar pine. When the brush country opened out again into the broad open graze called the Valley of the Witch, Cloud was almost within sight of his home camp.

To reach it he had to pass the old rancho which, though he was not living in it now, was the heart of his leases. It lay before him now, a mile up the valley, beside a twisting trickle of water. Here, within low enclosing walls, stood a rambling house built of adobe four feet thick, with low four-sloped roofs of grey shakes. Its plan was haphazard and without point, but a friendly ease of proportion, bequeathed to Indian adobe workers by their vanished gods, made it one with the

9

valley and the hills. In the serene clear light of the sunset, half-concealed by its pepper trees, the old house was lovely.

As Tom Cloud approached the rancho he became vaguely restless in the saddle and jogged a spur into the barrel of his pony. Lately this place had a certain unreality for him, which was odd, considering that he had lived in it for most of the two years he had been in Baja; until he had moved out a month ago in order that John Boyce and his wife, Kathleen, could be made comfortable.

It was Kathleen who gave the old house its unreality. The razor-back shoat snuffling along the outside of the wall and the nondescript hens flying up to roost in the pepper trees were the same as before. But he never passed this place—and he had to pass it eight or ten times a week—without a curious hunger to glimpse the figure of Kathleen.

This was a sensation objectionable to himself, as a rope is objectionable to a calf who has been caught up by a kicking hind leg. Once or twice a week he stopped in to see if there was anything the Boyces needed.

Whether he did this against his will, or merely against his better judgment, he could not have decided for the life of him.

He had not meant to stop tonight. But as he drew abreast he saw that there was a reined-down pony in front of the door, and he knew at once that Old Beard was here. No one but Old Beard rode so good or so out-moded a saddle on such worthless stock.

Cloud had been wanting to see Beard, which ordinarily meant a ride such as kills a day. He leaned low to open the gate, and rode within the low walls.

For a moment he waited in the saddle, his pony's nose overhanging the low broad steps; then Kathleen Boyce came, light-footed, to his stirrup, and Tom Cloud sat with his hat in his hands, slack with the strange sense of humbleness this woman always put upon him.

Kathleen Boyce was black-haired and blue-eyed; there was Irish blood there, and Spanish too, perhaps. As she stepped out into the last long flat rays of the sunset the red-gold light wrapped itself around her, making her an ethereal thing. There always was a magic in the sunset light in the Valley of the Witch; it turned the brown hills a ruddy gold, and made them look flat and vertical, as if they were cut out of cardboard and stood up. The trees and the house threw mile-long shadows, and every commonplace thing took on a strange disturbing beauty. The same stage-like effect touched Kathleen Boyce, making her face radiant with softly golden light, and weaving red-gold glints into her hair: so that in the sunset magic this woman was the heart of all loveliness.

"Howdy, Mrs. Boyce."

She looked at him now with the unreadable, faintly slant-eyed gaze that always meant trouble.

"Don't get so familiar," she told him. She imitated his sober face and slow voice. "You're supposed to say, 'Howdy, Mam.' "

"Shucks now, you're fooling with me, Mrs. Boyce."

"My name's Kathleen."

"Kathleen," he repeated. He was praying to his gods that she could not guess how many nights that name had sung in his head. "Right pretty name, considering that it's straight mountainy mick."

She smiled at him and said something in some soft

11

unworldly tongue that might have been Celtic for all he knew.

He stepped down, grounding his rawhide reins. Mrs. Boyce took his arm, subtly causing him to walk into the house before he had decided to go in at all. He drew a deep breath, tremendously stirred by the momentary pressure of her shoulder. It always profoundly touched him that this woman was glad to see him. But he couldn't get used to the ease of out-country women with men. Ranch-born western men kept their hands off of women—or if they did not, it was to be understood that they were on the make; and western women stood aloof.

But this woman was neither eastern nor western, but something entirely new to him.

He knew that her father had been a hell-roaring desert prospector named Kilcayne—a ten-striker whose name Tom Cloud had known before he ever saw or heard of Kathleen. But Kathleen was no mining-camp child. Where had she learned all her languages? Every word she spoke in her own language, for that matter, marked her as out-country—far out-country.

Cloud supposed that the fortunes which The Kilcayne had stormed out of the stubborn hills accounted for some of the difference—but not all.

"I saw Old Beard's rigging on that cayuse out there," Cloud said. "I've been kind of wanting to see Beard; and I thought—"

"We were just feeding him," Kathleen Boyce told him. "Of course you'll have pot-luck with us. Won't you? Because I positively won't hear of—"

Here John Boyce came into the main room from an opposite door.

John Boyce, nearly as tall as Cloud, had a bland, thin

face, its features irregular; the eyes were watchful and faintly sardonic. It was an expressive face—only, Cloud had discovered, it expressed exactly what its owner wished it to express, never anything more. But the measure of the man never fully appeared until he spoke.

The voice of this man had an exact, controlled modulation that made Tom Cloud's slow words, somehow, seem to blurt and stumble.

Cloud said, "Hello, John."

"Good evening."

Cloud did not know what was wrong with the way Boyce said that. The man's manner was not condescending; it did not seem to conceal an aloof disapproval; there was no suggestion of a blade behind that could slice if its owner let himself loose it. But Cloud experienced an edgy resentment. He had surmised before now that Boyce disliked being his guest in this house Cloud had lent them. But there was no livable habitation on the neighboring Kilcayne properties which Boyce was investigating; and Boyce could not help himself because of Kathleen.

Kathleen started to speak, but Boyce forestalled her. "You've eaten?" he asked Cloud.

"Yes," Cloud lied.

"Ah." Boyce turned away to the old cupboard in the corner. His unhurried, smoothly efficient hands set down a tumbler, half filled it with whisky. "In that case I'll be with you presently." Boyce waved a half weary, half light salute, and Cloud found himself holding the glass as Boyce went out again, strolling.

Cloud stood uneasy, his eyes on the glass in his hands, while slow dust storms blew through his head.

He was suppressing an impulse to smash the glass

against the wall.

Kathleen said, "Tom—I don't think he means to be rude."

"You don't think—look here—you've been married how long? Three years? And you don't know, for sure?"

Kathleen Boyce hesitated. "You see—he's been awfully eager to talk to Old Beard; he's anxious to find out what Beard knows about mining law down here—which should be a lot."

"Should be." Cloud couldn't picture even John Boyce getting information out of Old Beard. "Well, that being the case, maybe I'd better be drifting on, Mrs. Boyce."

"My name's Kathleen," she told him again. "Don't be angry any more."

"Didn't go to cause comment." He hesitated, glanced at Kathleen; then poured down at a swallow the whisky Boyce had given him.

Kathleen Boyce took him by a wrist, walked him to a chair, made him sit down.

"It's funny," she said. "We're living in your house, on your land; you found us our hill guides, and our landmarks—even our mules. During the last month you've been as much a friend to us as ever a man could be. And yet, sometimes I think you're the most distant man I've ever known; and I don't know you at all."

She offered him cigarettes in a gourd, but he was already rolling one of his own. Cloud let his eyes wander through the door, out across the brown hills whose far-flung, inscrutable folds were somehow draining away everything that made Tom Cloud of any importance in the world. He realized that he was weary, and for a moment Juan Amador touched his mind.

14

"Seems like a westerner sometimes seems that way to other people."

"I was born in Silver City. I've a right to call myself a westerner."

A fugitive gleam of humor went through his eyes. "Silver City? Wonder if you knew a man named Hochmeyer, Mrs. Boyce, ran a—"

Suddenly Kathleen Boyce was on her feet, straight and slim, furious as a little hawk. Her voice dropped to an impassioned husky whisper, cutting him down. "If ever you—call me Mrs. Boyce again—I'll lace you with your own romal!"

He was silent for a moment, amazed at her outburst. He had never seen her blaze up before; and stronger than his surprise was his observation of how strikingly lovely she looked, with fire in her eyes, and her slim body poised with the tense grace of an ocelot. "I'm sorry," he said at last, "Kathleen."

She sat down, picked up a cigarette and lit it with an impatient, deprecatory gesture. "Don't mind me. I'm the one that's sorry."

Cloud fumbled. "Seems like something's bothering you," he offered.

He spoke clumsily, he thought, in flat, level tones; but something in him always reached out gently, tenderly, to this woman, wrapping her in; he couldn't prevent some shadow of that from getting into his voice. And she responded to it now, tacitly.

"I like to have you come here," she told him. "Do you know why?"

"Can't imagine."

"Because you always seem so calm, and steady, and somehow easy-going; as if you had always been master

15

of every circumstance you ever met."

He set his poker-face, and hoped that he didn't look too flabbergasted. He was thinking of today's disaster in the deep brush; and behind that to many another failure to come to grips with those who were draining the life out of the Flying K. He was thinking of nights he had sat upon hilltops with his rifle across his knees, watching some obscure, suspected pass; while somewhere else, miles away, a little bunch of ten or a dozen Flying K steers trickled out of his range, gently pressed by quiet riders. He was thinking of Juan.

"You give me confidence," she said; "as if everything would come out all right, some day."

He started to say, "Didn't hardly realize—"

"Tom—I've got to get John out of here!"

He considered this, looking down at his own hands, tough with rope burns that had seared through his gloves; hands that had fought a thousand broncs, tied down ten thousand cow critters. He had thought the cow knowledge behind those hands could whip any cow country on earth—and the gaunt, rugged brush of Baja was swallowing him up. Easy to see why John Boyce, a mining man, with a background of Pittsburgh smelters and polo, should be lost and baffled in these desert hills. And a baffled man is not pleasant to live with.

"I guess I know, Kathleen."

"Do you?" An unreadable question. "Do you?"

Suddenly Tom Cloud made an ugly discovery. Until this moment he had never admitted to himself that he more than vaguely disliked John Boyce; but with the raw edge of perception which the death of Juan Amador had put upon his nerves, Cloud now knew that he hated this man. And in the same instant he knew why. The

16

smooth courtesy which he had never seen broken, the suave bland face that had never been tortured by sun or sleet, the too easily flowing voice with its vast fund of accurate words—these he could have accepted.

He hated John Boyce because Boyce possessed Kathleen.

CHAPTER 3

"We've got to sell these holdings," Kathleen Boyce went on presently.

"Poor time for it," he managed to say.

"I know. But—I don't know if you know this, Tom—this mineral land is—all there is."

"I kind of thought—he—"

"Not a penny, Tom! You don't know what it means to a man like that. Four generations on top of the world; Boyce was a name to build railroads with—they could stop wars, or start wars. And now—nothing."

"Nothing at all?"

"Only this. This little range of hills, that you've seen."

"Your range of hills," he said.

It was a funny thing, an ironic thing to think that John Boyce, son of a man who had once signed a check for ten million, should have nothing to look to now but a questionable mineralized range of hills belonging to his wife. Men named Boyce had been breeding thoroughbred horses when old Kilcayne had been begging a stake from the bartenders of Tucson. And now the ultimate seed of all the Boyces scratched desperately through the last leavings of the mountain

17

man, Kilcayne.

"Tom," Kathleen said, "do you know if there is any metal there?"

"There's no fortune there just for picking it up. You don't get the guts out of the mountains so easy—not any more. It takes plenty tough men—maybe long-lived men—to fight those mountains down. You see—well— oh, I don't know."

"I know," she said slowly. "I know. I think you and I both know. You and I—we had our roots in the rocks."

He looked at her curiously. Sometimes, as now, he would have given a herd of blood bulls to know what far places had given her the languages she spoke, the lifting grace of her walk, even the movements of her hands. Yet—after all, she was the daughter of The Kilcayne. If by any chance she could reach back and sense the sweating, back-breaking toil in the rock—

"This—this place isn't fair to him, Tom. He—" She stopped.

He sat silent, and his rope-strong hands did not move. He wanted to tell her that he understood; that he knew where John Boyce began, and where he left off. But he could only sit poker-faced in the grip of a malignant trap. He dared not look at her now; she was speaking to him, but he did not know what she said. When he looked at her; when he listened to her faintly husky voice, he knew that this woman was his destiny—the destiny that he had missed.

Not that he doubted himself; he had taken women from other men before. But by the code to which he was born, no advance was possible here without an implied dishonor to the woman herself. The women who had sometimes shared his blankets had had no faith in them;

18

yet Tom Cloud still, from some obscure source, believed in the loyalty of women.

Kathleen Boyce said in a toneless voice, "It isn't my fault if my father's hill country is all we have left."

"No," Cloud said; "no." Through his mind, without connection, drifted the face of Juan Amador who was dead, the ghosts of four hundred head of missing cattle, and the white, gently dazzling shoulders of this woman at whom he dared not look. His eyes, wandering in an effort not to meet hers, roamed over the altered contours of this room in which he had lived until the Boyces came. It had been a barren room then, open to the sweep of the dust-laden wind, for men who have slept often in bed-rolls are uneasy within walls. And though Cloud was a man who kept his leather and steel in beautiful working shape, his quarters always looked like a saddle shop. Thus this room was strange to him, now.

It was barren yet, in furniture, and in everything that costs money. But with worthless things such as can be won away from Indians for a few centavos, this room had been made new. In one corner hung a chain of the corn ears that burros eat, a slash of such colors as Cloud had never suspected before—bright as blood, blue as the sea, black as midnight, opalescent in pink and gold, for Mexican corn can show the colors of everything on earth. On the floor were serapes—worn, weathered serapes that proud vaqueros had been glad to get rid of—but warm and mellow with old, forgotten herb dyes, memorizing the colors of long gone sunsets. And on one wall hung the horned skull of a mountain sheep, deep-etched by the seasons.

Cloud had leaned down from the saddle to pick up

19

that head, and had brought it in to Kathleen as a momentary curiosity, never supposing anybody would ever want to hang it up. But now that the weathered spread of horns rested here the desert came friendly into the room, taking away the sense of war between man and the land of the broken crags.

But it was when Tom Cloud's eyes rested on his old reata, still hung on a peg where he had left it—that was too much. The worn-out rawhide was frayed from running through his hands, deep-stained with his own sweat, yet it was still here, a part of the room in which this woman lived.

"If there's any way," she was saying, "any way you can help us to get a—cash offer—for the Kilcayne property—in God's name, Tom, will you do what you can?" She was speaking in dead level tones, as one whose emotion is dead after long contention.

"So you can get out of here?" he said.

"So I can get him out of here."

He said, slowly, "I don't know as I can bring myself to want you gone."

Then he heard her say, almost inaudibly, "And I don't want to go."

He hazarded a quick glance at her. Too late he knew that he should have kept his eyes on the desert hills. His grey eyes, that had backed a raise of a thousand blues without any change of expression—the gates behind them failed him now. Without being able to look away, he knew that he had betrayed himself, that this girl was able to read him, clear to the bottom of his soul.

Then suddenly he knew something else. The blue eyes under the black lashes of Kathleen Boyce had lost their barriers as had his own. For a moment as their eyes met it was as if they had stood stark naked in front of each other, with no concealment possible.

Cloud came to his feet, and he stood over her, poised on the high heels of his boots, head down like a wolfed steer. "You—by the good God!—you're breaking me up, you hear?"

"You think it's easy for me?"

He held her eyes one second more; and in that moment he knew that this woman was his own; that whether she ever in the world slept in his arms or not—whether or not he ever again so much as touched her hand—this woman was his, more than she would ever belong to anyone else again. Then he turned away, and stood looking at the twilight on the desert hills, while yet all he could see was the unmistakable thing that had been in her eyes.

"Listen," he said, not looking at her any more. "You mean to stay with this man?"

"Yes," Kathleen said.

"No matter what comes?"

"Yes," said Kathleen again.

He said nothing, and the silence between them drew out until it became unbearable. "You've got to help me," she said at last, levelly. "You're the only one I can turn to."

"Help you? Dear God!"

"I've got to get rid of this mining stuff. I've got to get him out of here." She added, in hardly more than a whisper, "I've got to get out of here myself."

He didn't answer at once. He wasn't going to promise what he couldn't do. "Might take time," he said finally. "I've got a scrap on my hands, Kathleen."

Kathleen's voice hurt him like the stroke of a blade.

21

"Time," she cried out, "time—Mother of God, Tom—"

She was suddenly silent. In the rear of the house had sounded the scrape of a pushed-back bench. That would be Old Beard—profligate with other people's dinners, but infinitely chary of his information and advice—ending John Boyce's probings into the practical applications of Mexican mining law. In a few more seconds the door opened, and John Boyce stood back courteously to let Old Beard into the room.

Tom Cloud, but few others, knew that Old Beard's first name was Willard. Nobody called him Bill, now that his own generation was gone from around him. His face was a crinkled but expressionless mask, decorated with a mustache that may once have had a gallant buffalo-horn hook, but was now only a sort of mouth-portiere, draped noncommittally around a pipe stem. Only the eyes were significant, They were of a pale nondescript green, very old; but they contained an implacable peace. Men have founded religions on less than the unshakable look of peace in the eyes of Old Beard. Others with much the same attribute have been brutally shot dead by bystanders, out of sheer annoyance.

Old Beard had been shot in four places, but evidently it was the others who were dead, for Beard was here. Instead of a religion, he had founded herds whose incredible numbers were known only to himself. Miraculously, he lost no calves by thievery or misbranding, and his cattle prospered.

He had further founded—perhaps accidentally—a little churchless village of his own, based upon the semi-skilled peons who worked for him. Beard liked to employ family folk, such as would raise their own pork,

22

right under their beds. It was only partly true that his village was composed of Beard's illegitimate descendants. Cloud had once visited Beard's remote village. He knew that Beard's own adobe had a porch like an American farm house, and on the porch was a black walnut spring rocker with most of the stuffing out. Beside the door was nailed a hank of black hair that looked like horse tail, in which Beard hung up his comb. The fact that Tom Cloud understood Beard better than anyone else did was perhaps due to this: Cloud had recognized that the hank of hair in which Beard hung up his comb was not a horse tail at all, but a human scalp lock.

"Howdy, Mr. Beard," Tom said.

"Why, hello, son." Tom Cloud, to him, was only one of a long series of gringo cattlemen who bucked the Mexican game, came seeking the advice which Old Beard no longer gave—and presently drifted back whence they came. Beard himself had become a Mexican citizen, long ago.

"You've made yourself comfortable, I hope?" John Boyce said with a pleasantness of no value to Cloud.

Cloud knew that he was poker-faced once more, now that he was against males. "Right tolerable, for sure," he said.

There was a moment of awkward silence. After all, what speech could be common to these four—an old man long buried in Baja hills, a young cattleman whom those hills were bleeding to death, a polo player from Pittsburgh, and a girl whom no one of them understood?

Boyce, always at his ease, strolled to a window, taking note of passing riders whom the other men had heard but ignored. "There goes your organization, Cloud."

23

"*Bueno*," Cloud said.

"Just two descendants of Montezuma," Boyce described those he watched pass. "Both on the same— yes, doubtless they regard it as a horse."

"Mexican vaqueros are the best saddle and rope hands in the world, Boyce."

"What are those enormous baskets? Oh, those are their hats. Hats in hand. That, I imagine, is a tribute; I advise you to throw a geranium, Kathleen."

"Boyce," said Tom Cloud, "I already know you hate this country."

"Not at all," Boyce insisted. "I vastly admire it. What a scene for Diego Rivera to paint forty feet tall on the side of an abattoir! He'd call it 'The Spirit of Tuesday, Triumphing over Agriculture.' "

"John, for heaven's sake—" Kathleen began.

"The simple dignity of the authentically unwashed," the pleasant tones of Boyce went on. He seemed speaking to himself. "What a gravity in their vacant faces, as they—"

"The thing on the led horse," Cloud said in a flat voice, "is the body of a man."

He heard Kathleen's breath catch in her teeth. Again there was quiet here, backed by the griping bawl and squeak of the lonely burro in the corral—a crudely absurd antiphone.

John Boyce for a moment stood perfectly motionless; then he made an impatient, almost exasperated gesture. "I'm sorry, Cloud," he said.

"That's all right."

"Dead," Old Beard said mildly. "Another dead? Sometimes I think— Who is it this time, Cloud?"

"My foreman; he caught a knife in the throat."

24

Kathleen cried out sharply. "Tom! How did it happen?"

"Today we rode over a hill and caught some cow thieves branding a calf of mine, deep in the brush. Juan Amador pulled his gun and whaled into them; we aimed to stampede them into the open. Seems like one of them laid low in the cover, and threw his knife as Juan busted in."

"I believe," Kathleen said, "that this is the most lawless, wildly unreasonable country on the face of the earth!"

"Oh, shucks, now," Beard protested. "I think this is a real friendly country. Once you get the hang of the situation."

Suddenly Cloud felt unable to listen any longer to the suave satiric voice of John Boyce, or the mild mouthings of Old Beard. It was simply too much for him just now to be with these others in the same room with Kathleen Boyce.

"I'll be pushing on," he said; "I've been kind of wanting to talk to you, Beard, but there's no hurry, I guess."

Unexpectedly Old Beard said, "I was fixing to up-stakes anyway. I'll side-ride you a piece."

Going out, Cloud glanced once more at Kathleen; she met his eyes, and for a moment he thought he saw in hers a confirming shadow of what he had seen there a little while before.

CHAPTER 4

AS CLOUD RODE AWAY BESIDE OLD BEARD, KATHLEEN stood for a few moments, leaning her head against the doorjamb, watching the receding riders. A lost, draining

25

away sensation was pulling at her heart, as if she were being left entirely alone in this strange place; except that to be alone with John Boyce nowadays was just a little worse than being altogether alone.

As she turned back into the darkening room she was feeling the sudden chill that descends upon Baja when the sun is gone; and all the life and light were going out of her face, leaving it touched by a constraint that might have risen from a faint dread. John Boyce was sitting on the edge of a chair, perfectly still, his eyes fixed upon Kathleen.

He appeared relaxed, and his face carried no readable meaning; but in the thickening dusk it seemed to her that its pale, almost luminous oval shone with a vaguely baleful cast. He never tanned like other men.

She moved toward a lamp, feeling the urgent need of light, but stopped, remembering that the lamps in this room were dry. They never had anything any more, except what Tom Cloud sent them. Kathleen turned to the fireplace, but no one had brought in any wood, and this was cold and empty too.

She faced John Boyce, her arms tight against her sides. "In heaven's name, John—in heaven's name, don't look at me like that!"

Boyce regarded her a moment more, then smiled unpleasantly, and got up to get the brandy bottle. In some men that gesture would have offered hope of a mellower mood later on, but there was no hope of that with Boyce. He was a cold drinker. When he drank, which now was nearly every day, he put down impossible quantities of whatever liquor was at hand. Yet he never flushed or staggered, and instead of thickening, his words increased their precision.

His eyes were glowing with a queer somber light in a face gone bloodless, and there was a disturbing suggestion of an ordered madness in his speech.

"Too bad," he said now, "that you couldn't persuade him to stay."

She pretended that she believed he meant Beard. "I thought you had finished talking to him. Was he able to tell you the boundaries of the *Dos*—"

In liquor Boyce was both unapproachable and inescapable. "I imagine, though," he said, "that he stays longer when I am gone."

Kathleen said in a strained voice, "If you're speaking of Tom Cloud—"

"Your perspicuity astounds me," Boyce said. "I was speaking of your—I started to say, your lover; but I imagine that is yet to come. Convenient for you, isn't it, that I have to spend so much time grubbing in these infernal hills."

"John! Don't!"

John Boyce talked on in tones suavely modulated— treacherously so, for he had a command of words that could cut and burn like corroding acid. "What a pity," he said, purring almost sympathetically, "that he doesn't return your infatuation. I'm afraid you'll have to be even more obvious than you've already become. I suggest that you invent a ruse whereby you appear before him wearing a bath towel. That's the sort of display to which these simple souls react."

Dark spots of red had appeared over Kathleen's cheekbones; in the failed light they looked like charcoal smudges. This was not a new thing he was beginning. She stared at him a moment, then moved abruptly to go out of the room.

27

He stopped her. "I believe I was speaking to you."

"I'm going to build a fire."

"I'll take care of that." He stepped to a window. "Pepe! *El lumbre!*"

Kathleen took two quick steps to gain the inner door—a gesture of escape; but Boyce whirled and caught her arm above the elbow. "You're overwrought, my dear," he said in those velvety intonations. "You've allowed your—friend to affect you too strongly, under the circumstances. Nothing so unnerves a woman as too strong an unrequited desire. You must try to control your instincts. Sit here."

He made her sit down, with every appearance of gentleness; but when he had released her his finger marks showed upon her bare arm like scars. She sat motionless, her face hopeless, her eyes sad and quiet on the distant hills. No use to try to escape him, or to shut herself away until his mood turned; it might last for days. She had learned that to be quiet, and to wait, was the easiest way.

There was a perfunctory knock, and a little round-bodied man with a brown moon-shaped face came in laden with wood. He kneeled at the fireplace and began the leisurely laying of a blaze. Boyce began talking again, ignoring the *mozo*.

"If physical display fails—but of course it won't. I was going to suggest that you play upon his sympathy. But after all, he's anything but intelligent."

"John," Kathleen said, "you're being completely, unutterably vicious."

"I'm only trying to be helpful." He poured himself more brandy, stirred it about with a circular motion of the glass, and sniffed its villainous bouquet ironically.

28

"I'm afraid you must pardon me if I cannot conceal that I am ever so slightly revolted. I had hardly supposed that you would be so entranced by a set of back muscles. How do you tell whether you're embracing him or one of those execrable plugs he rides? Or can you? Or do you feel that it matters?"

There were little white patches at the corners of Kathleen's nostrils, but she said, "I think that when you're in a mood like this, nothing that you say matters at all."

"But I imagine," Boyce went on, as if to himself, "that I may still expect, usually, to find you here. Somehow I'm perfectly sure that Cloud won't be fool enough to take you, however you may expose the opportunity."

Kathleen turned on him sharply, desperation in her eyes, but he spoke quickly. "And now you're going to tell me that you *will* leave, that you *will* go to him, odor of the stable and all. Save your breath, Kathleen."

She faltered and turned away. It was the most terrible characteristic of this man that he could, many and many times, read her thoughts with an eerie accuracy.

"You see, my dear," he said in tones of factitious caress, "you could conceal things from me once; you cannot any more. The process of reading you is perfectly effortless. Everything about you is much more plainly exposed to the mind than as if you were naked."

Kathleen shuddered, turning weak and sick. She had inherited an all but imperishable tenacity from The Kilcayne. With it she had tried to make something lasting and decent of her marriage with this man. But she knew that she was nearly spent.

"I'm not leaving you," she said. "Not yet. Once you

29

were a presentable thing—more than presentable. You're not any more. That may be partly my fault. So I mean to stay with you until you're on your feet again. But once I'm convinced that you won't go utterly to pieces as soon as I leave you—then I'm going to leave you. Not for Tom Cloud, not for any man. Just leave you. Because living with you is not tolerable any more."

"Pleasant to have the reassurance," Boyce murmured. He looked amused, and drank again. "Of course—I realize that it's unfair to blame you for the tastes you've inherited from the unwashed Kilcayne."

Kathleen's face was white. "You're just a little cowardly, I think. I can't imagine your saying a thing like that in the hearing of my father, or my brother, if they were alive. Even Tom Cloud, whom I scarcely know, would break you in his hands."

"A typical Kilcayne conception," Boyce agreed impersonally. "Yet perhaps I am unjust. After all, you don't know—do you?—that The Kilcayne was your father at all."

"What can you mean by that?" Kathleen stood up abruptly, endurance at an end.

"It seems unlikely," he said soothingly, "that a woman who could surrender to the preposterous Kilcayne could have been very particular."

Suddenly Kathleen's breath caught in her throat, and she struck him across the face with all her strength.

His ironic, impersonally tormenting smile did not change, nor the peculiar fixed staring of his eyes, somber and faintly mad. It seemed to Kathleen that the blow shook the rigid poise of his head no more than as if he had been struck by a ghost, and her soft slender fingers left no mark on his already pallid face. She

30

turned and fled, and hid herself in her own room; and when she had barred the door, gently folded herself into a little heap on the floor. She hid her face tight in her arms, sobbing erratically, and wishing she were dead.

She would have gone with Tom Cloud then, if he had come. For a little while she felt an overpowering necessity to go to him, now, at once, to find him wherever he might be. It was only later, when she had washed her face with cold water, and the strained beating of her heart had quieted with fatigue, that she knew this to be a thing she could not do, now or ever.

In the ultimate, she knew with perfect certainty that she could never go to any man while she was driven and helpless and defeated. A mating should be a consummation that was the heart of peace; a gentle and happy thing, radiant and serene. She could never make it the refuge of a disordered retreat. To go to Tom Cloud now would have been like going to him unclean.

CHAPTER 5

JOGGING STIRRUP TO STIRRUP WITH OLD BEARD, Cloud was silent for a little way. Beard knew things that might be invaluable to Cloud; but Cloud didn't know how to open him up.

"When do you figure Boyce will be leaving?" Old Beard asked.

"Boyce hasn't told me he was leaving at all."

"Me neither, come to think of it; I just figured he'd be getting out."

"You watch us all come and go, don't you?" Cloud said with a visible annoyance.

31

"Boyce ain't hardly the man to go at the Kilcayne property," Beard said. "He ain't of any mind to settle into the country, and try to learn it. All he wants is to loot the country and get out. Well, he'll get out, all right, but it'll be him that's looted. Them rocky Cayugas can loot the heart out of a little man like him."

Tom Cloud growled, "This country sure is long on loot."

Beard said nothing for a little while. He was not a notably silent man, as lonely men go; but when you tried to find out something from him that would be some good to you, he dried up, "I was kind of hoping we might ketch some early rain," he responded at last.

Cloud spoke out bluntly. "You know why I'm here. This new U. S. duty on beef runs higher than the price of cows in Arizona. It's just plain smashed hell out of the cattlemen below the border—Baja especially, because Baja cattlemen can't reach the Mexico City market. Naturally the price of leases went to hell in a barrel."

Beard waited, regarding him without expression.

"Me, I was willing to bet that this big import duty would be dropped off again. Maybe not right away; but within ten years. I had a fair-sized stake. I figured I could buy more cows and leases with it here than I'd see in a lifetime any place else. In ten years my cattle should build up to where I'll be one of the strongest cattlemen in North America. Then if the import duty drops off, I ought to be able to take the world by the tail and crack it like a whip."

"If," said Old Beard.

"I took that chance."

"Well?"

"You know what's happened," Cloud said with a sort of slow, casual fury. "Build up, hell! I've had a beef shrinkage fit to bust the old Ten-In-Texas. It's worse than it used to be fifty years back, in the old wild days. And I'm damned if I can get my teeth into it."

"Takes time to learn a country," Beard said vaguely. "I mind when I first come down here, forty year ago. For a while it looked like—"

Cloud would not be led off. "Putting cattle into this country is like pouring water on sand," he said, speaking more bitterly than anyone down there had ever heard him speak. "If I just lost a calf once in a while I wouldn't mind. But they're game to flood all Mexico with beef jerky, if my herds hold out. God knows where they get rid of it all! I figure I've lost eight hundred head this dry season."

"Seems a mite high," Beard offered.

"If this was Arizona, a man could go at 'em and clean 'em out. But what can a man do where the whole population sucks up loot like a sponge?"

"Who taught 'em?" Beard grinned.

Cloud was silent.

"Look around you," Beard suggested. "You see a middling rich cattle country. But look at the people. Shy on shoes—where would they get shoes? Shy on blankets: shy on quinine; shy on everything it takes money to buy. Some years they run a sixty per cent death loss among their little kids."

"Laziness," Cloud snapped.

"This morning," Beard told him, "riding down from yonder, I passed a man on the road. He had a hundred pounds of pottery on his back, and he was running.

33

Tonight, riding back, I'll pass him again—still running. Due to laziness."

"Well, what's your answer to it?"

"You shouldn't never turn in," Beard said, "without thanking God that these here is sure a peaceable people. All you got here that's American is some blood bulls. Everything else has come out of these people. That's why there ain't no shoes."

"I paid for everything I got here, by God!" Tom Cloud said.

"You bought from Americans. I'm asking where the land and cattle come from to start with? When a man is pushed far enough down, he tries to take back some of his own."

They rode a quarter of a mile in silence.

"Was you figuring to sell out?" Beard asked presently. "Because if you was, I'd kind of like—"

"I won't sell," Tom Cloud told him, "while I got one cow with a calf at her flank. If I've got to fight the whole country I'll fight it."

"Just how was you aiming to go about it?" Beard said in friendly curiosity.

"For one thing, there's a couple of questions I wanted to ask you."

Beard shook his head. "When you know every man and boy in this country by his first name, and who his folks was, and can talk in four, five of the dialects as good as they can themselves—then you'll begin to see ways of handling these little things that come up. Until then I can't help you, son. And by then you won't be asking me."

"What I wanted from you," Tom Cloud said, "was your dope on a man. You know a man they call El

Fuerte?"

The dusk was now very thick, and Tom Cloud was looking straight ahead; but he knew when Old Beard's eyes stole sideways to study him with a sudden acute intensity.

"Heard the name," Beard said in a noncommittal flat voice.

"Guadalupe Francisco Contreras is his right name, I think."

"Contreras y Canedo," Beard corrected him. "Where in all hell did you hook up with that *hombre,* Cloud?"

"He comes kind of recommended to me," Cloud said.

"Recommended? As a hired man for you?"

"As a cross between a foreman and a partner."

Through his aged teeth Beard whistled half a dozen bars of a tuneless song. "I suppose you realize that you'll make an enemy of Solano if you take El Fuerte in?"

"What the devil is Solano to me?"

"Solano is the biggest neighbor you've got, excepting maybe me. He's your biggest Mexican neighbor. There's no better cattleman, nor squarer shooter, on either side of the border than Solano."

"And what did Solano ever do for me?" Cloud demanded angrily. "If he expects to lay down the law on who I'll take on, he can go take a flying jump at himself."

They were at Cloud's corrals now. His pony swayed restlessly as he held it from heading in to the saddle rack. For a few moments both men were silent.

"El Fuerte has a blond daughter in Guadalajara," Beard said finally.

"What in all hell has that got to do with it?"

"Me, I don't know much," Beard mumbled. "It just run through my mind. But I'll say this: I'd think it over before I took this El Fuerte on." Old Beard had the inert patience of the hills—a patience that could wait out the plans of men, the destiny of a country, the slow wearing away of the hills themselves. "There's a type of tool that sometimes turns in a man's hands," he said. "If I was you I'd kind of let it work over in my mind a month or two."

"A month or two!" Cloud exploded. "Dear God!"

"Things down here sometimes take a little time," Beard admitted. He raised his hand in an Indian salute, and let his horse drift on.

CHAPTER 6

THE TURKEY-NECKED MAN WALKED OUT TO THE saddle rack as Cloud unbridled. He was wanting to know what was to be done with the body of Juan Amador.

"Take him to La Partida," Cloud told him shortly, "and have the storekeeper put him in a box. Then go to the church and see the sacristan about getting him into a grave, *pronto*."

"Tonight?"

"Certainly tonight. Get gone."

As the man moved off it occurred to Tom Cloud that Juan Amador had been a religious man, in his way. He called the vaquero back and gave him a crumpled bill. "Tell the *padre* we want three or four pesos worth of prayers."

Cloud turned away and walked past the corrals to the

36

hovel in which he lived. This place had been an outpost of the hacienda itself, established two miles away in order that its lord should not be troubled by the dust. Cloud had based a mile of fenced pasture upon these corrals, and used it for the weaning of calves—an innovation which the vaqueros considered a sign of crazy Americanism. Because there were always a few score head of young beeves in the process of weaning, Cloud's camp forever resounded with the bawling of the fence-separated cows and calves.

Here, under a few very tall, very scraggly pines, stood two squat adobes—one of a single room, which was a bunk house for the vaqueros, and one of two smaller rooms in which Tom Cloud slept among his saddles and his gear. Cooking was done by open fire and adobe oven, around the margin of a palmetto lean-to that was open on three sides to the hot dusty winds and infrequent rains. It did not occur to Cloud that these were poor quarters; he had everything he needed here.

Now he got from a screened box a strap of beef jerky like salty leather. He was chewing upon this, and drinking the dregs of coffee which the vaqueros had left, when Teco, the chop-headed Indian boy, came in.

"Where's El Fuerte?"

"*Señor*, who knows?"

"I sent you to get him," Cloud said sharply.

Teco withdrew behind his coffee-black eyes and waited, as unable to comprehend his tall boss as Cloud was unable to adjust himself to the passive yet latently explosive people of the brown valleys.

"Where did you look for him," Cloud demanded.

"At his camp, *señor*."

"Did you go to La Partida? Did you go up the river trail? Did you see if he had gone over to the Perez place? No? Where did you go?"

"To his camp, *señor*."

Cloud raised eyes to heaven.

"They didn't know where he went," the Indian boy said doggedly. "I left your word."

"Go follow the others to La Partida," Cloud told him, "and make them buy you a drink. Go on, get out of here!"

Cloud himself saddled a fresh horse, and moved out in a new direction over a little-used trail. Half an hour later, having made a short cut over a fold of the hills, he stepped down in front of a little adobe which commanded a segment of the valley plain. The place was small; but its fresh whitewash gave it a prosperous look, and the horses in the corral near by were very good.

After Cloud had knocked there was a brief delay, during which he could hear children being shooed out of the adobe's main room, before the door was opened by a well set up young man in the vaquero-like clothes of a small ranchero, He wore shoes, and smoked a cigar shaped like a cigarette.

This man occupied the typically Mexican office known as Judge of the Plains. Nobody was supposed to buy or sell a head of stock, or even kill a cow for beef, without his cognizance; the idea being to check cow stealing and dispute. While the office did not in itself seem to carry authority in crimes of violence, Hernandez served, in this district, as an official link with Mexicali.

"Hello, Hernandez."

Hernandez looked neither surprised nor altogether pleased. For a moment he seemed to hesitate. "This is your house," he said at last, using the standardized greeting. "Come in."

Cloud was admitted into a small room which had been built in the manner of an Indian pueblo, but was now more or less furnished with American golden oak of a mail-order type. Hernandez pulled forward a chair for Cloud, and himself sat down; then waited noncommittally. He seemed neither interested nor apprehensive, but behind his placid face could be sensed a stubborn reserve akin to hostility.

"One of my men has been killed," Cloud said, dropping into Spanish.

"Ay," said Hernandez sympathetically. His face was blandly pleasant, unmarred and unhardened by any trace of thought; a small, carefully tended mustache decorated it. His sleek hair, descending in short sideburns in front of his ears, somehow gave him a self-approving appearance, "Who is the unfortunate?"

Already Cloud had surmised that Hernandez was preinformed of the whole affair, but he answered with an accurate and compact version of what he knew. "Amador was killed by a thrown knife," he finished; "but the knife is gone."

"This was on your range?"

"Certainly it was on my range. It was at the mouth of Canyon del Lobo."

"But that part of your range is not fenced," Hernandez said instantly.

"No," Cloud admitted, and regarded Hernandez sardonically. Knowing nothing of the man's family connections, Cloud did not know what nepotism was responsible for his tenure. He had originally supposed that the young man held his office by temporary appointment; but Hernandez continued on and on— destined to be a permanent occupant, for all Cloud knew.

"Other rancheros," Hernandez pointed out with a faint show of what he may have meant for sternness, "have a right to seek their stock on your range, wherever it is not fenced. I do not see what right you had to attack these men."

"They were branding my calf."

"How do you know it was your calf? Did you have it earmarked? No? Then you would have to display this calf sucking one of your own correctly branded cows," Hernandez declared.

"No cow was there. She may be lying some place with a bullet in her head for all I know."

"Then you have no evidence that this was your calf at all. Maybe you can look at a calf and say 'this is my calf.' But no court in the world is going to believe you. It is not the law. Did you recognize these men you attacked?"

"The thieves? Juan Amador recognized them."

"But you say he is dead. Who else?"

"Nobody."

"The doubtful statement of a dead man, then," Hernandez argued. "Well—who did he say they were?"

"He gave three names—Gomez, Castro, and Perez."

"Those are names of honest and well known little rancheros," Hernandez fussed. "Everyone will speak for their characters. Which men of these names did Amador accuse?"

"As to that," Cloud said wearily, "there was no time

for him to say."

"It was your duty to obtain a statement from him."

"How did I know he was going to be murdered?"

Hernandez made an impatient gesture, got up, and produced paper and pen. "Well, I'll make up a report. Also you will have to send your vaqueros here to make their statements. That's all I can do, I suppose, unless someone wants to make a complaint against you."

"Against me?"

"Obviously, by your own story," said Hernandez, "you and your men unwarrantedly attacked a peaceable group of citizens. You set upon them brutally with force of arms, while they were working stock within their rights. The fact that one of your number was killed in this act only makes your offense more great. The men you attacked have a serious action against you if they wish to press it. But all I can do is to send my report, after making what investigation I am supposed to make. Further investigation will be made by the rurales when they come."

"And when is that?" Cloud demanded.

"I expect them to make a tour here in about six weeks."

Cloud sighed deeply and fell silent. He had been through the whole sterile rigmarole on a similar occasion eight months before, and knew what it amounted to. That the thieves themselves should proceed against him was not to be feared; but neither could anything official be accomplished against the killer of Juan Amador. The rurales were sound men, notably scrupulous, surprisingly efficient; but all *paisanos* named Perez, or Gomez, or Castro would be found armed with alibis, and the whole country would

41

stand behind them. The rurales would be helpless in the face of a blank and passive resistance.

"If you wish any other action on this—" Hernandez began.

"I don't expect any action," Cloud told the Judge of the Plains shortly. "I'm here only because such things are supposed to be reported."

Hernandez grunted and began to take down Cloud's statement with a gummed and sputtering pen. "You are forever complaining," he reprimanded Cloud. "Always you imagine that you lose cattle. But when you are called upon for evidence, even what little you present is overwhelmingly discredited by testimony of our own citizens in good standing. It does not sit well that a foreigner of vast wealth, coming here for the purpose of exploiting our people, should always be a focus of disorder. It cannot be permitted, in this day and age, in our great country, that—"

Cloud got himself out of there, and rode off swearing. He felt the desperation of a man floundering shoulder deep in a quicksand. He could get his hands on nothing, come to grips with nothing. No enemy ever openly attacked him, none so much as showed his face; yet slowly his far-flung brand, with all its promise of ultimate fortune, was being cut out from under him.

CHAPTER 7

A STRANGE, UNQUIET NIGHT HAD CLOSED DOWN BY the time Cloud got back to his camp. He lighted a kerosene lamp, got out a cracked deck of cards, and began to play solitaire on a table he had made from a pine slab. But as his hands methodically controlled the game, he was looking through and beyond the cards, staring into the face of his situation with more grim stubbornness then he had ever known.

More than anything in the world he wanted Kathleen Boyce; at least he knew that now. But his hidden, remaining belief in the loyalty of women tied his hands. Because he loved Kathleen, he could not have brought himself to make her the disproof of that lingering faith. Instinctively—and, he thought, finally—he put from his mind any possibility of ever possessing Kathleen Boyce.

But now, with an insight unusual to him, he perceived that Kathleen was boxed in a singularly unpleasant position. It was easy for Cloud to see how the suave, smoothly flowing ironies which Boyce delivered with such unanswerable courtesy could make life intolerable to anyone in harness with him for very long. Worse, now, because Boyce was trapped penniless in a country that he despised and hated—with his only resources a range of hills which promised no immediate return. Still worse because the stubborn hills themselves belonged to Kathleen.

Cloud had the American's belief in the power of money; he was certain that he could immediately have eased Kathleen's situation if his own resources had been in the clear. Most of his years had been spent in a canny, driving war to attain ascendancy in terms of cattle—and he had come a long way. Yet, for all his herds, he could hardly lay hands upon a dime. Now it gave him a sense of tied-down desperation to perceive that he was unable to do anything whatever to help this woman that he loved.

For several hours, as he sat there, the bawling of the

43

separated cows and calves went on for a mile along the fences. By ten o'clock the moon was up, and the bawling died down as the cows drifted off in search of feed. Half an hour after the cattle had quieted, the coyotes began to sing. The surrounding hills were heavily infested with them, and now they all sang to the moon for a period of twenty minutes, each brute sounding like a dozen, so that it seemed that every thorn bush hid its coyote, Every night the odd primitive rhythm of the cattle and the coyotes marked the hours, in this way.

After the coyotes hushed there fell a curious chill of moonlit quiet; and in this cool midnight silence Cloud's visitors came.

Cloud heard the horses come up, and he reached behind him to unhook his gunbelt from the wall. He laid it beside him on the bench and went on with his game; but when presently there was a knock at the slab door, he let one hand drop below the table top before he called out to his visitor to come in.

The door swung open a little way and a small figure slid into the room with an obsequious air of apology.

"I am del Pino," the man said.

Cloud assumed that this was someone stopping by for the night. "This is your house," he said in his poor imitation of the Baja idiom. "There's jerky in the lean-to, there."

"I am El Fuerte's secretary," the visitor said.

Of all the unexpected things that Cloud had met in this unexpected country, this remark was the most astonishing to him. Supposedly El Fuerte was a Sonora rancher of some means and very considerable experience, seeking a new cattle location. Cloud had

44

never ever seen El Fuerte dressed in anything but a poorly pressed business suit; but no one could mistake him for anything but a wandering man of the saddle. To think of El Fuerte possessed of a secretary was impossible.

"El Fuerte himself is here!" Del Pino sounded as if he could hardly believe the magnificence of his own announcement. "Sir, he will speak to you."

"Tell him to come on in," Cloud said.

"But he is in the saddle."

"Well, he hasn't grown fast to it, has he?"

"Como?"

Cloud shrugged. "Oh, all right." He was accustomed to making concessions, down here, for unclear reasons. He walked outside.

El Fuerte was a tall, even a massive figure in the saddle. In the darkness Cloud could not see his face.

"*Buenas noches*," Cloud said. "Won't you light?"

"No, *gracias,* not now." El Fuerte's voice was deep, full toned. "Me, I have a little ride to make, to see some men—a little matter of business. Always there is business."

"Kind of late for that, isn't it?" Cloud suggested. "Better step down and have a drink."

"Late? Ah, Mister—" there was a purring note in the voice—"for riding the night is often the most nice part of the day! Later, maybe, I would like the drink; a thousand thanks. But please not now."

Behind El Fuerte Cloud made out the figures of two other mounted men. Cloud had been to the camp of El Fuerte—it was an abandoned *casita* on the border of Old Beard's vast lands—only once, and therefore he did not recognize both of these others; but even in the

45

darkness he knew the tall, relaxed, but very straight figure of Bravo, a man of lean Indian build and features, but of a people which Cloud could not place.

"I wanted to talk to you," he told El Fuerte.

"I am honored, Mister," said El Fuerte with good-humored decorum. "I will be glad to talk to you very quick. First thing in the morning, maybe? Or even later tonight, if this thing does not take too long; you are not busy tonight?"

"My time's my own. I'll be here any time up to tomorrow noon, so far as I know."

"*Bueno*," said El Fuerte. "Then, Mister, *adios y gracias*!" He saluted flamboyantly, wheeling his horse. And now, although he had ridden in at a quiet enough pace, he slapped the spurs into his horse and was off at a run, his two riders after him. Del Pino was left afoot, hanging to the headstall of a poorly broke animal which tried to follow the others.

Cloud watched him with a faint amusement. "You're going to get left, aren't you?"

"Ay, this riding all over the place is not for me. If it won't trouble you too much, I'll wait for them here."

Cloud supposed that del Pino had not missed his suggestion that somebody have a drink. "Sure enough," he said. "Here—I'll boot your horse into the corral."

With his animal out of the way, del Pino apologetically, but not without a certain dignity, followed Cloud into his adobe.

Studying del Pino, Cloud saw a small wiry man with a brown ascetic face as nervously alert as that of a terrier; his clipped mustache was evidently copied after that of El Fuerte himself. Del Pino wore a neat black bow tie at the collar of a well worn but clean blue work

46

shirt; and a black broadcloth coat which gave the appearance of being his own, yet a little too large for him, as if he had been slightly diminished by the adversities of travel. His boots were those of a rider.

"El Fuerte was away when your message came in," del Pino said in English elaborately pronounced. "I myself knew of it only a little while ago. I assure you sir, that El Fuerte would have honored your message before this, had he been there."

"You say you are El Fuerte's—what?"

"Secretary. Do not misunderstand El Fuerte," del Pino urged. "Sir, El Fuerte is a man of great affairs."

Cloud, very much diverted, roused himself to get out a pale yellow bottle. "Sit down. Have a drink of tequila."

Del Pino balanced himself on the edge of a box across the table from Cloud. "I think, sir," he said, "that El Fuerte will have news for you in the morning. *Salud!*" He tipped the bottle handily.

"News for me?"

Del Pino leaned across the table with an air of the utmost secretive solemnity. "Sir, I think I may take the liberty of saying that El Fuerte is—taking himself a ride."

"A ride?"

"A ride. You see—El Fuerte has already heard of your misfortune."

Cloud stared at him. "Look here—you mean that El Fuerte is on the ride tonight because Juan Amador is dead?"

Del Pino shrugged deprecatingly. "When El Fuerte takes himself a ride in the moon, it is not for me to say wherefore or whereat. But I will say this, sir—the killer

47

of Juan Amador cannot hide himself from such a man as El Fuerte."

"Now wait a minute," Cloud drawled. "Who the devil told El Fuerte to draw cards in this game?"

"Cards, sir?"

"The death of Juan Amador is my affair. If El Fuerte wants to bust into this mess of trouble, looks like he ought to see me first!"

"I must explain to you, sir," said del Pino with dignity, "that for El Fuerte to see lawlessness is like for a fighting bull to see the red cape. The men who have killed your vaquero have done a lawless thing. El Fuerte is a great enemy of lawlessness, wherever lawlessness is to be met. He stamps it out like an antelope desecrating a rattlesnake. *Que hombre*! What a man!"

It seemed to Tom Cloud that he was being kidded, and his anger rose. "Look here, you," he said flatly. "I don't know where El Fuerte's gone, or who he has with him—"

"He has two of the greatest fighting men in Mexico with him," del Pino said meaningfully.

"I don't care if he has two of the greatest Mexican armies with him," Cloud said. "If he goes to raising hell up and down my lease he'll find himself run off the place by the scruff of the neck, by God!"

Del Pino looked unspeakably shocked. "You don't know what you're saying, *señor*, sir. El Fuerte is your friend!"

A sudden suspicion struck Tom Cloud. "Who is this El Fuerte?" he demanded. "Why is he here?"

Del Pino leaned forward with a hypnotic intensity. "El Fuerte," be said, "is the most extraordinary man who ever honored Baja. First of all, he is the greatest of the—how shall I translate—of the free rancheros?"

"And what the devil is a free ranchero?"

"A free ranchero," del Pino explained mystifyingly, "is a ranchero who is a ranchero wherever he is; he is not tied down to any one place—at least not for a very long time. Therefore he is a free ranchero."

"Oh," said Cloud.

"But he is much more than that," del Pino hurried on. "Above all, he is a great leader of men. It was a sad day for Mexico when Pancho Villa usurped the army that should have been El Fuerte's. But I tell you, sir, times will change. You will live to see the day when a man who is not a friend of El Fuerte is not anything in this country."

"And why," said Cloud ironically, "is this great man here?"

"Do not suppose, sir," said del Pino darkly, "that he is here because of that little misunderstanding in Sonora."

"So," said Cloud, "he was run out of Sonora?"

"I must make you understand, sir," said del Pino, "that El Fuerte is not run out of places. As a free ranchero—"

"What's he doing here?" Cloud demanded bluntly.

For a moment del Pino appeared confused. He hid his confusion behind another draught from the tequila bottle. "I will tell you the truth, sir," he said at last with an air of great frankness. Sorrow came into his terrier-like face, and he spread his hands with great deprecation. "El Fuerte," he said in a lugubrious hollow voice—"he is following the quail."

"Following the quail? Which quail?"

"I see you do not understand about quail. It seems, sir, that quail live by the eating of certain seeds. In

49

certain seasons they eat one kind of seed, in other seasons another, and in different places different seeds. This has a great effect upon their flavor. Now in Chihuahua—" Here del Pino went into a lengthy dissertation on what quail eat in Chihuahua. Never having interested himself in seeds of no importance as cattle fodder, Cloud did not get much out of this. "Me, I know nothing about quail," del Pino finished his dissertation. "But El Fuerte is different. He is a great authority on quail seeds. *Que hombre!*"

Cloud was staring at del Pino again, a solitaire card held suspended. "Great authority on quail seeds," he repeated blankly. He had never heard such nonsense in all his born days. He could hardly believe that he had heard correctly what del Pino said.

Suddenly the answer occurred to him—the only explanation possible to Tom Cloud's code of thought. The man who called himself del Pino was stark, raving mad.

When Cloud had decided this he felt better. The country in which he held his lease was only a few hundred miles from his native Arizona; yet sometimes the people about him gave him a sense of being lost in a new world of strange, mad conceptions. Sometimes this almost became too much for him. He was happy now to escape through the opinion that he was dealing with a lunatic.

Having decided this, Cloud dropped del Pino from his mind as effortlessly as he would have dropped a saddle. He turned another card, played the ace, deuce, trey of clubs. Deluded men were one of the many things that had no bearing upon Tom Cloud's relentlessly vigorous life.

"Perhaps it seems strange to you," del Pino was saying, "that a man of El Fuerte's great—what shall I say?—power. That a man of El Fuerte's great power should follow quail seeds all over the map of Mexico. Sir, I will be frank with you. Sometimes it seems strange to me. As secretary of El Fuerte, I have not been without my trials. If he had listened to me—" He raised eloquent arms toward the rafters, and solaced himself by communion with the tequila bottle.

Cloud played the jack of hearts, noted with an ironic eye the falling level of the tequila, and reached for the bottle. "*Salud!*" he said, barely touching the bottle to his lips; then set the bottle on the floor beside the high-spurred heel of his boot, out of del Pino's reach.

A mildly hurt look appeared in del Pino's eyes, but his remarkable flow of English words rushed ahead as if he had not noticed. "Sir," he said, "this following of the quail seeds has been the cross of my life. And other things, too. Once I remember El Fuerte was entering the important town of Ojo Caliente. You know the strategic importance of Ojo Caliente?"

"Sure," Cloud lied. He had never heard of it.

"It was when El Fuerte was a commander of artillery," del Pino amplified. "Two hundred men would have risen in that town at his word, each with his own horse and saddle. He could have had a regiment of cavalry, right there and then. And El Fuerte is a great leader of cavalry. *Que hombre,* with the cavalry! I ride ahead and fix it with the *alcalde* of that town, for a grand victorious entry, with processions. Then when all is prepared, I ride ahead with El Fuerte's guns—he had four field guns then, with caissons too—I go ahead to see that there is a proper receiving of El Fuerte, and

51

enough cheering. Everything is prepared for El Fuerte to appear, in the eyes of all that town, and be received in state at the house of the *alcalde*. What happens? Sir, I weep! El Fuerte does not show up!"

"He didn't?" said Tom Cloud politely.

"Sir, you will not believe me. El Fuerte reaches the edge of that town; and all is ready. But just then he sees a pretty peon girl leaning over a gate. He turns aside!"

"You don't mean to tell me," Cloud simulated concern.

"I did not find him," said del Pino, "until noon the next day. And of course then it was too late."

He looked at Tom Cloud so sorrowfully that Cloud made a half motion toward the tequila bottle; but thought better of it, and went on with his solitaire.

"That was not the only time," said del Pino. "There was the time when I arranged the parley with the four generals of Tres Rios. Sir, it was a turning point. I swear to you, he could have had Mexico then! I arrange this parley. All is prepared. But what happens?"

"El Fuerte didn't show up," said Tom Cloud.

"You are a reader of minds. I found out afterward—"

The urgent, nervous voice of del Pino ran on and on. He was giving Cloud other examples of the sufferings he had been through while with El Fuerte. Had he known it, Cloud was listening to an Odyssey—such an extraordinary series of events in the life of a man as perhaps he would never hear again. But Cloud could only think about Kathleen, and wonder where money was coming from. Del Pino's many-colored tale drifted unheard into the lamplight and cigarette smoke.

"Ay," he heard del Pino say at last, "I have talked a

long time."

Tom Cloud glanced at his tin clock; it was nearly half past one. "Fairly long," he agreed moderately.

"I think sometimes I am getting old," said del Pino wistfully. "Certainly it is very cold. But I tell you this, *señor*—sir: if there is anything you wish to know about what is what in this country, ask me—maybe I will know."

"Which pile is the jack of spades under?" Cloud asked.

"Under the third pile from the left, *señor*."

Cloud relented, and passed del Pino the tequila bottle. "Where did you learn all this language?" he demanded.

"A border man who does not have two countries has no countries at all."

"You're not talking border American."

"Me," said del Pino proudly, "I have read more than four hundred books."

"That explains it, all right!"

Del Pino swigged profoundly and set the bottle down. "Mr. Cloud, I bid you good night."

"You'll find the bunkhouse right over there," Cloud said. "But blankets—"

"I always carry a blanket with me," del Pino said with dignity. He left Cloud still playing solitaire, and worrying about the inexplicable interference of El Fuerte.

For what form El Fuerte's entrance into the situation might take, or what might be its motive, Cloud could not even imagine.

CHAPTER 8

THE TALL INDIAN BRAVO AND THE RIDER WHOM
Cloud had not recognized drew abreast of El Fuerte as
he pulled up upon a high moonlit point, many miles
from the Valley of the Witch. The night was very quiet,
now that the hoofs of their own ponies were still; and
for a little while the three sat silent, studying the
shallow little valley that lay below.

"So this is it," El Fuerte said. "I thought you said it
was a long way."

Bravo grunted. "You ride like a crazy man."

The ponies of all three were drenched with sweat;
they stood blowing, so that Bravo's chaps made a faint
flapping noise with the heave of his animal's ribs. El
Fuerte rode brutally hard, with the disregard of
horseflesh of a man who has always found the supply of
range ponies unfailing. He had a single cherished
mount, a beautiful palomino mare which he pampered
unspeakably, but all other horses which fell into his
hands found themselves in trouble. El Fuerte liked to
ride horses that were like terrified wild animals, and his
ponies were customarily worn out and traded off long
before they knew their business.

Carlos—this was the name of the third horseman—
thought that they had come to the wrong place. "This
pass leads no place! We've wasted our time."

"Del Pino is perfectly certain this is right."

"What does del Pino know about finding lost ways
through the hills?" They spoke in loose, slurring
Spanish that was set all through with words from more

54

than one obscure Indian dialect.

"He's not supposed to know about hills," said El Fuerte. "*You* are supposed to know about hills. Del Pino is only supposed to find out what the people know. And he does it most wonderful."

"If they come this way, it means there's much more to this than we thought," Carlos said. He was a man with a lithe young body and a strangely old face; even in the moonlight that face was a humorously wicked anomaly. "For look," he insisted, "we already know how much Flying K beef they take away to the south—jerky for all the little towns. But they can't cut back to the south, coming this way. That means they ship across the gulf to the mainland—maybe by lugger from Bahia Coyote. They're plucking him like a hen, *por Dios!*"

"The American is a fool," said Bravo.

"You forget the country's strange to him," El Fuerte argued mildly. "What could even I do in his place?"

"Plenty," said Bravo shortly.

"But look! His range runs kilos in all directions. On every side of him are all these little nobodies, that think his stuff is their own."

"Maybe it should be," grunted Carlos.

"His vaqueros are worthless and indifferent," El Fuerte defended Cloud. "The only big cattlemen near him are Old Beard and this Miguel Solano. Solano doesn't like the Americans. Old Beard has seen gringos come and go too many times; he doesn't care. The Judge of the Plains is a little fool—somebody's nephew by marriage. He's getting a profit out of this thievery himself, we'll pretty soon find out. What can the American do? He's helpless."

They were silent, not wishing to seem to argue with him; but their silence obviously reserved their own opinions.

"Del Pino was right, Carlos," Bravo said after a long time; "there's cattle coming."

"If he didn't keep weaning calves a man might be able to hear something," Carlos grumbled. "The hills are full of wet cows bawling."

"Something's bawling besides wet cows."

They were silent again, a long time. "I see them now," Bravo said at last. Far off down the little valley had appeared a dark irregularity in the moonlight, so distant that it did not yet seem to move.

"I've been watching them for ten minutes," said El Fuerte. He lied, and they knew he lied, but that was just the sort of thing that bound them to him. They idolized his exuberant braggadocio, the supreme audacity with which he carried all situations before him.

"It's a little bunch of twenty," Bravo sneered. "Yah! What a cheap business! I could empty his whole range in two nights."

"There are better ways to do business than that," said El Fuerte. "How many riders?"

"Four," said Carlos tentatively.

"Six," said Bravo.

El Fuerte was disappointed. "I've brought too many men," he said. "Either one of you could have handled this alone, *mi capitanes*." When he was holding them roughly in check, as he was tonight, he called them his *capitanes*, in which rank they had indeed served under him; it was only when he was well pleased with them that he called them *mozos* and cursed them lovingly.

"If we kill no riders," Carlos complained, "we'll get

nothing out of this at all—not even a gun or a—belt or a pocket knife."

"All that comes later. *Cristo!* You better remember what I said! Hit the horses only. You hit one of those men and I have your livers out!"

"I suppose," Carlos said uncertainly, "you have some reason; but—"

"*Perdido!* Never ask me if I have a reason!"

"My sights are no good in this light," Bravo mourned. "I suppose if a horse jumps forward when I shoot it, and I hit a man in the knee—"

"I promise you," said El Fuerte with sweetly gentle ferocity, "I'll have your liver out!"

The little herd came on slowly; the heavy force of riders worked them so quietly that the cattle hardly knew that they were no longer on the graze. Far out in front, continually stopping to wait, the point rider led the way. The other five riders pressed the stock gently, not so much forcing them to move as simply preventing them from moving any way but one.

The shuffle of hoofs and the click of horns was distinctly audible now, though the chief sound was the occasional bawl of some bothered steer. Now and then one of the rustlers slapped his chaps with his romal, to turn some animal which left the bunch.

"The point is too far ahead," El Fuerte said. "Carlos, you move up the valley a little way; get the horse of the point rider when Bravo and I open up on the others. As soon as you've fired, charge down on the cattle; stampede them right back over the riders. Bravo, wait until I fire. Then take the first man on each side. I'll handle the others. And I want to find out that you've hit your horses square in the eye—none of this shooting at

57

the head and hitting the neck!"

"Which eye?" Bravo growled.

"Do we follow," Carlos asked, "if some get away?"

El Fuerte turned on him slowly, with a great show of disgust. "Well, *Jesu—Cristo*! No! Just quietly shoot yourselves, before I find out!"

For another ten minutes they watched in silence the slow advance of the herd. Bravo drew his rifle from its saddle boot and gently eased a shell into the chamber. El Fuerte's horse whinnied, winding the rustlers' saddle stock; but the hills were full of loose ponies and it made no difference.

"Let's get off the skyline," El Fuerte ordered. "Carlos, take your post ahead."

Carlos moved away, the feet of his unshod pony quiet on the steeply sloping ground. El Fuerte and Bravo moved side by side ten yards down the hill, and came to rest again. El Fuerte eased himself to the ground, and with a braided hair rope tied his horse to a manzanita; Bravo followed suit. They attempted no other concealment.

Slowly, with what seemed an infinite deliberation, the herd came into the flats below them. Just before it came opposite there was a delay as some of the bunch faced about and stood staring stupidly, as if thinking of breaking back. The rustlers sat their horses silently for some minutes, waiting for the cattle to move on of their own accord. At last one of them slapped his chaps with his romal, and chanted a guttural "Hiyuh, hiyuh!" Dribbling along loosely, the little herd drew abreast.

El Fuerte waited until he judged that the point rider was opposite the position Carlos had taken; then, at last, his rifle came up, steadied for a long moment.

Nobody could have realized how quiet the night had been, how relatively still the movement of the cattle, until El Fuerte's shot smashed out. It seemed to blast the night wide open, re-echoing from the rocky hillsides with the irregular cacophonies of a five-gallon can falling down stairs. Below, the tail rider's horse went to its knees as if its front legs had been struck from under it; it seemed to hesitate there for a long instant before it fell sideways.

Instantly El Fuerte's rifle barrel swung, and he fired again; then, after an instant, a third time, this time following a swift-moving mark. A running horse somersaulted. One of the wing riders fired a return shot—they saw it flash against the dark background of the herd; then his horse, too, went down, a sliding mass.

They heard an exchange of shots from Carlos' position, then a quick staccato from his six-gun as he sprang into the saddle and charged down the slope. There were shouts and the whistling snorts of cattle; the shuffling of hoofs, which had been struck silent for an instant, suddenly began again, rising swiftly to a ground-shaking thunder as the cattle stampeded. El Fuerte turned, jerked savagely at the head of his plunging horse, and managed to mount.

"Carlos got the point horse," Bravo said.

But El Fuerte was swearing most magnificently. "We lost one!" he bellowed.

"Six horses are down," Bravo assured him.

"There was a seventh," said El Fuerte—"far in the rear."

"I didn't see him."

"I'm certain he was there."

CHAPTER 9

TOM CLOUD, HAVING WATCHED THE DOOR CLOSE UPON the little anomalous figure of del Pino, turned back to his solitaire game, and played it out without success. He rose, stretched, but found that he could not yawn, for there was in him no trace of sleep. He blew out the light, and in the dark Kathleen was immediately before his eyes, an insistent vision. Doggedly he rolled himself in his blankets; and eventually his saddle-tired muscles drained the blood from his head, and he partly slept.

Even as he lay more than half asleep, that night continued to be a strange night. He heard the coyote song strike up again at half past two, and continue for half an hour. Dozing, he waited for the bawling of the wet cows to begin, sounding up the dawn.

Then presently Cloud sat up in his bed, aware that he had been listening for some minutes to the muffled sound of horses approaching at a walk. He could not have described how it was he could tell the hoof beats of a ridden horse from the shuffling movement of cattle at a quarter mile, but when he had listened for a minute or two he knew that at least three, perhaps five ridden ponies were approaching from up-valley. Because the road from La Partida cut in down-valley, he knew that these could not be bringing his returning vaqueros. He swung to his feet, dressed, and belted on his gun.

Thus he was waiting at the corrals when El Fuerte rode in, his men trailing behind him in the last weak light of the slinking moon. Cloud, having made sure who it was, stepped out from the shadow of the pines and strolled toward the leader.

60

"Buenos dias, señor," Cloud said. "You seem to have had quite a ride."

Guadalupe Francisco Contreras y Canedo, better known as El Fuerte, stretched luxuriously in his saddle. "It was a very pretty ride," he agreed, letting a suggestion of a chuckle come into his throat. "A very fine ride. In more ways than one."

"Step down," Cloud said. "Step down and come in."

Preceding El Fuerte into the cabin, Tom Cloud relighted the kerosene lamp. Behind him El Fuerte lounged into the doorway and there paused, leaning against the jamb. For the first time, in decent light, Cloud saw El Fuerte dressed as a rider—a big and mightily robust man in soft leather chaps deep-scarred by the brush, broad sombrero with carved leather band, and leather cuffs eight inches deep. Even El Fuerte's vest was of leather, embroidered with carved leather traceries to represent a pattern of roses—brush-scarred, too, like the rest. He wore double gunbelts.

Although El Fuerte was no taller than Tom Cloud, his shoulders filled the doorway; in the yellow light of the lamp he seemed enormous. He no longer had the leanness of the young; he was thickening at the waist and a suggestion of heaviness was beginning to show about his muscular jowls. But Tom Cloud had never seen a man who looked so utterly inseparable from horseflesh as this man looked; and from the whole man radiated a sort of sleepy energy, unhurried, half somnolent, but somehow suggesting the latent possibility of remarkable explosions.

But it was the bland, deeply satisfied expression of El Fuerte's face which Tom Cloud was studying now. This man was dark as a saddle, though without the essential

61

underlying swarthiness which characterized Cloud's mestizos; he wore a mustache clipped short after the fashion set by Plutarco Calles, the uncrowned dictator of all Mexico, and under his mustache showed a flash of teeth as naturally strong and clean as the teeth of a badger. The shadow-dark eyes were no more than slits, faintly slanted, faintly smiling.

Regarding the face of El Fuerte in the lamplight, Cloud was reminded of a mountain lion which has fed well upon a kill. He remembered now the words of del Pino, which a few hours ago he had set aside as voiced by a man out of his mind: "El Fuerte will have news for you in the morning." He glanced past El Fuerte at the vague silhouettes of the two other riders now dismounting, and suspicion struck into him, hard and sharp.

"Let me ask one thing," Cloud said slowly. "What is it those riders of yours are carrying?"

The tall, full-bodied man who called himself El Fuerte allowed himself a slow grin beneath the mustache that looked like the mustache of the dictator. "*Ay, que lastima!*" he said. "What a pity! Those are empty saddles."

An electric shock went through Cloud. "You mean—"

"Ah no, my frand," El Fuerte said reassuringly. "We did not shoot the men. We shot the horses. The men ran home."

"What men?"

El Fuerte grinned again. "Not frands of yours. But tomorrow you better put those saddles on new horses, and send them to their owners with your compliments, I think."

"What are you talking about?"

"It will be a fine generous thing to do," El Fuerte explained, "but will cost you nothing; because they will have an anger, and they will turn the horses loose. The horses will then come back. A fine generous thing—and free."

It would have been apparent to anyone, as certainly it was apparent to El Fuerte, that Cloud did not follow this.

"You are wondering why I have done this thing, Mister," El Fuerte said. "I am a great enemy of lawlessness. I could not bear to see the owners of these saddles doing the lawless thing that they did. You see, Mister, they were borrowing your cattle. Who knows when they would pay them back?"

Tom Cloud stared at his visitor for a long moment. "I guess we'd better have breakfast," he said at last.

El Fuerte looked faintly disappointed; and Cloud, with an unaccustomed flash of hospitality, correctly read the disappointment. He grinned and set the tequila bottle on the table. El Fuerte waited, ceremoniously, until Cloud had rattled down a couple of tin cups beside the bottle. Then he poured himself a substantial drink.

"To an end of lawlessness," El Fuerte toasted unctuously. "Such a bad thing!"

Deliberately, Tom Cloud turned and walked out to the lean-to; stirred about in the little adobe fireplace where they cooked, and set a frying pan to sizzling. Unhurrying, but with movements made efficient by many repetitions, he prepared hot shredded jerky, brown beans, coffee; and drained the last of a shipment of baking powder for biscuits. This took him all of twelve minutes.

When the vital, monotonous food of Baja smoked as pleasantly as it ever would, he slammed five enamelware plates onto the pine slab table, and said, "Chuck's up."

Deprecatingly, but with assurance, El Fuerte dished out three generous plates, and set them outside upon the doorstep. "*Bueno!*" he said to the open air. Silently the plates disappeared into what remained of the night.

Cloud watched this ironically. "Personally," he said, "I never would figure to pay a man for his work, if he wasn't a good enough man to eat with me."

El Fuerte's smile was so easy, so convincing, that it was as if an old man spoke gently, deftly, to a child. "There are changes to make, Mister," he said, "when you change from one country to another. Maybe I show you some of those changes sometime—no?"

Cloud shrugged, dished two more plates of jerky and beans, slid the depleted tequila bottle to El Fuerte. "*Quien sabe?*" he said without expression.

"*Quien sabe?*" El Fuerte murmured. For a little while they ate in silence—Cloud sparingly and without relish, El Fuerte with gusto.

"Now look here," said Cloud without prelude. "I want to know what happened tonight."

"It is like this," said El Fuerte. He allowed himself a small grin in retrospect, flashing the glint of teeth under the clipped mustache. "Yesterday you lost a man."

"Juan Amador," Cloud supplied; "the best foreman that ever forked a horse in Mexico."

"For a gringo," El Fuerte added casually.

"He worked for a gringo," Cloud admitted. "I suppose you people will always call me a gringo. But he worked like a man."

64

"*Bueno,*" said El Fuerte. "Today—yesterday, it is now—you found him dead."

"With a knife wound in his throat."

"Yes. Well, I went out to see what I could find out. I am sorry. I only found out a little. But still—I brought you empty saddles, my frand!"

"I want to know a little more about that, El Fuerte," Cloud said without expression.

"You do not wonder," El Fuerte said with mild disappointment, "how I knew Juan Amador was kill?"

Tom Cloud flared up at him, unexpectedly to himself. "How do I know how you people know what you know? You've got a grapevine telegraph that jumps over desert hills like wildfire. Maybe you do it with mirrors—I don't know."

"No mirrors. I have never been in Baja before—but I know this country, Mister."

For a moment Tom Cloud looked at El Fuerte hard and belligerently, seeing the big frame, the neatly clipped mustache, the slightly slanted, sleepy eyes; seeing what he could not understand; then he relaxed.

"Well—you knew it. And then—?"

El Fuerte shrugged, very slightly, and spoke as if in confidence. "Mister, am I child? These men I have with me—are they with me because they are childs? I sent two scouts over the hills—your hills. When they came back, they named to me a place. Tonight I went to that place. So, I found what I found."

"Just a minute," Cloud picked him up. "What do you mean, 'They named to you a place?' "

"It is not natural to the world," said El Fuerte, "that those who steal your cattle should rest, on a night when you, they think, will be at a wake for your dead man!"

65

"So you went to the most likely place for cattle stealing?"

"Ah, Mister, no! To the most *not* likely place! Are these people fools? Mister, these people were a hundred years old when you were born."

At first, Cloud could not swallow this. But—there were the empty saddles, brought in by this extraordinary man who called himself El Fuerte.

"Come on, come on," Cloud demanded frontally. "What happened then?"

"The word of Juan Amador's death—it came to me late. I swear to you, Mister, it did not come until I was eating my—night lonch. But so soon I heard, I dropped my knife and spoon. For I know this country, Mister, and I know what will happen then. I call for saddle and horse."

El Fuerte paused to fill his mouth full of beans, then went on briskly. "We go to the place we have think . . ."

Under pressure of his narrative the words of El Fuerte came raggedly, his English becoming somewhat skip-stop. But Tom Cloud, knowing the desert hills, and—above all—knowing action wherever it might break,—got the whole picture plain and clear.

He could see the thin clean moonlight on the brush, hear the half-hushed "Hiyuh, hiyuh!" of the vaqueros, and the shuffle of driven cattle as they straggled off through some crack in the hills. Then—the crack of guns, the weird whistling scream of a horse gone down; stampede of cattle, more blast and blaze of the short guns—and at the last the shadow-like figures of El Fuerte and his two men, looting the saddles from the cow-thief horses they had killed.

And, if any of El Fuerte's story seemed braggadocio.

or unlikely—there was that pile of saddles now outside Cloud's door, bringing all that story into the focus of near reality.

Cloud was silent for a full minute when El Fuerte was done. Then abruptly he demanded—"*Whose saddles did you get?*"

El Fuerte made a casual, even an airy gesture. "What does it matter? Have you any frands—but me?"

The sharp answer that offered itself to this evasion died in Cloud's throat. El Fuerte's implication was true; it had long seemed to him that every man's hand was against him here. It mattered very little whether or not Beard was right in saying that the people of the land were taking back their own. Certainly, Cloud knew, there were few about him, besides Beard and Solano, whom he could trust.

"Tomorrow, if you furnish new horses," El Fuerte said, "my men will take the saddles back where they belong. Not that it is a secret, Mister. I think we will find the saddles belong to—" Rapidly he tossed off half a dozen names, the names of small, not-too-distant neighbors whom Cloud had long suspected. They contributed nothing to Cloud's information.

The boss of the Flying K got up, coffee cup in hand, and stood looking out the door at the dark Valley of the Witch. Over the desert hills a faint light was showing; two or three cows were bawling far down the mile-long fence, and from up the valley answered the hopeful blat of half a dozen calves. Watching the light come over the round brown hills that were like the breasts of Indian women asleep, Cloud sipped his steaming coffee, and wondered where he got off.

He was checking over the story that this man called

El Fuerte had told him, no longer questioning its truth, but probing the meaning of this raid that had broken the back of a raid. He was asking himself what manner of man this might be, who stepped into another man's war without asking or being asked, yet had put these seven or eight saddles at his feet.

And now as the slow cold light came over the eastern hills a new thing came into Tom Cloud. Always he had had his roots deep in the grasslands, living close to the land, closer than the cattle themselves; and now it was as if a new strength flowed upward into him from this land in which he had struggled to sink his roots for two years in vain. Perhaps he could not yet read this land and its people; but it seemed to him now that the land itself had given him a tool for its own cleavage.

He turned from the cold light of dawn once more to the light of kerosene. El Fuerte was watching him, perhaps a little narrowly.

"Contreras," Tom Cloud said, "I need a new cow boss."

"*Si*, Mister?"

"I understand you are looking for cattle land—or an interest in cattle land."

"*Verdad*, Mister."

"Make me a proposition."

El Fuerte drank the rest of his coffee, and it took him perhaps fifteen seconds, but no more. It may be that the measure of this man is to be found in this: that all his life he had been taught to barter and trade, cautiously and without hurry, though it took all day; but now he did not try to dicker with this tall Arizonan, but made at once an offer that was first and last.

"I want two things here," he said. "First, I want one-half

the increase of the cattle, for not less than two years."

"Way things are going," Cloud grunted, "there ain't any increase."

"Me, I take care of that."

"And the other thing?"

"Fire these worthless men you have. Out of your pocket, hire men that I will bring you. At half again the wages."

"The same wages," Cloud bargained.

"*Bueno,* then."

"Done," said Cloud.

"Let us make a writing."

As he set his hand to the agreement, Cloud knew that he might be riding over dangerous ground. But the spirit of war and power that had come into him with the early light was strengthening now as he took into his hand this new tool with which to fight the stubborn land. Suddenly, as never before, he was glad that he had crossed the border into this country of strangers; as if, after all, his destiny might lie here—a war—like destiny though it might be.

CHAPTER 10

CONTRERAS Y CANEDO, CALLED EL FUERTE, MOVED IN upon Tom Cloud's camp late that afternoon. And here, for Tom Cloud, began new surprises.

In the first place, El Fuerte's removal into the Flying K camp required no less than six pack horses—most of which Cloud recognized as Flying K horses, evidently caught up on the range by El Fuerte's own ropers. And those horses were not led under pack as a mere form; they were loaded high and wide, loaded until they

69

shuffled and stumbled, raising a dust that could be seen for four miles.

Obsequiously and gently, but with his usual gay assurance, El Fuerte moved Cloud's stray effects entirely out of the smaller adobe's second room, installing himself therein. Yet that decent-sized second room seemed no more than a pigeon-hole by the time El Fuerte's pack animals were unloaded.

Prominent in El Fuerte's furnishings, and very interesting to Cloud, were twenty or thirty small wooden cases labeled "CANNED TOMATOES! *¡Que No Agarre!* DO NOT TOUCH!"

"What in all hell—" Cloud protested.

"Mister," said El Fuerte expansively, "I would not fool you. I would not fool you for anything in the world! Those are not the canned tomatoes. Those, they are a few necessary shells."

"Shells?"

"For different size gun," El Fuerte explained.

"What the devil do we want with forty different sizes of ca'tridge?"

"We have not yet unloaded the other three *caballos*," El Fuerte pointed out. "Anyway, suppose a man—he finds a gun. What good if he cannot find shells?"

From the pack horses now came a singularly large and varied collection of guns; and though many of these were hunting weapons, Cloud counted no less than fifteen heavy caliber rifles of various makes. A number of long boxes carried in with care might have contained further rifles for all Cloud knew.

"You sure go in for weapons," Cloud said drily.

"Some are trophies," El Fuerte explained, "some are the souvenir, and some are my hunting guns. Those others I just happen to have with me; I did not know what to do with them. You see, a friend gives them to me to keep for him."

"Seems like more guns than anybody could find any use for."

El Fuerte sighed. "In times like this, it never hurts any man to know where there is a few good guns. Mister, in this world things are very uncertain."

Cloud was thinking of Beard's hint—that there is such a thing as a tool that will turn in a man's hand. He admitted to himself that he knew less than nothing about El Fuerte; even that Beard might have been right that he was taking some obscure sort of long chance in bringing El Fuerte into his brand. But as he turned away he grinned. He was amused by El Fuerte's arsenal; very likely, he supposed, El Fuerte had taken some kind of part in the North Mexican revolution of four years before, and still clung to some of the tools of the trade from which he had been driven. He did not believe then that any situation could arise—at least not here in his own camp—in which he would not be able to control the men about him. Tom Cloud was a man who believed in himself.

Not all of El Fuerte's belongings consisted of the materials of war. Among the possessions which El Fuerte was moving in were other items varied and unusual. Two long-legged game chickens appeared in small hampers woven of sticks and rawhide. There was a case of whisky whose labels alleged it to be American, though why American Cloud could not conceive. There was a small live pig, and a light *metate* for grinding corn by hand, and a wash boiler evidently used for making huge quantities of coffee. Most of these possessions, except the live pig and the fighting cocks, were stacked neatly in El Fuerte's room, and covered over with travel-worn but finely woven old ponchos of all the colors in the rainbow, and two besides.

While this was being done, Cloud had a chance to get a better look at El Fuerte's followers than he had had before. The most striking of these was the tall Indian called Bravo. Except for a broad belt elaborately embroidered in red and gold thread, this rider was dressed like any border cowboy. But the lean face of the man, with its high bony nose, and thin-lipped mouth loosely set in a broad straight line, was made striking by its effect of contemptuous cruelty; and the small unresting eyes were somehow snake-like, rather than human.

The other was a little bow-legged man whose prematurely seamed countenance showed a self-sufficient sense of humor and a watchful wit. This was the man named Carlos; his history Cloud could not even guess.

"These are good men," said El Fuerte. "One of the first things we do, Mister—I urge this very much—we get rid of these riders you have. Mister, they are no good. But we can hire these men of mine instead. These men can get more work out of a horse than any men in Mexico. They will work the cattle twice better, I promise you. Sometimes maybe they will be useful in other ways."

Thinking of the quick information that El Fuerte had somehow obtained in the case of Juan Amador's death, Cloud thought that he knew at least a part of what that last suggestion might mean. Almost exultantly, he felt that he was getting into a position to get somewhere at last.

72

Del Pino appeared last of all, an hour behind the pack train that had brought El Fuerte's singularly assorted possessions. He rode a little black saddle mule, and was leading a beautiful golden palomino mare with pure silver mane and tail.

Ahead of him, del Pino was pushing one more pack animal—a burro which appeared to be loaded with a couple of long water kegs, covered with blankets patterned in black and white.

"You sure have a mighty complete outfit, El Fuerte," Cloud commented. "Even carrying your own water?"

El Fuerte was silent for a moment. "You see that mare?" he said finally with expansive pride. "That is the finest she-mare in all Mexico. Now there is this about palominos: they do not know how to eat."

"Eat?" Cloud repeated.

"In the hills they starve," El Fuerte explained what he meant. "But this mare I have made to know how to rustle for herself in the rocks."

"Broke to eat, is she?"

"Yes, Mister," said El Fuerte with more than a blow of pride. "Me—I teached her!"

When del Pino had turned the palomino mare into Bravo's hands he seemed for a moment to hesitate. Then, with ostentatious indifference, he led the burro behind the house. Cloud experienced a sudden clutch of curiosity. He waited two minutes, then strolled casually to the back of the house. Del Pino had cast off the ropes which packed the burro.

"Those are the funniest shaped liquor kegs I ever saw," Cloud commented.

For a moment a faint confusion seemed to be suggested by the immobility of del Pino's face. He

73

fiddled pointlessly with the pack saddle, visibly wishing that Cloud would go away and let him unpack alone. "*Señor*, sir," he said, "these are not whisky kegs."

"Then what in all hell are they?"

"These are—the drums."

"Drums? Come off!"

Del Pino threw back the black and white blankets and showed him. Cloud saw a pair of three-foot wooden tubes a foot and a half in diameter, black with age, and covered all over with a scratched-on design. They had heads of rawhide.

"Well, I'll be—" Cloud began.

"Sometimes," del Pino mumbled, "it is not possible to know always what will be useful, maybe."

Tom Cloud gave it up and went to the corral side of the house again. Bravo was just finishing the saddling of the palomino mare, with El Fuerte's rig; El Fuerte's heavily silvered black saddle and elaborate bridle made the mare the most barbarically magnificent mount Tom Cloud had ever seen in the southwest. El Fuerte swung leisurely into the saddle and the mare became very still and watchful, head high.

"I have one little ride to do, Mister," El Fuerte said. "I will see you pretty soon."

"We better figure to eat pretty quick."

"*Bueno*." El Fuerte called out some order to Bravo in a language that was neither English nor Spanish, but something Cloud did not understand; then turned his horse and went down-valley at a quick singlefoot.

Immediately El Fuerte's four men swung aboard the horses which they had not unsaddled, and turned up-valley.

Suddenly it was borne in upon Cloud that nothing

74

these people did was clear to him. On a sudden impatient impulse he shouted after them. "Where the devil you going?"

Del Pino wheeled his black mule courteously. "We look at the country," he said with a blank face. "We look at the country and the cattle, so that tomorrow's work will go more quick." They put their animals into a run, sloping quickly out of earshot.

Cloud went and stood in the door of the adobe, listening to the bawling of the weanlings and thinking about starting a fire for supper. But his eyes were on the elegantly mounted figure of El Fuerte, moving off down-valley. He was about to turn inside when he saw in the clear twilight that El Fuerte had paused at the quarter mile to speak to a rider who came swiftly up the valley. He saw them exchange a word or two briefly from the saddle, then El Fuerte proceeded down-valley, and the other came on.

Suddenly Tom Cloud forgot about supper. Old Beard was coming in on a tired horse at a shambling lope.

CHAPTER 11

OLD BEARD RODE LIKE A CENTAUR, BUT AS HE EASED down from the saddle in front of Tom Cloud's door a certain stiffness of the joints was noticeable; after all he was very old. By the last of the failing light Tom Cloud saw that the pale nondescriptly green eyes for once did not give their usual effect of great peace. Old Beard looked a little worried, a little sour.

"Come on in," Cloud invited. "Pretty soon now we're going to eat."

75

Old Beard stood for half a minute looking about him, his hand still on the horn of his saddle, then he pulled his pipe out of his mustache. "Well, I see he's already moved in on you," he said wearily.

"Just this afternoon!"

Beard stood motionless a moment more, staring vaguely up the valley, after the fashion of the old; then let go the saddle and walked slowly and stiffly into the house.

Cloud lighted the kerosene lamp. "Set down," he suggested, and Beard obeyed.

"In a way," Beard said, "it seems like I've come too late."

"What do you mean by that?"

"Cloud," said Old Beard, "what is it you're trying to do here?"

"Run cattle," Cloud said promptly.

"Yep. I seen you was running cattle. But I'm asking you something different now. I'm asking you straight— is that all you're aiming at?"

"You know damn well that's all I'm aiming at," Cloud said impatiently. "Beard, I want to know what you mean by that question."

"Well, I'll tell you," Beard said with reluctance. "It kind of seems to some of us that you're a little different organized here than what's necessary for just running stock."

Cloud grinned sardonically on one side of his face. "A little too much on the warrior side to suit you, huh?"

Beard looked uncomfortable; he knew well enough that he was upon uneasy ground. "There's people that kind of feel that there wasn't hardly any call to—"

"You know why I got El Fuerte in here," Cloud told him. "I came down here for the long pull; I paid for my range rights and I paid for my cattle; I paid my way in everything. I never asked any odds from you or Solano or anybody else. All I've asked of anybody was what was due and coming to me."

Slowly Beard refilled and lighted his pipe. "But your cattle ain't increasing," he said. "And so you got sore."

"Plenty," Cloud grunted. "And I'm not lying down, either."

"Son," said Old Beard, "ten years is a very short time to learn about running cattle in Baja. You can't hurry things down here, my boy, like you can the other side of the line."

"I admit it's panned out that I don't know how to run cattle down here," Cloud said harshly. "But I aim to get men in here that do know how."

"So you rung in El Fuerte," Beard said.

"I'm trying El Fuerte. If he don't work, I'll get somebody else—and keep trying, until I'm beat and broke."

"Way things are," Old Beard said through a concealing screen of smoke, "I don't know if your outfit or any outfit can last through a good siege of El Fuerte—let alone trying on any others later."

Cloud opened his mouth to reply sharply, but closed it again and considered. In the silence the bellowing of the weanlings and their unhappy cows bore down heavily, seeming to fill the valley with mournful sound. "Yesterday," Cloud said, "I came to you and asked your advice about El Fuerte. Seemed like you didn't want to give me any advice. That's all right. That's up to you. But—"

"Maybe I kept my mouth shut a little too hasty," Beard admitted; and there was another silence.

"Beard," Cloud stated, "there's something on your mind."

The old man shifted stiffly, leaned back against the wall and crossed his knees. "Did it seem to you, maybe," he said at last, "that this El Fuerte was a little bit over-anxious to make this hook-up with you?"

"No," said Cloud.

"So anxious even," Beard elaborated, "that he took it into his own hands to come onto your lease, with his own riders, and start working for you, and riding guard on your stock—before you and him even come to terms?"

Cloud made an impatient gesture. Repeatedly it annoyed him that Old Beard—like El Fuerte himself—seemed to command some unknown grapevine telegraph system.

"Well?" he demanded sharply.

"There's all ways a man has to look at a thing," Beard said. "Yesterday we was speaking of Solano—the biggest Mexican cattleman in all this part of Baja. Maybe, you gathered that I thought it was kind of bad medicine to go rooting up unpleasantness with Solano—the squarest shooting neighbor you got."

"Well?"

Old Beard leaned forward to tap Cloud's knee with the bowl of his pipe. "Cloud," he said, "turn back! You can clear your skirts of this thing, and square yourself with Solano, even yet. With me to help you. But youngster, turn back! There's more war than you're looking for in this thing."

"I'm not looking for any war," Cloud said dryly; "but I'm not refusing any either. If I've got to fight for my rights, I'm ready."

Old Beard leaned back. "If you want to go warring against Solano, I can't stop you," he said, as shortly as Cloud had ever heard him speak. "But the country won't hold the two of you—not if you stick with this El Fuerte after what's happened."

"If I haven't got the right to—" Cloud stopped suddenly, a new suspicion as to Beard's meaning entering his mind. "Maybe," he said slowly, "I don't know what you're talking about, Beard."

"I'm speaking of Jose Solano. He was a wild foolish kid, hard to control. But he was Solano's son. A man's son is his son."

Cloud jerked suddenly alert. "Was?" he repeated.

"You mean to set there and tell me you don't know what's busted?" Beard said, nonplussed. For a moment more the bellowing of the cattle bore down dull and heavy, wave upon wave of dismal echoless sound. "Jose Solano," Beard said at last, "rode in to La Partida last night shot through the body, half dead in the saddle; this morning he died."

Tom Cloud absorbed the shock of this news not all at once, but slowly. The unexpectedness of this country, the violence of its uncertainties, had never played about him more hostilely, more threateningly than now. More than ever he felt himself a man fighting blindly in a dust cloud against elusive but deadly shadows. Through the haze of smoke that Beard kept pouring out in front of him he heard the old man say, "Now will you turn back?"

For a moment more Cloud was silent, and there were many pictures in his mind. He saw again the face of Juan Amador who was dead, and the smiling face of El

79

Fuerte, and he heard the easy, delicately ironical tones of John Boyce. But mostly now he saw again the eyes of Kathleen, as she had looked at him with an unspeakable appeal.

Suddenly his temper thrust up like the frosted edge of a blade. "Hell, no! If they want trouble they can have trouble. Now, and all the time, from here out!"

"Solano—"

"Damn Solano! He never raised a hand to help me in his life. And neither did you, by God! Smoke that over."

For a moment Old Beard sat as if he had been struck; then he came to his feet with a movement astonishingly agile. Behind the fog of smoke the old eyes took on a queer luminous blaze.

"You damned young fool, if you aim to—"

His voice stopped, checked by a curious thing. Across the earthen floor spun a small object that turned out to be a black, twisted cigarette; it made a little fiery pinwheel through the shadows as it slid twirling, then stopped against a table leg and smoked. In the rear doorway behind Tom Cloud stood El Fuerte, leaning relaxed, his thumbs hooked in his broad belt. He was smiling faintly, and his eyes were sleepy; but Cloud had a quick eerie sense that El Fuerte had been just outside that door for a long time.

For what seemed minutes the eyes of Old Beard and the sleepy smiling eyes of El Fuerte met and held; and it was Old Beard who turned away.

Beard flicked a quick glance through the other door. There was something in that jerk of the old man's eyes that made Cloud's eyes follow; and now he saw that fifteen paces away, leaning against the trunk of one of the giant trees, the man Carlos stood, a rifle dangling

80

casually in the crook of his arm. A peculiarly wicked gleam of humor showed in Carlos' seamed face; but what was more noticeable to Cloud was the fact that in spite of his unobtrusive distance the rifle clearly commanded the segment of the room in which Beard stood. Somehow Cloud knew at once that Bravo was somewhere in the rear, just as casually commanding a different segment of the room from a little way off. For a moment it gave Cloud a queer eerie sensation to see how El Fuerte's followers—apparently without need of prearrangement or command—covered their captain foresightedly at the first sign of clash. Cloud wondered if sometime he would find himself under the eyes of those inconspicuous, watching rifles.

"I'll be moving on," said Old Beard tonelessly. He moved deliberately, leisurely toward the door.

When he was gone El Fuerte picked up the black twisted cigarette which he had spun across the floor and stuck it between his good teeth—all of which were now showing in the most merrily triumphant grin that Cloud had ever seen.

Cloud stood motionless until the slogging beat of hoofs died away, as Old Beard moved off, down the valley. Then he swung about abruptly to face El Fuerte, "Why the devil didn't you tell me that you and your people killed Solano's son?"

El Fuerte sat down on the table, took the black twisted cigarette from between his teeth and studied the upward curl of its smoke until his face had subsided into an expression of sincere sobriety. "By heaven, Mister," he said, "I swear I tell you the truth. I do not know it myself until this noon."

"Until this noon," Cloud echoed, a curious note of

strain going through his voice. "What's the matter with you, man? Isn't a killing here on my own land worth mentioning?"

El Fuerte looked him in the eyes with an appearance of ingenuous frankness. "This is an unfortunate thing," he said, "but it is not perfectly unusual, Mister. Me, I have learned this—if a man, or a man's son, he rides on a night raid with cow thieves, Mister, he is taking a fearful chance."

"Which of you killed him?" Cloud demanded flatly.

"That I do not know. Me, I did not even know a man was hit."

"Do you realize that there'll be all hell to pay for this?"

"Mister, I do not see why."

"You don't, huh? With Solano the biggest Mexican cattleman in—"

"See what he must prove," said El Fuerte reasonably. "First he must get the other cow thieves to swear that last night they are stealing beef and somebody is shooting at them. But who? Then he must prove that his son is also stealing beef, or else why is he shot? Mister, I do not even know myself that this is what happen."

"You know hooting well that is exactly what happened!"

El Fuerte shrugged. "I cannot prove it myself, even I. Maybe young Solano shoot himself. Maybe he is found in the wrong bed; that too is a very fine way to get shot. Maybe even old Solano gets mad and shoots—"

"Bunk," said Cloud,

El Fuerte turned serious. "We cannot run cattle, Mister, if we must guarantee that cow thieves are perfectly safe among our things. It is impossible! Now I

82

would like to know what you expect here, Mister?"

Cloud considered for a moment, lit a cigarette, and grinned. "I expect to fight 'em right down into the ground," he said. "You already heard me tell Old Beard that. But just the same—how are we going to handle Solano?"

"It's his move, Mister."

"And when he moves?"

"Then is soon enough to handle it, I think." El Fuerte stood up, shot the cigarette stub out the doorway, and stretched luxuriously, as a man stretches who is pleased with himself and the world. "We better wash our faces, Mister. What horse you want Bravo catch for you? We are going some place."

"When? Now?"

"Mrs. Boyce, she says you and me come call tonight."

"So that's where you went," Cloud commented.

"Who? Me? No. I only ride past, Mister. But a man must stop a minute sometimes to say 'dios' to a neighbor, no? Me, I change my clothes now."

Cloud stood in the doorway between their two rooms and watched El Fuerte unpack a suede jacket heavily decorated with a tracery of carved leather. He was faintly amused by El Fuerte's social arrangement, and a little restive. He had always thought of Kathleen as belonging to a different world—one that had no relationship to the dusty, bawling herds that were El Fuerte's background. It was impossible for Cloud to imagine the two in the same room, in the same conversation.

Briefly he debated as to whether or not he would accompany El Fuerte. Then suddenly he knew that he was sick and tired of the smell of brown beans simmering, and the close inward press of the thick adobe walls. He turned away to take a cold bath by means of a bucket of water and a dipper, and put on clean clothes.

CHAPTER 12

THE TALL INDIAN BRAVO RODE BEHIND THEM AS THEY jogged the two miles to the hacienda, for a curious feature of El Fuerte's beautiful horsemanship was that it did not seem to include an ability to tie the palomino horse, if there was anywhere a lesser man to do it for him. When they had given their reins to Bravo, Kathleen Boyce let them into the main room of the house.

El Fuerte, quietly gorgeous in his brown suede, bowed obsequiously to Kathleen; then, with the propriety of the Spanish stranger, appeared to ignore her utterly.

"Do you mind if it's a little dark?" Kathleen said; for the room was lighted only by the fire that burned under a bronze hood in the corner of the room. "The kerosene is all gone."

"I send for kerosene," El Fuerte said instantly. "Bravo!"

"No, no, please don't do that. I really like just the firelight. Don't you, sometimes?"

"Very much, me," El Fuerte agreed. "Bravo, go away."

John Boyce, sitting in the shadows in white flannels, rose and nodded. "A coolish evening," he suggested.

"Coming on winter pretty quick," Cloud agreed.

84

"How odd," said Boyce.

Seeing no sense in this remark, Cloud did not answer it. He was taking advantage of the poor light to look at Kathleen. After a saddle day of steaming horses and thick white dust, to look at Kathleen was to obtain an effect of cool cleanliness, unbelievably refreshing. In the little light her blue eyes looked nearly black, and very deep; but sometimes they caught the red-gold flicker of the fire, as if somewhere within them lived half-hidden points of flame.

"How are the various cows?" John Boyce said.

"They stood the summer pretty good; they'll be all right if we get rain."

El Fuerte was strolling about the room now, looking at the objects in it. The flickering firelight glinted on certain metal buttons, and the silver studs of his belt. Almost caressingly he reached out to touch a serape so ancient that he probably would not have deigned to throw it over the back of a mule.

"This—" El Fuerte's low tones boomed softly through the room like a gentle touch upon a big drum— "this is like my mother's house."

It was a bald-faced lie, and Tom Cloud knew it; but though the courtesy of El Fuerte was removed a thousand miles from the courtesy of John Boyce, there was a certain deep-grounded instinct there, like the instinct of a cow pony which places its feet with instant surety over uncertain ground.

"Won't you sit down," said John Boyce. He did not offer them anything to drink, but Kathleen brought brandy with a tray of cheap blue Mexican glass, and presently the odd undercurrent of strain in this room was eased somewhat.

85

El Fuerte tested an ancient rawhide chair to see if it would sustain his considerable weight, then sprawled comfortably upon it with that odd combination of grace and indefinable awkwardness which marks all horsemen.

"I didn't suppose," Kathleen Boyce said, "that it would ever get so cold here in Baja as it sometimes does, at night."

"Me, I think it is strange, too," said El Fuerte.

"I don't see how the palm trees live in La Partida."

"Very strange," agreed El Fuerte. "I did not expect such things about palm trees."

"Land of surprises," Boyce murmured.

"It is very hard to get some of our people to work when it is cold," El Fuerte said.

"How true," said Boyce. "And in the heat—impossible. Don't you find it so, *señor*—ah—"

"Contreras," El Fuerte supplied. "Contreras y Canedo. I remember once we plan to take a small city. We plan to take it by storm with the cavalry, for the artillery is empty. Suddenly it turns cold. The heart goes out of our people. Yet we can not wait, or the city will not be surprise. Me, I must lead the cavalry attack. Of one thousand men, I find at my back only fifty."

"Did you take the town?" Kathleen prompted.

"Ah, yes. But with what difficulty!"

"Amazing," said John Boyce without expression. "There must have been a furious resistance."

"Tremendous," El Fuerte agreed without resentment. "I remember one time other. It is while we are still with Villa. The enemy is all around us. Then suddenly it turn cold. But maybe this is not interest to you. Me, I talk too much, very often."

86

Cloud saw that Kathleen was about to speak, but John Boyce was before her. "I understand that the Colorado sugar beet crop is very inferior this year," he said to Tom Cloud.

Cloud did not answer, and a thorny silence came upon that strangely assorted group. El Fuerte's eyes seemed lost, sleepy, in the fire.

"This is one of the most remarkable countries I've ever known," Kathleen said at last, with a visible effort. "I'd give almost anything, I think, to know this country as you must know it, *señor*."

"Me? I don't know this country," said El Fuerte, rousing himself slightly. "I am in it two months only."

"I meant, to know Mexico," Kathleen said.

"Mexico is very many different things," said El Fuerte. "I would not say that I know very much all of Mexico. Only just before I come here, I see a thing I do not understand. I am in the Yaqui country. The Yaquis are a fighting people. For four hundred years they fight everyone, unbeaten. Me, I try to learn some of the Yaqui tongue; but this thing I do not understand. I sit apart on a hill while the Yaquis dance. All night long they dance, singing a sorrow song. Now why do they dance? Nobody is dead; there is no war, it is not time for rain, the corn is very good. Me, I don't know."

"What kind of a dance was it?" Kathleen asked.

In more involved descriptions, El Fuerte's English appeared to flounder; but he tried to answer her. He spoke slowly, often groping for words. And yet a born story teller was in this man. As he talked he managed to bring to the side of this little fire a vision of other fires, many of them, tall and slender in the blue-black dark. The drums were booming in broken intricate rhythms, their thunder filling a cup of the hills under the vast empty night; and among the fires trailed in and out long lines of people, half naked people, with bowed heads. For a reason lost in ancient mystery, they wailed a strange off-key chant—a song that was old when Cortez came, a song as old as the coyote song, and as little understood.

John Boyce's face was faintly weary, faintly ironic; Tom Cloud sat relatively unmoved by the account of what he would have called an Indian shindig.

But in the eyes of Kathleen Boyce was an interest like a wistful hunger.

"I wonder," she said, "if ever in my life I will hear such a song."

El Fuerte opened his sleepy eyes. "You would like to hear that song?" he said courteously. He came to his feet and went quickly to the door, his big silver-marked spurs ringing nobly.

He sent a low whistle into the night, and they could hear Bravo trotting across the sandy loam. El Fuerte gave an order in an unknown tongue.

"I have learned that song. I sing that song very good," El Fuerte said expansively, turning away from the door. He seated himself, this time on a bench with his back to the shadows and the blackness of the open door. "You shall hear this song." Suddenly a perturbed question came into his face. "You do not understand any Yaqui words?" he asked Kathleen.

"Not a word."

"That is too bad," said El Fuerte with evident relief.

Tom Cloud stirred with a minor annoyance; for he knew by this that the song which El Fuerte was going to sing was not truly a grief song, but a hunger song of a

88

peculiar kind. And for reasons vague to himself he already resented the unknown song, as a liberty no less presumptuous because Kathleen did not understand what it meant.

"Seems like—" he began.

But now Bravo stepped into the door; he placed in El Fuerte's hands a guitar, and a great lariat-like coil which the others did not recognize.

This latter object looked like a string of big white beads. As El Fuerte took it, the coil spoke aloud, with a rustling sound something like the talking of wind in dry brush.

"These are the rattles," said El Fuerte proudly. "There is a butterfly called the butterfly of the four mirrors, and these are the little houses of that butterfly. Only they are rattles now." He wrapped the long string of dry cocoons about a forearm and took up the guitar.

Almost idly El Fuerte began to work upon the instrument; and though it was a big guitar, his huge body and big hands made it look small. But the curious thing was that he struck no strings, not then nor later, but only beat with his fingers an odd fluttering tattoo upon the resonant box.

Thus the guitar began to speak like the sound of distant drums.

For perhaps three minutes El Fuerte seemed to be warming up that drum beat, while the rattles whispered irregularly. Then there came into the tattoo a subtle, syncopated undercurrent, gradually growing stronger until the soundbox of the guitar boomed and thumped with a compelling tom-tom rhythm.

Without rising in strength it seemed to fill the room, holding them all in a dull hypnotism of sound.

89

Then softly El Fuerte began to sing, drawn-out wailing words to a tune that made a strange savage use of what was in truth a conception of the diatonic scale:

"Ay, doraka manja hane . . .
Ay, doraka, wahma brone . . ."

The song cried and whimpered huskily through broken, suspended phrases, over and over dying away behind the sustaining drum pulse; while the coil of butterfly rattles talked huskily, sometimes marking the beat, sometimes varying it, but never still.

"I tell you what this part of the song means," El Fuerte spoke through the distant travail of the drums. "It is called 'The Sorrows of the Chief.' It says—'He is crying like the river . . . He is crying like the sea . . . He is crying like a woman, alone . . .' "

The beat changed, became slower, heavier, seeming to sink into a deeper, duller key; but the illusion of far-off booming drums strengthened, so that the insistent beat seemed to press outward against the walls. It was as if a deep, hopeless hunger had come into the drums, an unassuageable torment. But when the song began again it was high and thin and crying; so that though El Fuerte's voice lost none of its timbre, there were women singing in that room, heartbroken, the age-old victims of an unsatisfied desire that was the essence of all pain.

The song wailed and sobbed and ached, so that into that hacienda in the Valley of the Witch there came a sense of strain almost unendurable; the strain of a keyed-up violin string that is ready to break.

The high, thin variation trailed off, losing itself in the

90

insistent rising of the drums and the dry, hysterical rustling of the rattles. When El Fuerte began to sing again his voice was deep and strong. El Fuerte's face looked half asleep, very faintly smiling; but dark fires were behind the sleepy eyes, and his voice seemed not to come from him but through him, the voice of the deep-bosomed desert hills themselves. *"Charanda, randa lo . . . karev charanda lo!"* Subtly, the song strengthened and rose, following the irrepressible, increasing violence of the drums.

It was not possible that fingers tapping a guitar box could fill a long room with booming sound; yet that was what El Fuerte could do, playing his guitar without ever touching a string. Into the song came the smothered violence of war, the violence of a defeated hunger which, unsatisfied, turns to destruction, frustrated but unconquerable. The drums filled the room with their heavy tom-tom beat of war and hunger, and the rattles seemed to storm, crashing against the drum-thunder, weaving behind it, like ragged mountain winds. And strong above the rattles and the drums rose the Yaqui song, a terrible and savage song, a song of defeat that cried out against defeat, a song that cursed all gods and wished for death, yet bristled with a myriad weapons of stone and bone.

When the song that had smashed itself against the adobe walls subsided once more, its long dying was like the rushing away of vast waters that have broken and destroyed their barriers; an unsatisfied subsidence, full-bodied and insatiable, dying only because the peak of its strength was past.

Cloud was frowning, made angry and resentful by a thing that had swayed him against his will. The mad,

91

savage rhythms, rising slowly, with almost a surreptitious stealth, had come into forgotten primitive fibres of his body against his will; instinctively he drew himself out of it, denying the luring passion of the drums, and looked at the others.

El Fuerte, still half smiling, even though he sang, seemed almost to sleep. Only glancing at this man whom he had made his partner, Cloud studied John Boyce. To his own surprise he found that he had to peer through the shadows even to find John Boyce.

The man had somehow become a pale, thin nonentity, as if he in large part no longer existed. It was almost as if Boyce had left the room.

But Kathleen—it was when Cloud looked at Kathleen that he came down to earth, turning hard and sober. Kathleen Boyce sat relaxed to the point of languor, and her face was a composed mask; but within the relaxed curve of her body Cloud sensed a curious rigidity. Her eyes were slitted pools, no more expressive than a pencil mark; but behind them Cloud somehow knew that there was stirring a deep, hypnotic—fear.

The song had lost itself at last in the drums, and the drums themselves were dying away, fluttering and pulsing still, but fading into silence; and the rattles were once more only a whisper, the death-plaint of a wind that had whipped itself out in the dry brush. Suddenly an irrelevant sentence passed through Cloud's head, without connection or explanation.

It was a sentence spoken by Old Beard: "He has a blond daughter in Guadalajara."

Cloud shrugged his lean shoulders, impatient with the meaningless wanderings of his own mind. He had no least idea why that sentence of Old Beard's should have passed through his head. And at this time in his life it would have been impossible for Cloud even to imagine that a circumstance—or a man—would ever arise such as he could not master, if put to an open test of strength.

The last phrases of the rattles and the illusory drums were still whispering in that long room as John Boyce spoke. "Most remarkable," he said. "I freely admit that I have seldom heard—"

"Listen!" Kathleen snapped him off.

Looking at El Fuerte, Cloud saw that his whole frame, without seeming to move, had become suddenly alert; his fingers hung motionless over the belly of the guitar, and the rattles were still. Behind El Fuerte the tall figure of Bravo stood motionless as a post, faintly silhouetted by the firelight as a golden shadow against the blackness of the door. His head was cocked toward that door like a listening wolf.

And now from far off in the night came a strange unexpected sound—thin and far, heard and yet not heard, as if some wind spirit echoed the sound that a little while before had filled that room within the adobe walls. Far away in the hills a voice was answering, drawn-out and wailing, echoing a phrase of El Fuerte's song.

◆◆◆

"Charanda, hobran lo—
Karev, karev charanda . . ."

So distant, so near to stillness itself that it would never have been heard, except as an echo of the song that had gone before . . .

There was nothing but sincerity in the surprise that

93

came into El Fuerte's face.

He turned slowly to look over his shoulder at Bravo, and they exchanged a long unreadable stare. El Fuerte's lips formed a soundless word.

Bravo hesitated a moment more, his face a blank. Then he turned and stepped out into the night. The sound of his feet moved slowly away from the house; but when he was a little distance off they heard him start running toward the horses.

El Fuerte began sounding the strings that had been silent until now.

"I also know other songs," he said. "Would you like to hear a little Spanish song, called—"

"What was that?" John Boyce demanded. "What was that echo in the hills?"

El Fuerte hesitated; but it was plain that he could not deny what they had all heard. He shrugged in expressive evasion. "*Quien sabe?* A drunken peon maybe? Who knows? This little song is called—"

Cloud rose abruptly. "We've got to be pulling out. Long day tomorrow. We have to start a cattle count."

The casual impatience of his departure was partly frustrated, for it seemed necessary that El Fuerte slowly sip one more glass of brandy before they took to the horses; but when this was done Cloud got El Fuerte moving, and they pushed out into the night.

Afterward Cloud remembered that Kathleen had not spoken one word more after the echo from the hills.

CHAPTER 13

AFTER TWO YEARS OF CATTLE OWNERSHIP IN BAJA, Cloud recognized that the alien people among whom he found himself were a mystery to him yet. He could learn their language, could deal with them and work among them; but he still could not comprehend the multiple civilization which was behind them, nor the workings of their minds, nor their methods nor their ways.

Consequently he did not know what form of reprisal to expect from Solano, whose son had been killed in the act of stealing Tom Cloud's cattle. And though he did not worry very greatly, the threat of war with Solano hung over the Flying K constantly, never fading for an hour; like the shadow of a mountain which has been prophesied to fall.

El Fuerte said no more about the matter, and Tom Cloud did not question him. They started the cattle count which was necessary to the terms of their partnership, and pushed it forward vigorously, not sparing horseflesh; and in the course of the next two weeks Cloud found that he was getting to know his new associates a good deal better.

From the start there was no doubt whatsoever as to the high efficiency of the new personnel. El Fuerte's riders had an unfailing instinct for rooting out the little deer—wild bunches of cattle which had long ago learned to lose themselves in the deep brush of Baja. They trailed like hounds, and found lost cattle as if the big buzzards in the sky were helping them with their bird's-eye view of all the hills. With the born cattleman's ability to recognize, individually,

95

incredible numbers of his own head, Cloud was able to judge accurately the precision of the count; and he was forced to admit that he had never seen anything like El Fuerte's riders. By El Fuerte's interpretation of their contract he was paying these two what he had paid four riders before; but they seemed to be worth it.

And El Fuerte himself was proving to be one of the finest horsemen Cloud had ever known. The Flying K's new help might be a little hard on horseflesh, a little rough with the stock, but there was no question about their competence in the saddle. El Fuerte especially had that gift of delicate horsemanship which enabled him to space the running stride of his horse, so that even on a pony gone wild with a craze to run, he could plant that pony's feet upon sound ground among the broken rocks of the steep slopes.

But although in riding with these men Tom Cloud presently lost the feeling that he was teamed up with strangers, he realized constantly that there was much about El Fuerte that he did not know. Often he puzzled over small circumstances, such as the incident at the Boyce house when El Fuerte's Yaqui song had been answered by a distant voice in the hills. When he had waited a long time for something to turn up which would at least partly answer certain of these questions, Cloud overstepped his habitual silences to ask El Fuerte outright.

They were returning down the long trail that followed the Valley of the Witch; they had worked a long way off that day, and the valley brimmed with dusk under a red sky. Cloud and El Fuerte rode stirrup to stirrup half a furlong behind the others, their ponies at the slow jog so easy on horseflesh, and so hard on all riders except those who have spent their lives on horseback.

"That was a kind of outstanding song you sung over at the Boyces' that night, El Fuerte," Cloud said. "I don't know as I ever heard just the likes of that song before."

"You like that song?"

"That was a whole lot of song," Cloud agreed. Then, cautiously, "Sort of funny the way somebody answered back that song from out in the hills."

"Yes, that is a funny thing."

"I kind of thought at the time," Cloud forced the issue, "that maybe that was a signal of some kind."

"No, no," El Fuerte assured him. "I am just as surprised as you."

"Did Bravo find out who it was?"

"No, Mister. When I hear that song answer back, I have a quick hunch—maybe out there is the kind of man we can use. 'Bravo, go get him.' "

"Use for what?" Cloud asked curiously.

"I don't know, Mister. Always there is use for a man. But Bravo finds nobody."

"What the devil do you suppose he answered that song for?"

The proud expansive grin that came so easily to El Fuerte spread slowly over his features now, showing his good teeth. "Mister," he said, "when you sing *al corazon de la tierra,* the heart of the earth answers you."

Cloud considered this obscure statement. Up ahead, the tall Indian Bravo, and Carlos, the man whose face had the odd texture of a withered apple, were singing an interminable narrative song—

◆◆◆

97

"I see a stranger passing—
I know his joys and sorrows;
Another such as I am,
Whose life is all tomorrows . . ."

The tired ponies jogged on in the twilight, half asleep. Suddenly El Fuerte spoke. "Mister," he said exultantly, "when that song answers back, that is the greatest thing that happens to me in Baja!"

"But I thought you said—"

"I do not know who singed. But until then I do not feel I am a *paisano* of Baja. Never before I am on this soil; I think I am a stranger. But when that song answers back for me—then I know different, Mister!"

"I don't get you."

"Mister, I know then that all Mexican earth is my earth." Exuberantly he turned in the saddle to lean toward Cloud. "You know what I can do? I can take three, four good men at my back, and I can go to La Partida, and I can raise fifty men in one hour!"

"Raise fifty men? What—"

"I tell you, Mister, I can lope this horse through the street of La Partida, with my men behind me, and I can shout *'Rise, compadres! Sigamen rebeldes!'* And they jump in their saddles with their belts and their guns, and they don't know where I go, but they follow me. Fifty men? I can raise a hundred!"

"What in all hell would you want with fifty or a hundred men?" Cloud demanded.

"I tell you, if I can raise a hundred men, I can raise a thousand."

"But what for?" Cloud insisted.

For a moment they looked at each other, El Fuerte

98

suddenly as puzzled as Cloud. Then El Fuerte grinned a little and settled back in his saddle. "Mister," he said, "we are a very old people. There are those among us who are a thousand years old when you are born. But our country is in the making."

They jogged along in silence, Cloud puzzling. Then suddenly he saw light; and at last became clear to him a hundred things about El Fuerte which any Mexican would have known in the first place. El Fuerte was one of those remarkable Mexican figures, half politico and half bandit, who devote themselves to an unassuageable ambition to rule.

Probably he was some vagabond hill-general without any troops. Certainly he was an occasional insurgent; perhaps an habitual one. Cloud grinned crookedly to himself in the dusk, tickled that he had hit at last upon the key to the character of his new partner.

"Don't forget this," he told El Fuerte: "we're here to run cattle. The cattle come first—likewise last, and all the time!"

"You bet we run cattle," El Fuerte agreed without reserve. "You and me, we run plenty cattle! Maybe some day we run more cattle than Mexico ever see before in one brand."

Cloud's identification of El Fuerte's mainspring amused him more than a little. Coming from a country of individualists, he had no comprehension of the political surge that constantly swayed the Mexican people. Yet somehow he was pleased, happy to have in his hands this turbulent, wide-swinging weapon against the peculiar odds which he had so long faced alone in Baja.

"What the devil does del Pino do with himself?" he

demanded suddenly. Not once had El Fuerte's "secretary" ridden with them in working the stock.

El Fuerte hesitated for a noticeably long moment. "Oh," he brushed the matter aside, "he fixes the saddles, he does errands to the town; he can help us keep books. He has been with me the long time. I give him a peso or two sometimes—not much. Mostly—he just rests."

Cloud knew that del Pino did not mostly rest. He was, in fact, seldom to be found at the camp. El Fuerte's little hanger-on remained an unimportant but singularly complete mystery to Cloud.

"Seems to ride out quite a bit."

"Maybe he make love," El Fuerte suggested.

Cloud got a grin out of this picture of del Pino, but found it impossible to accept. As he rode on he was wishing that he knew more about these new associates who had become his hope in Baja; and he was wondering where del Pino was.

CHAPTER 14

AS IT HAPPENED, DEL PINO WAS ON THE RIDE. HE HAD, in fact, been on the ride for nearly twelve solid hours, and he was a very saddle-weary little man. Del Pino did not have the natural ability of Bravo and Carlos at finding wild forgotten passes in the hills, but he did have a great flair for nosing out human habitations; and there was hardly an adobe, however humble, in the entire La Partida district that he had not been in by now.

Almost any place else del Pino would have passed for a saddle-hardened horseman. But because he had been town bred, and had hardly been on a horse until after he was twenty years old, he ranked among El Fuerte's people as no horseman at all. Next to El Fuerte's preoccupation with quail seeds and such like luxuries of life, the everlasting riding of horses was the cross of del Pino's existence. He was subject to rheumatic pains in the right knee, not serious when on the ground, but utter torture toward the end of a long day's ride.

Riding with El Fuerte this was not so bad, for El Fuerte led out most of the time at the lope, which is easy to sit; but alone del Pino did not have the nerve to wear out ponies like that, so punished himself by interminable trotting.

Much less painful, but limiting his activities in the long run, was the too fulsome hospitality of Baja. Only an iron stomach sustained him, for it was impossible to establish cordial relations with a household whose food and drink you refused. Fortunately for the development of his projects, del Pino had an unusually ravenous appetite, and no little capacity for drink. Even the most poverty stricken and starving family always had something or other which they insisted that he consume. He recognized that cumulative dyspepsia was going to undermine his naturally wiry constitution, but could see no help for it.

Del Pino, jogging uncomfortably homeward to the Flying K camp in the sunset, hesitated at the foot of a little, twisting goat trail that led up a gully three miles from the Flying K camp. What he wanted to do was to press on home, and get out of his infernal saddle; but his practiced eye told him that some obscure sort of habitation was at the head of that little trail, and his peculiarly selective conscience bore down hard. The people who lived here would be of small importance—

only squatters upon Tom Cloud's land; but del Pino had schooled himself to be interested in all alike. He sighed deeply, and turned his horse upward.

The trail was even longer than he feared; but he came out, at the end of twenty minutes, upon a mean little *jacal*, half dug-out, half of wattles plastered up with mud. Before it an aged man sat cross-legged beside a bed of coals. He was stewing something in an earthen pot, and though he regarded del Pino acutely, like an animal, he did not speak.

Better built than the hovel was a mud affair six feet tall and shaped like a beehive. When del Pino saw this he knew that the old man was a charcoal burner, in a small way. Somewhere about would be a burro or two, and big pack-baskets black with dust.

"*Señor*," said del Pino in such tones of respect that an astonished suspicion flickered in the old man's eyes, "I have ridden a long way, and my throat is very full of dust. I am wondering now if a cup of water would be too much to ask?"

The old man tossed coarse grey hair out of his eyes—he had a full head of it, whacked off peculiarly all round—and indicated an encrusted olla that stood against the house. In this del Pino found a gourd dipper, and he drank sparingly, but with simulated avidity. It was green and mucky, evidently from some cow-wallow up the gully, but—"Ah, that's fine!" said del Pino. He leaned against the shanty, as if too weary to regain the saddle; and the old man said nothing at all.

"My father was a charcoal burner, from time to time," del Pino lied. "It is a very honorable profession, too little appreciated, nowadays. Ordinary rancheros think entirely too much of trees that they would never use

102

themselves anyway."

"True," said the old charcoal burner sourly. He had been uprooted from other people's timber too often to have any liking for strangers prowling about his camp.

"Here, though," del Pino assured him, "you will never be molested."

"Who says no?"

"My own *capitan* is now the partner of the Americano who owns this lease. I would not drink your water, friend, and fail to put in for you if any question came up." Already del Pino knew more about this man than the charcoal burner might have supposed. By the ancient hawk face, by the accent of his Spanish, by the knife-whacked cut of his hair, del Pino had recognized the old man's race. Because it was a fighting race, and because such an old man must somewhere have many sons, del Pino was interested. It is by means of interrelated families, and nameless clans based upon cousinships, that squads, and companies, and regiments are formed when the people rise. A summoning-together of relatives is worth twenty fiery crosses, any old day, as no one knew better than del Pino.

"And who is your *capitan*?" the old man demanded.

"Guadalupe Francisco Contreras y Canedo," del Pino intoned—"called El Fuerte!"

"Some place I have heard the name. Perhaps, once with Pancho Villa—" he eyed del Pino speculatively.

"*Si, si*! That's where! The greatest captain of artillery, the most valiant captain of cavalry, that ever rode for a downtrodden people!"

"Would he be that tall one that's new here, the one—"

"The one who rides the beautiful palomino horse."

103

"A fine figure of a man," the charcoal burner admitted. Suddenly he eyed del Pino narrowly again. "And who is it that sings Yaqui songs down there?" he asked.

For a fraction of an instant del Pino hesitated. In time he remembered what El Fuerte had told him of that evening in the Boyce house, when El Fuerte had sung the Yaqui Sorrows of the Chief—and a voice had answered from the hills. "Who but El Fuerte," he said reverently. "*Ay, doraka wahma brone*—"

A little red flame leaped up behind the old man's eyes. "*Ay, doraka korem ked*— You speak the language of the people?" he challenged, changing to a new tongue.

"No, *señor*," del Pino said sadly, though he had understood the old man well enough. "I am too stupid, me." He didn't want to get switched into a dialect in which he was, at best, ineloquent. "But El Fuerte—he speaks it like a born son of the hills. I've heard that he is related to your people," he fabricated; "but I don't know. Tell me—are there others of you here?"

"Why do you ask that?"

"One night El Fuerte sang the Sorrows of the Chief, and a voice took up the song in the hills."

The old man permitted himself a slow, deep grin, "*Yo*," he murmured, tapping his chest with his thumb. "I was coming back from La Partida; I try to sell my charcoal down there. I answered the song."

Eagerly now the old man got to his feet, went into the hovel, and brought out another earthen plate. Generously he heaped it with stew.

The stew proved to be of fresh young beef, absolutely white hot with *chili pequeños*. Del Pino accepted it with

104

voluble deprecations, and an urgent squeam of the stomach. It was the twelfth time he had eaten that day. But he scooped at it with a curled bit of *tortilla,* and most manfully swallowed it down.

For a little time the two squatted on their heels and ate in silence.

"How are all things going with you, *compadre?*" del Pino asked at last, smothering a hiccough.

"Ay, not well. I was barely able to buy this bit of beef in the town."

Del Pino laid a hand on the old man's arm. Well enough he knew that the beef had never seen the town, nor any money either. "Buy no more," he said gravely. "Remember that *mi capitan* is now partner in this Flying K. Never in all his life has he begrudged a bit of beef to the poor. Though of course you understand that doesn't go for large families . . ."

"Very few of his like are left, then," said the old man bitterly. "The country has gone to the devil. I work forever, and I'm begrudged a few cents. None of the great *patrones* are left, and nobody has any money, not even two centavos. The food is taxed out of the people's mouths. Babies die in the streets of the towns, and if this goes on the world is going to end. I tell you, if Villa were alive, this thing wouldn't go on. If he should ride through again, ten thousand of us would follow at the word!"

"You still ride?" del Pino asked.

"Do I still ride?" the old man flung back at him with fierce scorn. "I can wear down a hundred of the like you find in the towns and *milpas* today, and it won't take me two weeks to do it! I can take my four sons at my back, and I can hurry and raid like a wild dog pack—and be

105

gone again like a shadow. I tell you, I can do more than that! I can—"

"*Four sons*?" del Pino cried out.

"I have had nine sons. Five are dead, the other four to the south, in the mines. I can—"

"Could you get them here?"

"Could I get them—for what?"

Del Pino leaned close to him, his voice dropped to a fierce whisper.

"Scout troops! Scout troops, as the people rise!"

"Rise? Who rises?"

"How long would it take you to gather your sons?"

"A week; with a good horse."

"There will be no lack of horses."

"What is this thing?" the old man demanded.

Del Pino gazed steadily, somberly, into his eyes. "*El hombre* has come," he said with a deep gravity. "The man, the leader, has come. I can't say any more. Be ready. Be ready, and speak to no one of what I have said. The time is not far away."

He sank back on his heels, and they regarded each other for a long minute. "One more raid," said the old man at last. Lurid memories were glowing in his eyes, suggestive of an ancient submerged ferocity that made del Pino uneasy. "One more long-riding raid—and I think I would be ready to die."

Del Pino got up stiffly, creakingly mounted his horse. "Be ready," he said again with a maximum of grave mystery. "And meanwhile I'll tell no one that I've been here."

He rode off down the goat trail, exultant in the dusk. Swallowing another hiccough, he filled his lungs, and blew out his cheeks. Four Yaqui scouts—five, counting

106

the old man; he did not doubt that he would really get them when the time came, either.

He shuddered when he thought that he almost had not gone up that goat trail; and it had been so easy, after the riding part was done.

He was very weary, but very much pleased with himself, too. He had had a good day. He had, in fact, been doing very well for almost three weeks. Only the hard ones—the near little neighbors who had done so well with the Flying K beef—had had to be handled by El Fuerte himself. Those El Fuerte had first had to put the fear of God into, and then show them the way to better things.

But the Cattlemen's Protective Society—an idea of del Pino's—had been an inspiration. El Fuerte now had it organized until it was a cross between a secret fraternity and a squadron of light horse.

Del Pino esteemed the soil fertile, the time ripe. He was certain that El Fuerte was safe, this time, from the lure of the quail.

Now, if only no woman interfered—

CHAPTER 15

BECAUSE ALL HIS LIFE CLOUD HAD BEEN ACCUSTOMED to forcing success against all manner of difficulties, he did not worry too much about Solano. If he was uneasy, it was because he knew that trouble was inevitable; he could not understand Solano's silence, his apparent blank inactivity. Sometimes he sounded out El Fuerte about this. El Fuerte always answered with a gesture of sublime confidence. "That we will handle—when it comes the time."

Cloud was of the opinion that trouble in this quarter was already overdue. Yet two weeks more passed, and they had finished the cattle count, and dropped into the monotonous routine of the daily work, before at last Solano came.

By a curious circumstance, Cloud was away when he came, and no one but del Pino was at the camp of the Flying K. Solano came alone, and unarmed. Del Pino, that earnest little man, seated himself in the door of the room in which El Fuerte lived with his many unaccounted-for guns; he would not be moved, and nothing could be learned from him. Solano had no recourse but to wait. El Fuerte was riding, as he always was riding; lately Tom Cloud had not always known the trails nor the purposes of those rides.

And Tom Cloud—he was at the hacienda of the Valley of the Witch. In the three weeks since El Fuerte had joined him, Cloud had visited the *casa* of the Boyces seldom; and the few times that he had been there he had not set foot to the ground. He could not keep himself from stopping at that house sometimes as he rode past, as he must ride past. All day long, every day, it seemed to him that his eyes found an empty world because they were not filled with the slender, infinitely vital figure of Kathleen Boyce; all night long her slim figure haunted him through hunger dreams, so that often El Fuerte, who woke a dozen times a night, found him smoking on the edge of his bunk, grim and taciturn, unable to sleep.

Too much to ask that he should not occasionally turn aside in passing to jump his pony over the low adobe walls. As he sat his horse there, he could not know what

108

a tall, clean-shouldered figure he was against the sky. He could see the impressive swagger of El Fuerte, but his own leaner, harder timbre he could not suspect. Because he was one man against many, in a strange land with strange codes, he saw himself as a half-discredited bulldog, but nothing more.

When Kathleen came to the door in answer to the slam of his pony's hoofs upon the baked ground, he sometimes found himself all but unable to speak. Usually it was at sunset, as he returned from his long saddle labors; and the same horizontal light that had showed her to him the day of Juan Amador's death painted her in unreal beauty against the adobe of the old hacienda. It seemed to him then that all he had missed in his life was hidden in the shadowy blue eyes of this woman he would never possess. Holding his face as expressionless as the rock of the desert hills, he would drink in with his eyes the firm clean line of her shoulders, the soft, subtly expressive warmth of her lips, the smooth, gentle outline of her body as she stood in that red-gold light that was like no other light in the world.

"Need anything?" he would say, not offering to dismount.

She no longer teased him; she had turned shy, silent as Cloud himself. "No, Tom."

"Everything all right?"

"Everything's all right, Tom."

"Okay." Then he would turn his horse, jump it outside the adobe walls, and ride on without looking back.

So it went, while they were counting cattle, and one week more.

But this night it was different. When Cloud had come in and washed the heavy white dust from his eyelids, he wolfed his jerky as he always did; but as the last of the sun went out of the world beyond the western hills he found himself unable to rest. He was dog-tired, half hammered to pieces by the hard-gaited jug-head he had ridden for fourteen hours; yet when he threw himself upon his back in his bunk his blankets seemed to crawl beneath him, and the eternal bawling of the weanling calves for once prodded him out of all semblance of rest.

He came to his feet and drank more coffee made from what was left of the grounds. Del Pino, always loitering awake, reached hopefully for the pinochle deck; but Cloud, having drawn cards, found that he could not successfully read his own hand. Slowly, with a dark reluctance, he took up saddle and rope, and went out into the night.

It was foolish to tell himself that he only meant to ride past the house where she lived; that if only he could look for a little while at the roof that sheltered her he would be able to sleep. He asked himself nothing, but only saddled—and rode, chin on his chest, never even wondering by what signs his pony knew where it was expected to go, had to go.

Thus Tom Cloud rode to the ancient hacienda in the Valley of the Witch, and presently sat his horse staring at that house in which he used to live; and it was as if his own soul had left his body and hidden there.

Within the old adobe walls was a little flickering light—the light of a fire under the bronze hood, although Cloud had long since sent this house kerosene;

and the living light of that short-lived fire told him that someone was awake here.

When you have ridden range horses for a long time, you sometimes don't know what you do to make a horse answer the impulse that has passed through your head. And now the pony between Tom Cloud's thighs went loping forward, while Cloud would still have sworn that he sat motionless in the saddle. It jumped those low adobe walls as if the devil had it by the throat, and came to a stop before the door of the ancient adobe with a dull sound of hoofs in dry dust.

For a moment the pony stood still, wary and waiting, and all up and down the Valley of the Witch there was no sound; for it was between the crying of the calves and the song of the coyotes, and the valley was still. Then the door opened, and Kathleen stood silhouetted against the fire's little light.

"Child, child," said Tom Cloud from the saddle, and his leathery words somehow carried the soul of all tenderness—"haven't I told you how to open the door at night? Serape over your right shoulder, gun under the serape in your right hand—"

Kathleen said in a low voice: "I knew it was you."

That silenced him; and for a moment he sat motionless, until she said, "Aren't you going to step down?"

He dismounted slowly, like a man in the grip of a destiny that moves him against his will.

"John didn't get back from the hills," Kathleen said.

Tom Cloud checked almost on the threshold. "John not back?"

"No."

"I can't come in here."

111

Kathleen hesitated; and when she spoke her voice was faintly mocking, but very gentle. "It's stuffy in here, anyway. Would you like just to—look at the night a minute?" She caught up a poncho, threw it about her shoulders. Side by side, without any words, they walked along the barren, sandy ground within the walls, under the great drooping trees. She slipped a hand through his arm; and presently they came to rest leaning upon the adobe wall, backs to the waning moon, looking down the shadowy valley that had turned silver and mysterious in the night.

It seemed to Cloud that he must say something—anything—to get out of the grip of the quiet.

"John finding anything in those old Cayuga shafts?" he asked.

"Not so very much, I'm afraid. He's working hard, Tom. And he really knows rock. There's metal there, all right; but it's the kind that takes money and time to get, Maybe we could get the capital; but I'm beginning to think we—don't have the time."

He didn't ask her what she meant by that, and the silence wrapped them in again. There was something sad, brokenhearted, in all that quiet.

Kathleen said, "You never say anything to me any more. You ride up and say, 'Everything all right?' and you ride away again. You never even tell me what you've done during the day."

"Well—I don't think I do anything, special."

"What did you do today, for instance?"

"Well—we rode up the Boca Grande; and we found a little bunch we missed before, and them we tallied; and we got hold of twenty-two strapping calves, bigger than their mammies, and we sent Bravo and Carlos to run

112

cows and all back to—"

He trailed off and stopped, frustrated by the inconsequence of his own words.

"And—?" Kathleen prompted.

Cloud stared across the barren hills; and the coyote song was beginning, a thin, high yapping and chattering, waking the night.

"And all the long day I couldn't think of anything but you," he said slowly.

"Tom, Tom—" Kathleen began.

Cloud stood motionless, but he was turning rigid, no longer conscious of the aged adobe on which he leaned, nor the dark valley at which he looked. He was aware only of this woman beside him; against his will she filled his eyes, his brain, his whole body, even when he was not looking at her.

He did not need to look at her to feel the color of her eyes, the faint subtle quirk of her lips as she smiled, the smooth, clean curve of her body as she leaned against the wall.

He knew the faint, elusive scent of her hair . . .

He heard her say, "Tom—" and stop.

Vaguely he said—"I rode up the Boca Grande—"

Suddenly Tom Cloud covered his face with his hands. *"God Almighty, Kathleen!* This can't go on!"

There was a long moment of quiet in which neither one of them heard the wordless clamor of the coyote song. Then Cloud turned, and took his hands away from his face, which was left an expressionless mask.

"I don't know as this is so easy for me, Kathleen," he said.

Kathleen Boyce stood quiet in the faint light by the adobe wall; and the pressing dark made her seem very

113

slim and frail, more frail than she was.

"Maybe it isn't easy for me, either, Tom."

"Kathleen, what are you saying?"

"Do you think it's easy," Kathleen said, not looking at him, "to be with him—often every second of the day—to take care of his breakfast, to see his bed is made, to live—interwoven with the nearest intimacies of his life—and all the time loving another man?"

Cloud repeated in a voice taut as a cinch—"Loving another man—"

Kathleen cried out, "As if my heart would break!"

Cloud turned swiftly, not noticing that she shrank away from him as his hands caught her shoulders.

"Listen," he ordered her; "Kathleen, listen to me!"

"No, no—" A swift, inexplicable panic was upon her.

The arms that had laced out ten thousand ropes, and jerked into submission more broncs than he could remember—they took her against him, holding her motionless.

"Tom, in God's name—"

With one hand he turned her face upward, and his mouth smothered the words upon her lips. For an instant Kathleen Boyce stood rigid.

Then, all at once she seemed to go to pieces, so that she was able to break away; not by physical strength, but simply by going dead in Cloud's arms, so that he no longer held Kathleen, or any woman at all.

"Tom, there isn't any—future to this."

"To hell with the future," Cloud said.

Wearily she shook her head. "It won't work. Nothing under heaven can make it work!"

He turned away. Even here in the three-quarters dark, dimly silhouetted against the valley, he was a figure all

114

of clean pliant muscle, somehow competent still. The years behind him had built him too well to let him look beaten now. He leaned on the wall again, staring down the valley while he tried to pull himself together.

"Be still," he said. "Kathleen, be still!" And in a minute more he knew that he was still Tom Cloud, saddle man. He made himself relax, and turned to her once more.

"I think," Kathleen said, "you'd better go now."

"Yeah; I'll be moving along." His voice was harshly casual. "I'll be seeing you in a couple of days."

"I'm sorry, Tom," she said. "Try to forget what I said."

She stood watching him, half visible in the shadow of the pepper trees, as he stepped aboard his horse. He waved his hat, jumped the pony over the adobe wall, and was gone.

For half a mile Tom Cloud let his pony race back toward the corrals as if the wolves were at its heels; then he pulled it down to the customary jog trot of the range. His head was not swimming now; he was cool and steady. But he was wondering if the day was coming when he would have to kill John Boyce.

CHAPTER 16

THE EMPTY POLE OF THE SADDLE RACK TOLD CLOUD that El Fuerte and his vaqueros were not at camp as he rode in. To be gone at various odd hours of the night had become a custom with El Fuerte since he had joined the Flying K. El Fuerte called his night rides "patrols"; they were, he said, supposed to guard against the raids which had been a drain upon the

115

Flying K until he had come. Sometimes Cloud had ridden with El Fuerte on these patrols; but nothing ever happened on these occasions and he had presently given it up.

Unsaddling, Tom Cloud noticed that the lamp was lit in his own room of the smaller adobe; through the open door he could see the long shadows the yellow light cast upon the earthen floor. He supposed that del Pino was there, laboring away obscurely. For among the curious things which Cloud had discovered about del Pino were that del Pino considered himself a lawyer—had at one time, at least, held a license as such; and that del Pino was writing a book. It was to be called, "The Truth About Mexico; or, The Wrongs of My Country." Del Pino liked to work in the comparative privacy of Cloud's room, whenever he was tolerated there, and sometimes he had read to Cloud passages of his great work: "*O patria mia*! Can it be, in this advanced day and age—"

But now as Cloud swung his saddle onto the pole and kicked free his pony, a figure appeared out of the dark at his elbow.

"It's me," del Pino said in a strained whisper.

Cloud studied him curiously, wondering at del Pino's furtive caution. He was about to demand what was the matter when suddenly he stiffened. Out of the corner of his eye he had seen one of the shadows move, in the lamplight within his room.

He gripped del Pino's shoulder so sharply that the little man almost collapsed. "Who's in there?"

"Sir," said del Pino in tones of consternation, "it is Solano!"

"How many are with him?"

116

"Sir, he's alone. But, ay, *carramba!* I don't like his looks!"

Cloud hitched the heavy gunbelt which he nowadays never rode without, bringing it around so that the big holster hung in front of his thigh. "All right. You stay around out here. If El Fuerte comes in, go out and meet him; warn him and send him in."

"Si, señor."

Cloud walked squarely to the door of the little adobe and stepped inside, looking like the boss of four haciendas come home; which, after all, was what he was.

As he entered, a tall, very lean man who had been sitting beside the slab table rose to his feet, slowly, with grave face and hard eyes—and yet with a certain air of courtesy.

"*Buenas noches*," Cloud said.

"Buenas noches, señor."

Solano was deep into middle age, but he bore himself erectly, with the easy rugged balance, akin to awkwardness, of a man who had ridden every day of his life, and would ride until he died. His long hands, without calluses but as brown as an Indian's, were steady as he dragged upon his cigarette.

"*Favor de sentarse*," said Cloud; and Solano sat down. Cloud saw that the back door was open, as well as the front and he shut it; then picked himself a place on the end of the bench, beside the slab table, and well out of line with either of the two windows. The front door he left open.

"I come upon a peculiar errand," said Solano in excellent English. Though he spoke slowly, with a trace of apology, he was not embarrassed.

117

Cloud watched Solano's face and waited. It was a cleanly chiseled face, line-carved by the weather; but though it was deeply bronzed, the features showed no suggestion of Indian blood. The nose was high-bridged and thin, the thin-lipped mouth set itself, at rest, into a line of enduring resignation. Above the mouth, the mustache was a narrow, neatly trimmed line of grey. Only the deep-socketed eyes, steady and direct, but without warmth, suggested that this man was not Cloud's guest out of friendship.

"I have run cattle in this country a long time," Solano said now.

His English was accurate, but accented heavily.

"I've been with cattle all my life, myself," Cloud said "though not down here."

"In some ways it is different, running cattle here than in your country," Solano went on. "Maybe not harder maybe not easier—but different."

"So I've noticed."

"Most Americans do not succeed here," Solano said. "And nowadays—I am afraid it is sometimes difficult for a man to hang on forever in a country that is not his own."

"What do you mean by that, Solano?"

"Let me be frank," Solano said. "So far as I know, you have always dealt fairly with everyone. I know that you bought your leases in good faith, and your cattle also. But this land that you have leased—it has an unfortunate history. I know that you have had trouble with some of the people here. By tradition—sometimes by tradition that was old even when my people came— certain of the people will always feel that this land is their own."

118

Cloud had to admit that there was much he did not know about the history of Baja, or its people. But Solano's view was so much like Old Beard's that an impatience rose in Cloud, very difficult to suppress.

"Now there comes to Baja this man who calls himself El Fuerte," said Solano.

"I thought you were coming to that."

"Naturally," Solano admitted gravely, "I came here to talk about El Fuerte. I ask you to believe that I come peaceably and in all good faith. You see, for example, that I am alone and unarmed."

"I'm not questioning your good faith," Cloud told him.

"You know who El Fuerte is?" Solano asked.

"What do you mean, do I know who he is? He's proved to me he's a cowman."

"In Mexico," Solano said, almost with contempt, "all men are cowmen; or if not cowmen, at least horsemen. That means nothing. But do you happen to know the life story of this man?"

"Where I come from," said Cloud, "we don't believe much in poking into the 'life story' of a man."

Solano shrugged eloquently. "But this is different. This El Fuerte has been a center of disturbance everywhere. When the country rises, I suppose everyone takes to one side or the other. But there is a large class of people in this country, *señor,* who will follow without sense or cause, wherever a man like this leads. And, this man is only too ready to lead. He is known over half of Mexico as a dangerous man to the peace of any state."

What Cloud could not understand was that Solano, who must certainly blame the death of his son upon the

Flying K, could sit here solemnly debating what amounted to Baja politics. It was true that the Flying K could hardly be held responsible, morally or otherwise, for the death of Jose Solano. But Solano could not be expected to allow for that; human nature just didn't work that way. Cloud began to wonder if Solano really knew just how his son had met his death.

"All I know," Cloud said. "is that he's a damn good cowman. That's enough for me, Solano."

Solano disregarded this. "*Señor*, I have told you—El Fuerte is much more than an ordinary revolutionary. Now I tell you that Baja is not the place for El Fuerte."

Cloud was beginning to lose patience again. "Well, he's here, isn't he?"

"That's why I have come."

"Now look here, Solano," Cloud said; "I came to you twice. My cattle were draining away on me; I came and asked your advice and your help. What did I get? Nothing at all, by God! If you had wanted to act like a neighbor of mine, maybe I wouldn't have had to call in this man to take over the job of stopping up the leaks. But when I came to you the second time—damnation! That time was the last! From here out I handle this my own way."

"I was sorry, *señor*," Solano said quickly. "But there were circumstances—"

"Circumstances!" Cloud snapped at him. "I've run into enough circumstances around here to load a pack mule down!"

Solano was silent while he lit a fresh cigarette. The faint tremor of the match as he lit it perhaps signified that he was not used to being spoken to in the tone used by Cloud but his face did not alter.

"*Señor*, El Fuerte cannot run Baja; when he tries it he will break himself—and if you persist in backing him, he will break you too, and nothing will be left of the Flying K or your leases, or anything else you have here, when he is done."

"I don't get your game," said Tom Cloud. "Play your hand, man! Then I'll play mine."

"I'm only telling you," Solano said soberly, "what will happen if you insist on backing El Fuerte. And I will tell you one thing more that will prove what I say, if you are willing to see. The rurales are on the way north. Within the week they will be in the Valley of the Witch."

"For what purpose?"

Solano made a quick meaningless gesture. "To make an examination," he evaded.

Cloud knew something about the rurales—the mounted police of Mexico—men in improvised uniforms on unimpressive mounts, but hand-picked men, every one of them, and good fighting men. Some of them could track through the brush country like Apaches; and they had proved repeatedly that they were game to track a man the length of Mexico and back again, once they had set themselves to run him down.

"It's time they came," Cloud said. "God knows I tried to get them here long before."

"They're coming now," said Solano drily. "I advise you—"

Cloud grinned a little on one side of his face.

"The time when I was asking you for advice is now past, Solano!"

A silence fell, while Solano studied his cigarette, and Cloud waited out his man.

"I'll say one thing more. I'll speak straight, *señor*. If you will not back this El Fuerte—"

"Back El Fuerte, hell! El Fuerte's backing me."

Solano shrugged.

"If you will drop El Fuerte, I can, within limits, be your friend. It may be that I can help you in some small way to solve your problems."

If Cloud's answer was delayed it was because he was, for the moment, considering Solano in a new light. Here was a man who had lost a son in what amounted to a skirmish with Cloud's men; yet gravely, with more than dignity, he appeared to be offering truce.

Cloud wondered if the old ranchero could possibly be laying a trap.

"The time for that is past," he said again.

For a moment Solano sat motionless. Then he raised somber, unreadable eyes to Cloud.

"*Señor*—" he began, "*señor*—"

As the curious thing that had happened to Old Beard now happened to Solano, Cloud found that he was not surprised. He had heard no sound as El Fuerte came to the door; yet somehow it seemed logical, even inevitable that he should be standing there.

And now the foolish little pinwheel made by the coal of a cigarette came sailing through the door, this time to drop in Solano's lap.

Solano stood up like a man struck with a whip, his face twisted with astonishment; and in the doorway stood El Fuerte, showing his strong teeth in the same exultant, infinitely triumphant grin that had faced down Old Beard.

As he stepped into the room, however, he appeared not quite so tall as usual, and Cloud saw that he was barefoot; evidently del Pino had met him, well out from the corrals, and he had hung his boots on his saddle before coming forward alone.

His broad brown feet made a splayed dusty track on the floor, as if he might have worn sandals once.

Moving leisurely across the room, El Fuerte unfastened the rear door and swung it wide. For an instant Cloud wondered why this was done. Then he remembered the day that El Fuerte had faced down Old Beard, and he saw again the face of Carlos, curiously wrinkled, yet wickedly humorous, as he stood a little way outside with his rifle in his hands, commanding a segment in the room; and he knew that once more the rifles of Carlos and Bravo were casually converged upon the interloper in this room, from somewhere outside in the dark.

El Fuerte went to the shelf where the tequila bottle stood, and half filled a tin cup; he regarded Solano brightly over the rust-marked rim.

After the first confrontation, Solano did not look at El Fuerte.

Stiffly he made a faint bow to Cloud.

"Adiós, señor."

"Hasta luego."

Solano went striding off into the night.

CHAPTER 17

"FUERTE," SAID CLOUD, "SIT DOWN."

With his bare heel El Fuerte crushed out the cigarette which had dropped to the floor as Solano stood up; then sat down where Solano had sat, locked his hands behind his head and sprawled luxuriously.

123

Cloud sat down behind his slab table and braced his elbows on it, hunching his shoulders. His big, angular frame looked tremendously solid, but it was a mobile solidity, like that of a tough hill pony that stands resting on a steep mountain side, ruggedly braced.

"I didn't hear you there," he said.

"I been there a long time," El Fuerte grinned. "That is *un hombre muy malo.* I thought maybe he starts trouble—who knows?"

"Then you heard most of what he said," Cloud suggested, beginning to roll a cigarette.

El Fuerte shrugged.

"How do I know how much I don't hear? I hear plenty, maybe. I don't know."

"There's a couple things about this that have got to be thrashed out," said Cloud bluntly.

El Fuerte's sleepy eyes widened a little. "You don't like something he says?"

"I took you in here," Cloud said, "because I was losing cattle. You're supposed to get half the increase in return for seeing that I don't lose any more. But the increase we're talking about is natural increase. There aren't going to be any sudden increases on dark nights, or by swinging the long rope!"

"The long rope?" El Fuerte questioned.

"I'm no rustler," Cloud told him flatly. "What I've lost by thievery, I've lost; I don't aim to turn thief myself to get it back. I don't know how long a rope you used in Chihuahua and Sonora, and I don't give a damn. But I've shot square so far, and I don't figure to team up with any rustler now. We may just as well understand that to begin with."

El Fuerte was neither bothered nor annoyed. "I think I

124

do not hear all Solano says. If he is missing cows—"

"He didn't say he was missing cows. But, by God, the idea was behind what he said, just as plain as a longhorn steer behind an ocotillo bush!"

El Fuerte waved a big hand reassuringly. "I think you imagine things."

"If Solano isn't afraid—"

"What do we care what makes Solano afraid? I will tell you the truth. In most places I would not make this contract with you, Mister, if I did not expect to take back at least the cattle we already lost."

"Take them back?"

"Just go and take," El Fuerte verified.

"My lost cattle are probably already drying in the wind for jerky. If you're talking about rustling stock to replace past losses, I say no, by God!"

"I speak of what is usually the way," El Fuerte explained mildly. "But here, Mister, this is not the country for that. The cowmen are too small, too many. Every one of them knows every cow he owns, when he looks her in the face."

Cloud stared at him ironically, stumped by El Fuerte's simple, practical, and wholly unethical explanation.

"We will long-rope no cattle, Mister," El Fuerte assured him. "Not Solano's nor Beard's, nor anybody's. I am glad you look at it this way you do. I was afraid you expected I could make the cattle increase a little faster than can be done here. Most places, yes; Baja— no, Mister."

Cloud shrugged, and lighted the cigarette which had hung idle in his fingers while El Fuerte spoke.

"Well, I'll say this for you—so far as I can see you've

125

stopped down on other folks stealing from us—at least for right now."

"There will be no more steal from us," El Fuerte said with conviction.

"You think you've taught them—"

El Fuerte fixed his sleepy eyes on Tom Cloud, eyes that could be at once drowsy and very watchful. "I think these little cowmen that have cause you all the trouble—they will soon prove to be our frands, Mister."

Cloud, studying El Fuerte, suddenly recalled that he could not trust the plausibility of this man's word. A conviction came upon him that El Fuerte had lied; that if he, Cloud, were to ride certain quarters of the range again in cattle count, he would find certain Flying K beeves he had never seen before. There are ways to make a cow deny her own calf, and drive it off so that it can be given an alien brand.

There was no question at all as to whether or not El Fuerte knew those ways.

Abruptly Cloud leaned across the table. "Fuerte," he ;aid slowly, "you have not told me the truth."

El Fuerte smiled. "About what, Mister?"

"Right now," said Cloud with utter conviction, "tonight, there's fresh-branded stock running under the Flying K that came in under the long rope."

For a moment El Fuerte looked faintly sulky, but a twinkle came into his eye. "Mister," he said reproachfully, "I think you go and look."

"You admit it, then?"

Sharply El Fuerte leaned forward, seeming to come fully awake for the first time; and now he spoke rapidly, with force, marking off his words with a rapping of knuckles on the slab table. "You want to know how it is

126

a man runs cattle in this country. You want to know what it is Beard knows and Solano knows that you do not know. And I come to show you how. I give you a simple rule, Mister. A man cannot win a fight on the defense. A man cannot win a frand if he is too easy. Now I have showed that the Flying K is not to be fooled with any more. We are at peace with those who stole our cattle, and they are our frands. I have done what was needed to do, and that part is all over. Mister—" there was a little smile on El Fuerte's face—"I do not hope to hear now that all things better be done your way."

Cloud's face darkened.

"You mean—"

"In calves," El Fuerte said, "in young beef—we have taken back some of our own."

Tom Cloud came to his feet, leaning across the table, his neck thickening as the blood rose to his head. "You fool!" he snarled at El Fuerte. He did not know whether Carlos and Bravo still watched from the outer dark, in positions from which their rifles could rake the room— and he did not, care. "You infernal fool! I tell you, the rurales are coming—they're already on their way!"

"Good," El Fuerte said.

"I sent for them twice," Cloud rushed ahead, his voice like a saw in tough wood. "Now that they come at last what will they find? A lot of fresh, raw Flying K brands on stock I've never even seen!"

El Fuerte regarded him with a weary tolerance that deepened the dark flush that had come into Tom Cloud's face. "And you think I cannot handle all that?"

"How the hell do I know how it will be handled? Damnation! They've got us dead in the wrong."

El Fuerte made a blank look of goat-like stupidity

127

spread over his face.

"Now you got me mixed up," he said.

"Mixed up?" Cloud bellowed at him.

"This right and wrong business," El Fuerte said. "First they take your cattle—that is wrong. Now we take some cattle back again—that is wrong too. Mister, who did own these cow animals?"

"In the first place, I was the loser," Cloud snapped at him. "But that doesn't square you for going out on your own say-so and long-roping as suits you. If these things can't be handled somewhere near according to the law, they can't be handled at all!"

"Oh, it's the law," murmured El Fuerte. "I thought you speak of right and wrong. *Bueno*. I think I am within my rights, Mister."

"You talk to me of rights," Cloud shouted at him. "Don't you forget I own this brand and this lease. If you don't work this rancho to suit me there's nothing to stop my putting you out of here!"

"Except the law," said El Fuerte reasonably. "Me, I got a contract under the law."

El Fuerte's composure was too much for Tom Cloud. "Damn the law!" he shouted. "By God, I'll—"

Once more El Fuerte made the look of utter imbecility come over his face. "Now I am mixed up again. First you say it is not right and wrong, it's the law. Then you say to hell with the law—you are going to be a lawless man, now. Mister, I think you make up these rules yourself."

For a moment they stared at each other; and now slowly the stupidity left El Fuerte's face, and though it remained almost as blank as before, El Fuerte's eyes faintly narrowed, and a glitter came into them for the

128

first time. With smooth movement he stood up on his heels and faced Cloud. "Do not go too far with me, Mister. Contempt for law is one thing in your country; but we will not stand for it here."

For a moment more they faced each other, Cloud dark-faced and blazing with a burst of the berserk temper so hard to raise, so hard to put down when once up; El Fuerte, blank-faced, faintly slant-eyed, waiting in arrested motion.

Then slowly Cloud relaxed. Somehow, he did not know just why, the situation had become ridiculous to him. A twinkle came into his eye; and after a moment more his face broke into a grin.

"Well, I'll be damned," he said.

El Fuerte's grin answered and he stuck out his hand.

"I think we can work along and handle these things fine, Mister," El Fuerte said.

Cloud chuckled and shook El Fuerte's hand. "I guess maybe," he agreed. "I guess maybe we will."

El Fuerte stretched lazily. "Mister," El Fuerte said, "we are going to go far, you and me. We understand each other, Mister. And we will show Baja a rancho like it has never seen. And maybe much more things, too," he added.

Cloud checked in the act of hanging up his gunbelt and eyed El Fuerte.

"Much more things?" he questioned.

"Mister, I think some day you and I will be greatest in Baja; and that day, maybe, Solano—and Old Beard, too, they will be far away."

Cloud regarded him ironically a moment more. "First we got to get some salt out in the up-country brush," he said prosaically. "There's cows up there never saw any salt in their lives."

129

He was starting to take off his shirt, getting ready to turn in.

El Fuerte picked up his hat. "I see you tomorrow," he said.

"Where the devil you going now?"

"I got one more little ride tonight."

"No more long-roping now!" Cloud warned him.

"Oh, no, Mister. Nothing like that, I promise you. This is just a little ride I make."

He flashed his quick grin, and was gone, his bare feet silent upon the dry earth.

CHAPTER 18

RIDING DOWN-VALLEY, EL FUERTE PRESENTLY TURNED aside into a dense manzanita thicket, and from its depths extracted an oil-cloth-wrapped guitar; for this was not the first time that El Fuerte had ridden down the Valley of the Witch feeling the need of strings and song. At least four times in the last three weeks El Fuerte had serenaded Kathleen Boyce; and almost automatically he had taken to planting the guitar in the thicket, since obviously it caused less comment to ride out with a rifle in his saddle boot than with a guitar on his back.

He rode on gaily, at a snappy trot, for by this time much of the night was gone; and in a quarter of an hour rounded a point of rocks into view of the Boyce hacienda. He began to clear his throat and hum to himself, selecting the songs he would sing. First a good swinging, swaggering song, like "*Rancho Grande*,"— that was to wake her up, for he was of no mind to be wasting his breath. Then a sad, sad song of grief over lost love, like *"Adiós,"* and finally a coaxing, yearning song, very emotional without being at all unhappy, for which *"Quisiera"* would do. Three songs would be plenty, the idea being to leave her wishing for more and wondering why he had stopped.

Sometime, El Fuerte supposed with flawless confidence, Kathleen would come to her window when he sang; sometime later, he would sit in the outside of her window embrasure, talking with her in whispers between songs. For when John Boyce was in the hills ransacking old lost shafts for some sign of the metal that might rebuild his fortunes, no one was around the old hacienda except Kathleen and a few mestizo servants, whom El Fuerte knew how to handle as well as he knew anything in the world. El Fuerte looked to the future happily, with a gentle surety.

He was debating with himself whether she would be offended if he made his version of the thundering *"Rancho Grande"* slightly *colorado,* and his eyes were fixed speculatively on the hacienda, when something that he saw there made him pull his horse up sharply.

Through the low-hanging pepper trees showed a little steady gleam of light. Someone was awake and up in the main house.

He hesitated, momentarily at a loss in the face of this minor mystery. For several minutes he sat quiet in the saddle, watching the light in the vague hope that it would go out, and thus eliminate itself as a mental problem. He was wondering if by any chance John Boyce would have returned from up-country in the middle of the night; and this annoyed him, as a discredit to his information to say nothing of an upset to his serenade.

131

Suddenly he dismounted, picketed his horse to a bush, and walked on toward the house, his high-heeled boots surprisingly silent on the sandy soil. Slowly he made a half circuit of the low garden wall, peering through the low drape of the pepper trees in an effort to get a view within. Through a window of the house he could see the high-trimmed lamp which lighted the main room; but not until he was almost directly in front could he make out any great part of the room itself.

The broad front door was open, wide, and El Fuerte, whose teeth were chattering slightly with the night chill, shivered a little at sight of this evidence of barbarism. It told him that John Boyce was there; for already El Fuerte had gathered that Boyce was a fresh air fiend at all hours—a thing utterly inexplicable to El Fuerte. Swearing under his breath, he shifted his position until he could see the gracefully sprawled figure of Boyce himself. Boyce occurpied the room's largest and most comfortable chair, and he was smoking slowly, as if with relish. Then, shifting a yard farther along the wall, El Fuerte brought into the picture the figure of Kathleen, and his gently chattering teeth shut with a click.

There were things about John Boyce which El Fuerte would never understand, and even more things that he would never understand about Kathleen. But in certain directions his intuitions could be as subtly accurate as those of a coyote or a wolf; and now, with his first glimpse of the figure of Kathleen, he knew instantly and certainly that she was under an all but unendurable strain, a strain that was twisting her to the cracking point.

Kathleen sat with her feet drawn up under her in an immense Spanish chair. It was a straight chair, built of hard flat planes of wood, with high useless arms, and its exaggerated size made her slim, huddled figure look tiny, like the wispy figure of a child. She was wearing some kind of a black robe; her hands, gripping one arm of the chair, showed very white against the black folds—but not so white as her face, with her dark soft hair all about it.

Her chin was in the hollow of one shoulder, as if the shoulder had come up in instinctive defense against something unseen within the room; but her face was turned squarely toward John Boyce. And she was perfectly still. He had never seen anyone so completely still, yet so taut, so unrelaxed.

John Boyce was talking. El Fuerte could not hear what he said. Those suave low tones so characteristic of Boyce probably did not carry out of the room, let alone across the twenty yards that separated the open door from the wall upon which El Fuerte leaned. And El Fuerte could only partly see the man's face. But without being able to see Boyce's expression El Fuerte knew about what it was. It would be faintly ironic, faintly smiling, in a way that should have got Boyce into trouble long before this.

El Fuerte knew also in what manner the low tones Boyce used would be flowing on and on, deceptively gentle, subtly accented by that perfectly modulated, perfectly controlled voice. The impish and impious eavesdropping of El Fuerte had all his life been entirely shameless—it may almost be said that he had gained his entire education from this practice; certainly he had often learned things that had surprised him no little. And this was not the first time since he had noticed Kathleen that he had stood surprisingly close to John Boyce,

133

unseen and unsuspected, listening to those modulated tones.

So now, without being able to distinguish Boyce's words, but with his eyes upon Kathleen, he knew what sort of thing John Boyce said. That man had a control of words which could work on another living being like a deceptive poison, destroying something subtly and gently, without ever any open attack. Starting from indirections, he could build a half concealed meaning that presently fastened itself dreadfully deep.

There was no doubt in El Fuerte's mind that Boyce could more than torment this woman—could strip her to the very bones of her soul.

He supposed now that Boyce was working on Kathleen because Tom Cloud had been there—for El Fuerte knew that Cloud had been there. Doubtless Boyce had pried that out of her; Boyce could pry at Kathleen until nothing within her remained concealed.

Kathleen said something in a low, intense voice, rapidly; and though the listener did not catch the words, they had the sound of a desperate pleading that still was without any hope.

El Fuerte leaned both elbows on the wall and slowly rolled one of his bitter cigarettes, for he felt the need of a drink, and tobacco would have to do. Then he stooped low behind the wall and lighted the cigarette, concealing the flame of the match in his armpit within his jacket. His hands were cold, and shaking a little with the chill of the night. Deliberately he squatted on his heels with his back to the wall and to the house, and drew a few deep drags, the coal of the cigarette hidden in his fist.

Then within the house a chair moved sharply on the floor, almost like the crying out of a voice, and El

Fuerte stood up, whirling, as if he had been cut with a bull whip.

Kathleen was standing very straight beside the Spanish chair, a slim, taut figure in her black robe. He could see her hands, fingers spread tensely, pressed tight against the sides of her thighs. Her hair was back from her face as if she faced into the wind, and for a moment her eyes were big dark smudges in the whiteness of her face. Then her mouth contorted, and even from the outer wall El Fuerte could see upon her cheek the glimmer of sudden tears.

She cried out, "No, no, no! I can't stand it any more . . ." Then abruptly she turned, and was gone out of El Fuerte's range of vision, out of the room.

El Fuerte stood looking, his eyes gone sleepy again under their heavy lids, at the almost placid figure of John Boyce, who continued to sit where he was, smoking. He still could not see Boyce's face. He sighed deeply. It was often his prideful belief that he was the only living man big enough to handle all things; and though sometimes he resented the necessity of taking care of all the most difficult things himself, he was almost joyful at the prospect of taking care of this thing now.

Cigarette trailing from his lips, he swung over the adobe wall and went through the garden toward the house; not in perfect silence, for now he wore his boots, but silently enough to evade the untrained ears of Boyce.

For a moment El Fuerte stood in the shadow outside the door. John Boyce seemed to meditate; his profile conveyed nothing—unless, in some obscure way, there was a suggestion of a queer, faint kind of a smile behind

135

a face that assuredly did not smile.

Then El Fuerte's black, twisted cigarette shot spinning across the floor, bounced once, and slid to rest just beyond the seated man.

Boyce's whole body jerked as he looked up; and though he had never before seen El Fuerte's trick of announcing himself with his cigarette, he must have known instantly what he would see. El Fuerte was lounging in the doorway, enormous on his high-heeled boots.

His heavy-lidded eyes roved idly about the room, and he was smiling a sleepy, contented, somehow faintly anticipatory smile.

For a moment there was silence there, except that half a furlong away El Fuerte's restless horse whinnied, and was answered from the little horse corral behind the house. Then Boyce demanded sharply, "Well—what do you want?"

The visitor's eyes ceased their wandering to rest for a moment or two on Boyce, without seeming really to see him; but El Fuerte did not reply. Instead he stepped into the room, lounging easily, and looked about him with a mild, genial curiosity, as if he had never seen the place before. For a moment he seemed to notice a neat hunting rifle that stood in the corner, almost within the reach of Boyce's hand; but then his eyes passed on, studying the vari-colored string of corn ears that hung against the old wall, the serapes, the old frayed reata. He strolled across the room to stand examining the sheep skull on the wall, as if it were a curiosity the like of which he had never seen; then passed on, pausing here and there to gaze at some trivial thing. He was still smiling.

Boyce had not moved from his chair, but now he spoke again, and this time his voice was easy and

136

controlled. "Do have a chair," he suggested. "It's a cool night; just the time for a drink."

El Fuerte continued his casual, strolling circuit of the room. He appeared to slouch, utterly lazy. Only, his boots made no sound on the floor, and there was something uncanny in that, infinitely disturbing.

And now in the new, tense quiet that was on that room could be heard a faint broken murmur that came from another part of the house: the smothered sound of a woman sobbing uncontrollably.

El Fuerte stopped now in front of a window; he adjusted one of the casements, as if to let in a little air, then stood gazing out into the night.

He hadn't spoken any word.

Unquestionably, Boyce knew exactly what he was up against, by then.

Suddenly he said in a queer, cracked whisper—"*In God's name what do you want?*"

If El Fuerte could see the face of John Boyce reflected in the pane of the window, he knew then that Boyce's face had gone white and rigid, with staring eyes—the face of a coward unexpectedly caught in a limitless cruelty. And once more in the silence that room heard the little muffled sound of a woman crying, crying terribly, as if she would never stop again.

Then John Boyce moved explosively, quick as a trapped animal, and his chair overturned as he snatched at the rifle in the corner.

El Fuerte did not turn from the window that he faced, did not seem to move at all. But his gun spoke from under his arm, with a heavy, smashing report.

The blurred reflection in the window pane showed the white face of John Boyce turn upward as his knees

137

sagged; then he collapsed suddenly, as if something within had snapped with an awful finality. He was down upon his face, his rifle under him in his hands.

The visitor holstered his gun, waved one hand in ironical salute; then stepped out through the window into the dark.

CHAPTER 19

THE KILLING OF JOHN BOYCE LEFT CLOUD CURIOUSLY dazed. The exigencies of the cattle business had trained him on the one hand to be forever on his guard against mischance, but on the other hand never to expect any accidental change for the better in an unpleasant situation. And he was forced to admit to himself that he could not regret the removal of John Boyce. In Cloud's opinion John Boyce had needed removing from the face of a pest-ridden earth if ever any man had. Kathleen had seemed unable to detach her loyalty from him in adversity; and Cloud had found at his command no means with which to help her. But the sudden and unexpected death of Boyce was the kind of stroke of providence that upset Cloud's calculations.

A prompt and vigorous investigation, in which El Fuerte co-operated with Cloud in every way, showed that a mule man was missing from the pack outfit with which Cloud had equipped Boyce. The missing man was the round-bodied, brown-faced little mestizo known as Pepe; he was the one whose duty it had been to lay Kathleen's fires when he was not out on the trail with Boyce.

Although Pepe was missing, Cloud found it

impossible at first to think of this man as a killer. He remembered Pepe as a well fed, dopy little man, sleepy-eyed and grinning; usually to be found flat on his back in the sun, and singing to himself—the very soul of carefree contentment and drowsy song. But Bravo, after trailing the fugitive two days into the hills, returned to report that the presumed killer was too clever and too swift to be caught by any methods he knew; and when it was further shown that Boyce, who was always nagging his packers savagely, had found occasion to thrash the man with his quirt, no one any longer questioned that Pepe was the killer of John Boyce.

Awkwardly, but with an appropriate reticence Cloud did what he could to make things easy for Kathleen. He did not believe that Kathleen could suffer any very great grief over a loss that could hardly be said to be a true loss at all. But he understood that Boyce's death, and the manner of his death, must be a tremendous shock to this sensitive and lonely girl. Swiftly he recognized that Kathleen wished to be alone; and he left her alone, contenting himself with making whatever provision he could for her physical comfort. She did not seem to want to think about the future, nor did she seem to have any immediate plans.

And now the arrival of the rurales gave Cloud something else with which to occupy his mind. They rode up the Valley of the Witch to Tom Cloud's camp three days after the killing of Boyce, a dozen brown-faced men variously mounted on tough little hill ponies or mountain mules. These men wore khaki shirts and military cord breeches, supplemented by a combination of puttees and elastic-sided shoes—an inexpensive representation of boots, such as Cloud had seen

139

nowhere else. They seemed to furnish their own hats, and indeed the rest of their equipment was entirely individual, where it was not altogether nondescript. They rode lounging in their saddles, after the Mexican fashion, silent easy-going men, packing rifles in worn saddle boots.

Cloud, knowing that the rurales were respected by all who had come in contact with them, studied their faces and saw that there was reason for this to be so. Some of them were obviously full-blooded Indians—dark, slenderly moulded men with surface lighted eyes; others had the olive skin of the Spaniard who has long ridden in the sun. But there was not a man among them whom Cloud would have marked as a futile man nor an uncourageous one. To a discerning eye they looked like what they were—a unit accurately adapted to the country they rode, an effective human weapon of enforcement.

Their *jefe* was a tall, well-shouldered man with a full mustache; he was short-worded, but very courteous.

"We are making our headquarters at La Partida," he told Cloud. "We will be in your country a few days; perhaps more. We hope that you may find us of service to you here. In any case, we hope that you will try to give us your cooperation, in whatever we may have to do . . ."

When the chief of rurales had learned all that was known of the killing of John Boyce, two of the unit were promptly dispatched on Pepe's trail; and when this was done the rurales turned their attention to other things.

For a week the rurales came and went. With Hernandez, the local Judge of the Plains, they rode the

140

hills and valleys, inspecting herds and brands, sometimes camping for a little with one or another of Cloud's neighbors. Cloud had no difficulty in observing a marked disquiet on the part of Bravo and Carlos while this went on. Nor was he free of a certain uneasiness himself. Never having found himself in a similar position before, he had no idea what complaints the rurales would dig up against the Flying K, nor what would be the resultant action. Only El Fuerte remained blandly indifferent to the presence of the mounted law.

It was the middle of the second week before Cloud learned of the strange thing that was happening. El Fuerte had been silent, or evasive, as to the activities of the rurales; but now one afternoon he came in from La Partida in jubilant and expansive mood. El Fuerte threw down his reins and swaggered into the adobe, beaming like a full moon, and poured himself a brimming tumbler of tequila.

"It's all over, my frand!" he told Cloud jubilantly. "My Cow Association stands like one man."

"Cow Association?" Cloud questioned. "What Cow Association?"

And now El Fuerte told him what he had done in some of those long rides for which he had not accounted to Cloud. Working with what miracle of persuasion Cloud could not imagine, El Fuerte had managed to organize every last one of the little enemies of the Flying K into a single solid band which called itself by a long, impressive name. Roughly translated, the name meant "The Rancheros' Patriotic and Self Protective Association." All those little hill rancheros who had so heavily drained Cloud's herds—and had in their own turn been levied on by El Fuerte himself—had been

141

visited by El Fuerte, enrolled by El Fuerte. Overriding enmities, race prejudices, and past wrongs, he had somehow united them all into one unbroken front against outside interference. It was a story replete with long-winded incidents, of little meaning in themselves, but building into a tale that was almost a physical monument to El Fuerte.

One by one the rurales had visited the little rancheros who had been the victims of El Fuerte's reprisals, and everywhere they had met the same impasse. The *paisanos* had lost no cattle; they had heard of no cattle stolen. They could not imagine where such a false rumor had begun—had in fact never heard of anything like it before, in all their lives. Confronted with definite proof of loss, in the form of a Flying K calf suckling a Spearhead cow—evidently a slip-up in El Fuerte's technique—the owner of the Spearhead blandly asserted that El Fuerte had bought the calf for the Flying K, paying an excellent price for it; and that, assuredly, they were all brotherly little friends together, here in this land of sweetness and light where no misunderstandings ever happened.

And that was as much help as the rurales got. Wherever they turned they met nothing but blank faces and the assurance that everything was going smoothly. The rurales were nobody's fools; they knew what was happening here as well as El Fuerte did. But El Fuerte had done his work well, and the instinctive Baja prejudice against governmental interference, as represented by riders who were strangers, held the ranks of the preposterous Rancheros' Association firmly united.

So at the end of two weeks the rurales went their way. Their *jefe* came to see Cloud before they left, and talked

142

to Cloud in his well-bred Spanish.

"You have no complaints to make?" the *jefe* asked, eyeing Cloud narrowly. "No reports of thievery or the like?"

"None," said Cloud, only too glad that the obstreperous El Fuerte had not dragged him into trouble.

"Nothing further to add concerning the death of Juan Amador?"

"On that, I've given you all I have."

"Then there's nothing we can do here," the *jefe* told him. "I'm sorry I must tell you that I find nothing in the Amador case to modify the original report of the Judge of the Plains. It is my belief that you have been wronged. But I have nothing to go on."

"I understand," Cloud said. "I know what you were up against, in that."

The other shrugged. "I have one bit of news for you," he said. "I have word that the murderer of your friend and countryman, John Boyce, has been captured by my men."

"Fair enough! Can you get a conviction?"

"It will not be needful. After my men had held him two or three days they were—ah—talking to him, one dark night; and he confessed."

"I suppose he'll be tried in Mexicali?"

"No, *señor*. I am sorry to say that the unfortunate tried to escape, and my men were forced to shoot him. *Ley del fuego, señor*. I have made the proper reports, which will be sent to your government. So that matter is ended."

"Your men have worked well," Cloud said somberly.

"Thank you. Now I wonder if I can give you a piece

143

of advice, *señor*."

"I didn't ask for it; but I'll be glad to hear it."

"You are an American. You do not know all our ways and customs here. Some of your neighbors are solid men—others are not truly your friends. Miguel Solano is a solid man. In case of doubt, if I were you, I would seek advice from him; only very carefully from certain others."

"Such as El Fuerte," Cloud supplied.

"Such as El Fuerte," the chief of rurales agreed. "But I do not think I would care to say any more, *señor*."

He accepted a drink from Cloud, and rode away. Cloud never saw him again. He had seen here what he was to see over and over again—sound and practical men, honorable and effective men, frustrated by a total lack of co-operation among the clannish peoples of the brown hills.

CHAPTER 20

CLOUD HAD NOT REALIZED UNTIL THE RURALES WERE gone how thoroughly they had taken up his mind. He was a one-track thinker always, accustomed to bear down on one thing at a time; and though the presence of the rurales had not called for any great activity on his part, the necessity of wary watchfulness had absorbed him. But now as they dropped once more into the monotonous routine of the daily work, Cloud's mind turned to Kathleen.

Not that he had neglected her; no day had passed that he had not stopped at her door at least once. He had made sure that the two Mexican women whom he had

144

put there were taking care of her, and that she needed nothing which he could obtain. If these daily visits had been only saddle visits, as brief and casual as his calls had been before the death of Boyce, this was partly because he had imagined it a kindness to Kathleen to let her be alone, at least for a little while.

But on the second day after the departure of the rurales, as Cloud sat looking down at Kathleen from the saddle, he was wondering if he had given her attention enough. He noticed now how thin she looked, and how remarkably pale. The reflected light of the southwestern sun had turned her skin the color of old ivory; and now he could see a little tracery of blue veins in her temples that had never been visible before.

She gave him a little smile, but the smile didn't have in it the quirky devilment that had always been characteristic of Kathleen.

"You ought to see the way they're fixing up La Partida for the fiesta," he told her. "Seems this is a *grito* fiesta, celebrating the 1910 revolution, or something; doesn't amount to much here, usually. But this year it looks like a real powwow. People are in from all the little hill villages with pottery, and baskets, and all kinds of junk. The houses are already all filled up, and they're sticking up thatch shelters all over the works—I bet there's going to be five or six hundred people. We'll ride down and take a look, if you want to."

"I'd love to."

Suddenly he stepped to the ground and his big hands cupped her shoulders gently. "Doggone if I believe you're getting enough to eat!"

"Why, how foolish!" she protested, drawing away from him. "Of course I am."

145

Abruptly he turned and loosened his pony's cinch; then went stomping through the house to the kitchen. Here a bag-like Indian woman, already middle-aged at twenty-five, stood placidly watching something stew on the top of the wood range.

"Beat it, Maria. I aim to cook supper myself."

He peered into the stew pot, and found there what might have been expected. He had sent over fresh beef that morning, and the woman appeared to have chosen from it what she conceived to be delicacies—part of the backbone, a section of windpipe, and other cartilaginous selections now boiling down into a mess. "Take this soap-boiling away," he told her grumpily, "and cook it for yourself outside. She can't eat that stuff."

He hunted until he found the tenderloin, which had been hung aside to be made into salt jerky. A stack of *tortillas* like cardboard wheels were racked up on the backstove, but a considerable search was necessary to unearth a can of baking powder he had brought here a week before. It had not been opened. "*Madre de Dios*," he muttered, and sailed the *tortillas* into the brandy-colored dusk.

"Now you sit down and let me do this," Kathleen protested. "I can make beautiful biscuits."

Cloud wondered if she really could. Certainly she did not seem to be much of a hand at taking care of herself. He made her sit down and leave the cooking alone. "I'll catch up a wet cow in the morning," he said. "From here out you have to drink milk all the time."

"Oh, you mustn't do that. I don't want you to bother about me."

"Sure, I'm going to bother about you."

She said, "You're so foolish; but you're terribly

146

sweet."

Once she had told him that she didn't want to leave the Valley of the Witch while he was here, but that was before Boyce had hit into his finish; it seemed very long ago. The death of Boyce should have meant the removal of the barrier between them, but instead it seemed to him that she had become a stranger, detached and unattainable. She would never meet his eyes any more, as she once had done.

Cloud thought he had never seen anyone appear quite so completely lost as Kathleen did. Her fragility made her more dear to him, as if she were a flower, or something perishable like that—to be treasured and cared for as precious beyond belief. Her slender hands were lying relaxed on the table before her, and now he covered both her hands with one. Her cool soft fingers lay motionless under his, unresisting, unresponsive, as if there was no life of any kind left in her any more.

A fear was on him that she was still here because she was broke. Much as he wanted her here, he didn't want her to stay for any such reason as that.

"I meant to tell you," he said. "I can give you a thousand for the *Pájaro de Plata* shaft, if you want."

He didn't know where the thousand was coming from, but it was worth that much to him to find out what was in her mind. "Of course we'd have to get it appraised."

She gently drew her hands away, as if they were faintly uncomfortable under his, as she added uncertainly, "We'll talk about it one of these days."

Cloud frowned as he set the tenderloin to sizzling over the open coals in the firebox of the stove. It occurred to him that he had left her alone too much, too

147

long. It would be easy for loneliness to become a ghastly thing for her, here in this house where John Boyce had died.

"How long since you've been away from this place?" he demanded suddenly.

"Yesterday. I rode to La Partida yesterday, with El Fuerte."

For some reason this took the wind out of Cloud. "With El Fuerte?" he repeated.

It was borne in upon him how little he knew about what El Fuerte did with his time. El Fuerte had contracted with Cloud to accomplish certain things, and he had proved himself effective. The cattle losses had stopped—some of them had even been recovered; and the peculiar cow association which had turned the rurales away seemed to consolidate and secure the position of the Flying K. Beyond this Cloud was willing to admit that it was none of his business where or when El Fuerte came and went. Yet a situation in which El Fuerte was able to form a preposterous cow association, without Cloud knowing anything about it until it was done, seemed to him slightly outlandish.

And now the casual revelation of El Fuerte's interest in Kathleen angered and disturbed him. Not that he had any sense of jealousy; this did not occur to him in connection with El Fuerte. But the association of El Fuerte and Kathleen in any picture whatever still seemed so anomalous to him that he was unable to accept it. Suddenly he wondered just how often El Fuerte was to be found at the hacienda.

"I guess he's around here about every day, isn't he?"

"Not every day."

Cloud stared at her. "Look, Kathleen. If he makes

148

himself a nuisance, I'll see that he stays out of here!"

"Oh, don't do that. He isn't a nuisance."

For a moment or two Cloud gave his attention to the stove. "This El Fuerte is quite a case," he said at last, a little drily.

"El Fuerte is Mexico."

"He's Mexican, all right."

"I don't just mean he's Mexican," Kathleen said; "I mean he's Mexico itself. In many ways he's like a child; but he has a great reckless valor, and a superb horsemanship, and gallantry, and a capacity for doing the most astonishing things—and all that is Mexico. Above all he has a great vital, primitive strength that is Mexico."

"*Que hombre*," Cloud quoted. "I don't get him, sometimes. El Fuerte—'the strong one!' Can you imagine the laugh a man would get in Arizona, going around calling himself 'the strong one'?"

"The word 'fuerte' means more than just strong," Kathleen objected. "It carries the idea of exuberance, and animal spirits, and gusto—all that sort of thing. A kind of general lustiness. There's a town in Zacatecas named El Fuerte, after him. Did you know that?"

"He told you that, did he?" Cloud started to tell her that he hadn't supposed El Fuerte was as old as that—the town having carried that name for more than a hundred years. But he checked himself, recognizing that he was close to bickering with her over a man whom he could not bring himself to regard as much more than his own hireling.

"You like this Mexico?" he asked uncertainly.

"You mean do I like El Fuerte?"

"You just said it was the same thing."

She seemed to consider this, her eyes wide and dark and lightless upon the fading hills. When she spoke her voice was very low, but there was more fire in it than it had held since the death of John Boyce.

"Sometimes I think I hate him!"

That night Cloud rode away from the hacienda deeply troubled.

CHAPTER 21

DEL PINO RETURNED THE NEXT DAY. CLOUD HAD NOT even known that he was gone. Because del Pino was a weak roper and an indifferent horseman, and made no pretense of holding up his end as a vaquero, Cloud paid small attention to El Fuerte's little "secretary." He had to think back before he was sure that he had not seen the man for more than a week.

But on this occasion del Pino's return to the Flying K was a very noticeable one, for no less than seventeen mounted men straggled into camp behind del Pino's black mule.

Ironically Cloud surveyed this cavalcade. They were a ragged and dusty lot, for the most part, many of them barefoot in their battered stirrups; their ponies were ratty, and most of them brought with them nothing except the gear they rode and the clothes on their backs. Yet they lounged in their dilapidated saddles with the nonchalant ease of true Mexican horsemen, and their brown, flattish faces were confident and unhumble.

"What the devil is all this?" Cloud demanded of del Pino. "Do you think I aim to feed—"

Del Pino shifted uneasily on his black mule. "These

150

are old friends of El Fuerte—they come for the fiesta. Here—El Fuerte will explain to you."

El Fuerte now came forward, grinning proudly and waving a greeting to the ragged horsemen with both hands. They grinned back at him and saluted loosely with wide swings of their arms. Cloud watched in silence while El Fuerte shook hands heartily with half a dozen of the foremost; this only ended when Bravo brought El Fuerte's saddled horse.

Cloud suffered a burst of annoyance at the nonchalant manner in which El Fuerte seemed to ignore the need for an explanation. "Look here!" he stopped El Fuerte. "I want to know what this is about."

"I was just about to explain," El Fuerte answered, still beaming. "These are old frands—some of them come a long way for the fiesta. I have invite them to camp on our land—the part that is nearest La Partida."

"And just eat freely into our beef," Cloud suggested sarcastically.

"You are generous, Mister," El Fuerte grinned, affecting obtuseness. "But I cannot permit you to do this thing. Every beef that they eat, it is tallied against my own share on the books—no, I insist on it. You see, sixty-two more are coming."

"*Sixty-two more—*"

El Fuerte stepped into the saddle and saluted Cloud gaily. "I see you soon. *Bueno, amigos!*" he shouted at the troop, jumping his pony into a run with the curious, disregard for horseflesh which marred his centaurship. The seventeen ragged ones spurred their horses after him with a shout, and away they all went thundering down the valley in a terrific cloud of dust.

"Put me in mind of a bunch of kids," Cloud

grumbled. He was half amused, half annoyed by El Fuerte's flamboyant example of Latin hospitality; but he supposed it was all right if El Fuerte paid for it.

Cloud had got hold of some more wire, and had meant to build fence that day, but evidently his hands were not figuring to work. Often he would have given a whole lot for half a dozen American rimrock cowboys, who didn't know what holidays were; but the immigration laws shut them out. He had learned by this time that there were one hundred and thirty-three holidays in the Mexican calendar, and half of Mexico observed them all. The capacity of these people for rest and celebration was a constant marvel to him. When occasion prompted, they could ride night and day, apparently without fatigue; they could run all day behind a pack burro. But when necessity was not snapping at their heels they were game to squat against a sunny wall interminably, drowsing and singing, apparently very happy.

Different from Americans; Americans lived marching, forever ridden by an urge to get some place. An American out of motion was as good as dead, and only began to live again when he got into action. Now that Cloud's crack vaqueros had laid themselves off, his first impulse was to go and build fence himself, anyway; but he knew that would be a mistake.

Leisurely Cloud shaved, put on a clean shirt and black neckerchief. He was saddling a horse, with the intention of riding down to see Kathleen, when Old Beard rode in.

Old Beard was sober faced, but not unfriendly. "Going to town?" he asked.

"Not me. Vaqueros went to town, damn it. Seems like

this fiesta is going to cut into the work."

"Liable to cut some deeper than that, son."

"Step down and come in."

Old Beard went through the form of getting off his horse, a sort of necessity to etiquette under the old ways; and he accepted a drink. Almost immediately he mounted again. Cloud realized that Beard was looking at him curiously—had been looking at him curiously ever since he had arrived.

"I'd go to La Partida, son, was I you," Beard said.

"Don't know as I've lost anything in La Partida," Cloud grunted. He resented this fiesta which had butted in on the building of his fence.

Beard eyed him oddly. "Might lose something in La Partida still yet," he remarked. He leaned slightly toward Cloud. "How deep are you in this, son?"

"How deep am I in what?"

Beard studied Cloud for what seemed a long time. Even when he had made up his mind he seemed unable to believe his own conclusion.

"Seems to me like something's gone almighty wrong around here, Cloud," Beard said at last. "Can't make up my mind whether to believe you, or not. If you ain't been to La Partida, you better go. You remember this same fiesta last year?"

"Wasn't much shakes, so far as I recall."

"No; La Partida's never had what you might call a pilgrimage fiesta—not heretofore. Generally the families in the town get out their pictures of Madero, and carry them in a procession up to the church, and kill a few pigs, and lie around all day eating and getting drunk; and at night they'd maybe have a dance, and the rancheros would come in from the country to some

153

extent, and they'd be a couple of fights, and somebody would get a knife in him. But that was all it come to. Until now."

"You think something's up?"

"Go to La Partida, Cloud."

"I was there a couple of days back. Sure is a pile of people there."

"How many would you say?"

"Oh, a couple of hundred," Cloud estimated.

"Go to La Partida," Old Beard said, harping incessantly on the same string. "Two hundred, hell! They wasn't nothing but seed."

"What do you figure goes on, Beard?"

"I know damn well what's going on," said Beard gloomily; "and if it's true you don't—which is hard to swaller—you better be finding out. The main fiesta day is tomorrow. But they've been building up to it for a week. If I know a damn thing about this country there's going to be a hell of an explosion, Cloud. I've been in this country a long time. I've been through seven main disturbances, besides a whole string of minor disorders. Every time I hoped I never would see another. But we're up against another now."

"You figure they aim to rise up, huh?"

"Rise up and boil over," Old Beard confirmed.

Cloud shrugged. "Let 'em," he said. "Let 'em boil over freely. By and by they'll simmer down again and settle back. They'll have to scrap it out among themselves. I'm here to run cattle; I reckon I can weather out a general ruction about as good as the rest of you can."

For a moment or two Old Beard stared at Cloud pityingly. Then suddenly he seemed to anger, and he

154

blazed up as Cloud had never seen him blaze up before. "In God's name, you young fool, won't anything wake you up?" The muscles of his ancient jaws quivered; he almost frothed at the mouth. "You're sitting on a powder keg, you hear me? And by God, the fuse is lit and whistling. Don't you know your own finish when you see it?"

"Horse feathers!" said Cloud.

Beard rose in his stirrups as if he would dive at the other. "Don't you horse feathers me, you squirt! You've let this thing build up under your own nose—blind as a bat and forty times as dopy. You've sheltered this thing and let it build strong right on your own ground, until the man don't live that can stop it now. But you're the one it's going to trample under—you hear me?"

Cloud was set back on his heels by the old man's fury. "What in all hell riled *you* up?" he said without heat.

Old Beard steadied himself and mopped his face with his neckerchief. "I guess nothing is ever going to wake you up," he said at last. "You could have saved yourself from being dragged into this, the time I warned you. And Solano could have stopped this, most any time, if he'd been of a mind. But he wasn't of a mind, for reasons you'll pretty soon see. He's give El Fuerte rope—and El Fuerte has furnished his own hanging. Solano sees his mistake now; El Fuerte's come too strong for him, and now it's too late. Solano'll be wiped out, most like. Only your neck is snarled in the rope too, my boy! Don't fool yourself that the Fuerte's two-for-a-nickel war will amount to a hoot. But when the Federals swarm in they'll lay waste to you quick enough! And

155

rightly, by God! The Flying K is through in Baja, Cloud."

"I guess it isn't going to bust the Flying K to have a few cows barbecued by a little pack of rebels."

"Little pack of rebels, hell," Beard said contemptuously. "Rebels come and rebels go. But damn it, it's your partner that's stirring this up—can't you get that through your thick head? The Federals will come down on him like a deadfall; maybe he'll be able to squirm out of it again, and maybe he won't. But you, you can't squirm out. You, you're nailed to the ground. Now tell me that you're an American citizen."

"Sure, I'm an American citizen; but—"

"So it may be you won't get shot. Well, personally, I'd go smoking over the border, was I in your boots, sooner than to put it to a test. But nothing in God's world will save your leases and your cows; you'll be barred out of Mexico for life. American citizenship doesn't cover coming down here and setting up a war against the government."

"What is it you want from me?" Cloud demanded. "You didn't come here to give me advice, Beard."

"Hell, no. It's too late for advice. I gave you your advice long ago. But I can't say I want anything from you either; not that I know of."

"Then what the devil are you here for?" Cloud snapped at him.

"Reckon maybe I was curious," Beard admitted.

"Curious? About what?"

"You," said Beard. "I've seen all kinds of damn fools in my time. But I admit you got me beat. I don't see yet how anybody could be such a damn fool as you've been. It seems so kind of ingenious and elaborate. A man doesn't let himself in for what you've let yourself in for, without he has a special talent for it."

"Come in again some time," said Cloud drily; and Beard, with a wave of his hand, put his horse down the trail.

A hundred yards away Beard turned in his saddle to shout back. He was grinning in a curious and not altogether pleasant way. "Stand from under, boy! And don't ever say I didn't warn you!"

CHAPTER 22

TOM CLOUD HAD BEEN BORN AND SPENT HIS CATTLE years but a few days' ride north of the border. But a couple of hundred miles leaves room for a whole lot of differences, in race, in habits of thought, in every viewpoint possible to man. With the proud provincialism characteristic of the western ranges, where the dry-land isolation of each brand schools each man to stand on his own legs, he and his kind had always taken lightly the tumultuous political activity that was always boiling up below the border.

Not that he held the Mexican riders in contempt; he had known and worked with too many good vaqueros from below the border for that. He knew their horsemanship, their natural skill with gun, knife, and rope—and especially he knew and respected the reckless heights of courage to which they could rise. But he came from a breed of men as unexcitable as any on earth; it was a breed that turned instinctively and always to individual action, never to cooperation. To hear that a thousand men had sprung to arms and were rampaging

157

across the face of Mexico in the name of revolution; and then to hear a month later that the entire show had been squelched, and the thousand had returned peacefully to their homes—this was the sort of repeated performance which Cloud had no means of understanding.

Thus, in common with most of his kind, he had never formed a very clear picture of the type of revolutionist which seems to breed so readily in Mexican soil. Certainly he had never taken the idea of revolution seriously. He found himself unable to take it seriously now.

He had recognized and taken into account the ambitions and war-like political tendencies of his extraordinary partner, and it had been his intention to watch carefully the development of this side of El Fuerte. Certainly it had been no part of Cloud's plan to become involved in political violence. He had meant to detach himself from El Fuerte long before any storm of this nature was ready to break. It was the time element that had tricked him.

Had Cloud ever felt it necessary to organize a revolution he would have gone at it methodically and carefully, as he laid his cattle plans; he would have given thought and long preparation to sources of money, to transportation, to commissariat resources; his plans would have struck their roots so deep that the preparation would have been one of years. But El Fuerte had been in Baja only a matter of months; it had never occurred to Cloud—it seemed incredible to him yet— that any proper revolt could be attempted by El Fuerte in so short a time.

Yet Old Beard had managed to shake up Cloud at last. When Beard had ridden away, Cloud squatted on his heels for the duration of a cigarette; and he was wondering if by any chance a swift turn of events had caught him asleep. Unbelieving yet, but with a certain grim sobriety now, he boarded the pony he had saddled, and went jogging down the seven miles to La Partida.

To his surprise, El Fuerte, riding a steaming horse, met him on the road a quarter of a mile outside of the little town.

"Good, good!" El Fuerte hailed him. "I come to look for you. There is much I want to show you here." He wheeled his horse and pointed back for La Partida at the run. To run his horse for no reason in the heat of the day made Cloud feel like a fool; but he spurred his pony into a lope, and together they charged headlong down upon the village.

La Partida was made up of three score adobe houses, set close together in two long, slightly irregular rows on either side of a broad street. Most of the houses were of two rooms and a lean-to, hardly better than huts. A few had the flat sod roofs of the pueblos, a few were tiled, some were roofed with shingles, and more with thatch. They stood tight together, their front walls continuous, splotched with the shade of the Partida palms. Those palms, tall and ancient-trunked, distinguished La Partida from all its sister villages; they were believed to have been set out long ago by an exiled priest from across the sea.

Beyond the double line of houses and of palms stood the little church, square across the end of the street. Its façade was plain, in the Spanish colonial style, and from it the plaster was chipping away in irregular patches, exposing its rounded adobe bricks; but it was made dignified and beautiful by its high carillon of five bells.

All this Cloud had seen many times before, but he

159

was accustomed to see it always in a somnolent state of sun upon sleeping dust, with hardly anything moving in the street except a few half naked children, an occasional burro or a pig. Never had he expected to see it as it was now, swarming everywhere with more people than could ever have packed themselves under its roofs. Two hundred people? There were more than a thousand here—perhaps several thousand, for all Cloud knew.

"I send a man to tell you to come," El Fuerte said. "But he sees you a long way off, and comes back to tell me you already come. So I come to meet you. I want to show you this great thing myself." He beamed and watched with unconcealed delight the wary questions in Cloud's face.

They pulled up their blowing horses as they neared the foot of La Partida's street. Before they could enter they had to pass through the welter of a dense encampment, where a hundred or more crude shelters had been improvised of blankets, bits of canvas, boughs, palm thatch, and grass. Thirty or forty men rose from their heels to watch them, and a ragged cheer went up as El Fuerte rode by. El Fuerte grinned, made his horse prance, and waved his hat.

They pushed on, stirrup to stirrup, into the thronged street. The people parted to let them pass, and closed behind them again, so that they were the constant center of a moving open space which traveled with them. As they passed along the broad band of dust, the doorways filled, and the crowd in the street increased to an unquiet river of brown faces. Here were stolid flat-faced Indians of the *milpas*, and the proud, faintly wolfish people of fighting Yaqui blood; lean sun-carved saddle

160

men, aged peons wizened under shags of coarse grey hair, clean-cut men of Spanish caste with Indian eyes. Lean-hipped vaqueros swaggered here, clanking their spurs, their eyes merry in the rich brown of their wind-burned faces; they wore the coarse blue work clothes of American cowboys, but flat-heeled shoes took the place of the half boots they could not afford. There were heavy-shouldered *cargadores,* probably from the railroad towns of the border; there were men recognizable as pottery and basket makers, stoop-shouldered from bending over wheel and reed. Sturdy bare-legged young women, with the loveliest soft, dark eyes in the world, hung together in tight little groups, very full of nervous laughter.

There was color in that crowd, sharp and living color that caught and split the brilliance of the sun, striking through the muffle of dust that rose from the ankle-deep street. The pajamas of the *mozos* were turned by the sun to glaring white patches, set in spots of shadow cast by the monstrous-peaked straw hats; the serapes folded upon their shoulders were bright color-scales of blue and red, white and black and gold, and the *rebozos* draped over the heads of the full-breasted women were of intricately woven patterns of white and blue.

And now La Partida had also a confused voice of song. The sour reek of *pulque* came from the doors of a dozen houses that had been turned into cantinas over night, and with the floating smell of alcohol came bursts of balladry, and that persistent, spirited, never-tiring beat of guitars that is forever present wherever Mexican people are gathered, so that among them no one is ever long out of earshot of song. It was a bright crowd, a gay and happy crowd, full of fiesta.

161

Yet behind it was poverty and an ill-equipped struggle for existence. That struggle showed in the grave, wrinkled eyes of the old men, in the premature aging of the women; and in all that crowd hardly anyone—except the vaqueros and such young women as had received gifts—wore shoes. They shuffled barefoot in the dust, or protected the soles of their feet with sandals made of old tire casings. Shapeless old women with stoically tragic eyes sat before the house walls cooking in pottery dishes on little clay charcoal stoves. From the humble cookery came an odor of *frijoles* boiling with ham rinds and garlic, the stinging pungence of chili pepper, the smell of frying beef that Cloud supposed was his own. They had set up improvised tables in the street itself, and motley rows of strangers joggled elbows here as they ate, all powdered with the dust.

And the eyes of all of them, young or old, drunken or carefree or vigilant, were upon the two riders who worked their way slowly up the street. Those eyes were curious upon Tom Cloud, but hungry upon El Fuerte with a fervor of idolatry that Cloud could not at first believe. They stood up as the riders passed, waving their hats in the air for El Fuerte; they stopped their songs and their vending to cheer El Fuerte. Tall men called out to him across the heads of the crowd to offer him jests of comradeship; bold young women reached out to touch the silver conchos of his chaparejos.

El Fuerte rode high in his square bucket stirrups, and the silver on his saddle and bridle flashed brilliant in the sun. He seemed to swell bigger than ever, straighter, broader, more powerful. His left hand worked gently on taut reins, making his pony fret and sidle and pick up its

162

two front feet. His right hand, heavily gloved, waved to everyone, everywhere. El Fuerte grinned broadly, showing all his teeth; his eyes laughed, the eyes of a man who knows when he is in his own country, and appreciated there.

Suddenly an uneasy chill went through Cloud; he could no longer refuse to see that he was looking at a born leader of this people, perhaps a great natural leader. El Fuerte leaned down to sweep up a pretty Indian girl with an arm about her waist, kissed her mouth, and set her down again—and the crowd cheered. There was nothing that he could do that did not please the hundreds who had come to this town, nothing which did not stir them to cheers.

El Fuerte kept pointing out particular men in the crowd.

"That's Julio Moreño—you hear more of him pretty soon . . . That's Manuel del Sol . . . That's Torreon, the black one; he brings forty men, or more . . . That's Alcazar—he has only twenty, but good horses . . . That's old Teotac, the Yaqui scout. *Recristo!* There's the old man that answers my Yaqui song that time—remember? A charcoal burner from the hills. *Ay, padrecito mio!* Are those your sons?"

"I never knew Baja had Yaquis," Cloud said.

"No, Mister; they don't grow here, much. But some of these come a long way."

Wonder as to what had brought all these people to La Partida left Cloud's mind, for now he knew. These people were the tinder of action—and El Fuerte was the flame. These people were here because El Fuerte was here; somehow some unknown password—perhaps even a command—had gone out over the long grapevine telegraphs to bring them here—started by del Pino and Bravo, no doubt, but self-perpetuating and self-multiplying, until there was no corner of the hills for a hundred miles where it was not known that a new and great leader called his people to La Partida!

Now an impromptu band gathered behind El Fuerte—first an excitable barefoot singer with a guitar, then four more, then two small boys who drummed intricate trap rhythms upon a box. An enormous bull fiddle was produced from somewhere; a *mozo* in pajamas carried one end of it, and a little wizened old man under an enormous hat staggered under the weight of the neck, sawing vigorously. They struck up a swinging military song, a marching, fighting song for cavalry; the beat of hoofs and the crack of rifles were in it, together with the wild long yells of hillmen on the warpath. All along the street voices took up that song, inchoate in note and tone, but full of a swinging, slashing rhythm. What had started out to be a ride through a street had spontaneously turned itself into a celebration, a demonstration, a triumph.

The thing Cloud was looking at was as surprising to him as if it had come in upon his own cow camp. As a matter of fact, his leases did not literally include La Partida, nor the stunted cornfields and ragged vineyards which gave the village its precarious existence; but the Flying K lands, spreading over hills and valleys, encircled La Partida in their long arms. Looking three directions from La Partida you saw little but Flying K leases. Although he hardly ever visited La Partida, Cloud had always felt a negative sense of proprietorship, as if he tolerated the somnolent village upon his own lands. He could not get over his

164

amazement that the sleepy, insignificant little town had been transformed over night into the center of something unbelievable.

He noticed something else about this crowd—that the women and children were few. The saddle type of men were predominant here; far more so than was justified by the character of the people and the land. El Fuerte spoke truly when he said that there were men here who had come a long way. Basically, perhaps, this was fiesta; but in its extension it was something more— something of unknown potentialities, that might be as dangerous as a giant diamond-back in coil.

CHAPTER 23

EL FUERTE'S SPONTANEOUS PROCESSION OF TRIUMPH proceeded the full length of the street; and ended at last before a house with a tile roof, a little more impressive than the others, set almost in the shadow of the church.

This was the house of the La Partida *alcalde,* and a new unrest came into Cloud as he saw that a dense concentration of unencumbered men had focussed here. He saw at once that a sort of headquarters had been formed here for El Fuerte—in the very heart of what official authority was available to this little town.

El Fuerte waved his hat once more to the crowd and swung down from the saddle; a dozen hands disputed for the honor of holding his horse. Cloud followed him as he stepped through the doorway into the cool interior of the tile-roofed adobe. A *cantina* had been set up here in the earthen-floored ell—evidently an exclusive one, for it was half filled with no one but spur-heeled

165

horsemen. They fell silent and moved quickly out of the way as El Fuerte strode through.

"Everybody out of here," El Fuerte ordered in Spanish; "bring in only the musicians—everyone else must go."

When half a dozen of the troubadours had been admitted the place was cleared of general riffraff, until only two of El Fuerte's own lieutenants remained—del Pino, and the pleat-faced Carlos. The shutters of the deep-set windows were already fastened against the heat of the day, and now as the heavy door was closed and barred the interior suddenly became crepuscular.

El Fuerte walked through the house to a little high-walled patio in the rear, where a shallow open cistern held a placid brown mirror of stagnant water. A lean-to of palm thatch here made a cool and airy place to eat and drink; the sun, splashing through crevices in the thatch, made scraps of brilliant light on the hard-beaten earth below. A fighting cock tied by one leg to a post fixed beady eyes on El Fuerte's feet, bristling combatively as the man flung himself into a splint and rawhide chair.

"Now we can talk," said El Fuerte.

Cloud sat down on the opposite side of a little table, rested his elbows on the edge, and looked poker-faced. At a wave of El Fuerte's hand the musicians went across the patio and set up shop in a stable shelter on the other side, squatting about in its dirty straw.

"El Fuerte," said Cloud, "I guess I better be knowing what goes on here."

El Fuerte grinned exuberantly. "What you think of it, eh?"

166

"I don't aim to think anything until I know more about it."

The *alcalde* appeared with his arms full; he was a little saddle-colored man with earnest unperceiving eyes and a bushy grey mustache. He set on the table a big pitcher of *pulque,* two big blue glasses, two little blue glasses, two pottery mugs, a bottle of golden tequila, two different wine bottles—

"There's a boy in the street selling little pieces from a roast calf's head, El Fuerte told the *alcalde.* "Bring the calf's head here."

"Si, señor."

El Fuerte took a stiff drag of tequila and chased it with the sour-smelling *pulque.* Even in the heat of the day nothing ever seemed to affect that man's head. Cloud himself took a stiff snort of the stronger liquor, then made his glass ring on the table top.

"El Fuerte, I realize it's you that got all these people here. Now I want to know what you figure to do with 'em."

El Fuerte smiled with great relish and spread his hands in jovial dissimulation. "How can I help it if they come? You think maybe they come because I am here? Maybe so."

"You sent for these people," Cloud insisted.

"Can I help it," El Fuerte said sententiously, "if wolves follow the lion, and coyotes follow the wolves?"

The troubadours in the shade of the stable shelter were beginning to sing again, crooningly, not too loudly, but with a rich sustained flutter of the guitars. They were gravitating naturally now into the songs of love and sorrow to which Mexican troubadours are

167

forever turning—esteemed especially suitable now as an accompaniment for the eating and drinking of distinguished gentlemen:

"*Nada espero, porque pienso—*"

"I hope for nothing, for I think
That your love is like a sigh—"

"What I want to know," Cloud persisted doggedly, "is what comes next."

El Fuerte leaned back with his hands locked behind his head. For a few moments he gazed unwinking, almost dreamily, into the blazing blue of the sky. "This is my country," he said. "This is my own country. I have stay too long away."

Suddenly, with a singularly cat-like movement, he let his chair down and leaned across the table toward Cloud. His face was exultant, his eyes glimmered. "Mister, I hold Baja in the cup of my hand—so!"

"What the devil are you talking about?"

"You don't know what I'm talking about?" El Fuerte chuckled. He hesitated, then lifted his head sharply, listening. "Come here with me—I show you something more!" He seized Cloud's arm and almost dragged him through the house to the door of the ell, which he flung wide.

From the foot of the street went up the long hazing yell of the vaquero, and a dust cloud shot up beyond the throng. Up the broad band of dust between the houses charged five horsemen, the tall figure of Bravo in the lead, the others strung out. The thud and slam of the hoofs upon the dust of the street rose to a rumble, then a drumming thunder that seemed to vibrate the massive adobe walls. The dust sprang up in a choking cloud, obscuring the rear horsemen, and before the roaring hoofs the throng parted alertly, but with that well calculated leisure of movement peculiar to people who have lived with horses all their lives.

But there was another sort of movement all up and down that street, a subtle instinctive movement, sensed rather than seen. There was no cheering now, and except for the rising thunder of the cavalcades there was sudden quiet. But men not in the way of the horses moved quickly, unconsciously, jerked suddenly alert. In the scant shade of the ancient palms Cloud saw half a dozen men take hurrying steps toward their picketed ponies. A standing horse reared high as a ragged youth seized the reins and vaulted into the saddle. And all up and down the street ran a queer electric thrill, as if an unheard answering drum-beat had sounded in the brains of all these people, a drum-beat that answered the thunder in the dust.

Suddenly Cloud remembered the words of El Fuerte—"I have only to gallop down a street with four or five men at my back, shouting 'Rise *compadres*'— and they will rise and follow, not asking who I fight or where I go!"

And now Cloud knew that what El Fuerte had said was true. Drum of running horses, hazing rebel yells, a few impassioned catch words of revolt, and these people would swarm into the saddle, wild-reckless and ready to fight—drawn irresistibly by the thunder in the dust.

El Fuerte's eyes were on the rush of the dust-ghosted riders, and there was a glow as of red fire behind his

169

eyes. He flung one arm about Tom Cloud's shoulders, clamping him in an affectionate and mighty grip. "This country is our country," he said, his voice purring. "There is nothing we cannot do here, my frand! Nothing!"

He waved gaily at Bravo, but shut the heavy door against the dust as the riders pulled up sliding, with froth-dripping curbs. Expansive and light on his feet, El Fuerte strolled back through the house again and dropped himself beside the table.

For a long moment Cloud stared at him. Outwardly he was still relaxed, at his ease; but within he had turned as taut as rawhide stretched to dry in the sun. No joke here now. No blur of distance to make a futile burst of revolt seem funny. No chance to laugh off a thing which, as Beard had pointed out, might well end in the destruction of everything Cloud owned. Nothing here now that was not real, immediate, inevitable. The explosive forces that La Partida contained were as real as the hard brown living flesh that filled the street, as real as the reek of sweating horses—as real as the blood that would drip into the dust if this horse people pitched themselves into a crazed war.

Cloud realized now that El Fuerte could raise five hundred armed and mounted men out of this district at a wave of his hat. No chance, either, to smile at the smallness of a revolt started with only five hundred men. Dodging and twisting in these broken hills, five hundred tough riders with a practiced guerrilla leader could cost any government millions of dollars before they were put down. And apparently El Fuerte had succeeded in bringing here enough hard-fighting and ruthless Yaquis to form the keen edge of his blade.

Tom Cloud spoke with repressed violence. "You're crazy! By God, you listen to me! I tell you there isn't anything can be gained by this!"

El Fuerte smiled. "And—why not, Mister?"

"Maybe you can raise a mob on horseback here that can raise a whole lot of hell; I've got no doubt of that. But that doesn't mean that the state of Baja will rise behind you—not by a hell of a sight!"

"Look at it," El Fuerte urged him reasonably. "Your country has put a terrible tariff on beef. These people have nothing but beef. They can sell it nowhere. They cannot even ship to Mexico City—Chihuahua is so much more close. So now these people have nothing left. They can eat their cows and make clothes of leather, maybe—that is all. Yet the tremendous taxes bear down harder than ever—and no fruit of those taxes is ever seen. They are a people in a trap. They will rise and fight—all of them, to the last *mozo*—at a word. Many months they are ready to fight; a leader is all they need." He leaned across the table and tapped himself on the chest. "Today you see. You have see them cheer and sing when I just ride in the street. I ask you—am I such a leader? No?"

"You can't make an army," Cloud objected, "even if they all rise. You have no discipline, no training."

"I have an army that can ride and shoot and fear nothing; and they know every crack in these hills—every water hole and blind canyon, even in the dark."

"You haven't any way to move them; even to move the length of the peninsula would be a matter of weeks."

"We have all the horses in Baja—something the enemy will not have. And horses are the only means of travel over most of Baja."

171

"You haven't any means of supply."

"We have our beef. That is all we have anyway—meat. Nobody will notice any change."

"But, damn it," Cloud raved, "they can cut off your peninsula here so that not so much as a grain of salt comes in from outside—they can blockade you until—"

"Nothing comes in now," El Fuerte said, still very reasonable. "Since your country's cow tariff went on, Baja is cut off from the world."

Cloud knew that this was so. He was at a loss for an argument which would show El Fuerte the madness of his plans.

"I know what you think," said El Fuerte. "You think that one drilled regiment can sweep the peninsula. That is nonsense, Mister. In this country I can make a fool of an enemy that outnumbers me ten to one. But suppose you are right. Suppose one crack regiment can sweep me out of here. Mister, at this time that regiment cannot be sent! You do not know this. Two important states are on the verge of revolt. The Federals must hold every available man ready at their borders. For if those big states rise, it is no question of a little outbreak in a distant province like this. It means the central government fights for its life. They can send no men here!"

"Well, what then?" Cloud demanded harshly. "You think you can secede, and form a separate nation out of Baja? Or maybe you think you can take Baja and subdue all of the rest of the country? This is all rubbish, El Fuerte. Other states have other leaders, strong as you. You can't stand out long against a nation that runs from here pretty near to the equator. Maybe you'd be top dog here for a while; but what the devil's your object? There

172

isn't even any loot! And as soon as the Federals can turn their attention here you'll be kicked out to hell and gone—if you live. There isn't any future to it, El Fuerte."

El Fuerte chuckled. "You just cannot understand politics, Mister. Mister, you see before you the next governor of Baja. For how is a country like this to be held together? By letting each state be ruled by its strongest man—the man who controls the people. When I am governor of Baja all will be safe and sound here again— and three regiments from here will join the Federals in their other troubles elsewhere. This they will see."

"I don't believe it," said Cloud flatly.

El Fuerte shrugged. "Look at the central government. Look, at the cabinet—all made of generals. And what is a general? A general is a man whose people will follow him at his word. These people do not understand things that happen very well, Mister. They cannot read. They do not even trust flags—anybody can seize a flag. They must trust a man, a leader. When a man can show an army that trusts only him, then he is a general; then he is taken into the central government. In this way this country is governed. And it is a very good way."

El Fuerte spread his hands and leaned back. To the best of Cloud's belief everything that El Fuerte had said was so.

"How do you plan to strike?" Cloud asked.

"We seize Ensenada—we can get rifles there. A few troops from Mexicali then move to save Ensenada. We leave Ensenada in the hands of its own people, and, move like shadows through the hills, in two nights, and strike Mexicali. As you know, the central government is run by one man who holds no office, but is dictator. To

173

this man a wire is sent, saying that a leaderless revolt seizes everything—please send help. The dictator is angry. He—"

"Why a leaderless revolt?"

"You think these little politicians want the dictator to know that there is any leader stronger than themselves? Very well. Now I wire the dictator; I say that I go among the rebels, and I talk them sense, and I now seize everything in the name of the dictator himself. And everything is now in order except that the people do not let the old governor come back—and I am waiting his orders with respect. Right away he finds out from spies that it is El Fuerte the people want. All is cheering in the streets. And all is fixed."

"Suppose the dictator orders you to turn everything back to the regular officials?"

"That is the best we hope," said El Fuerte. "Then I turn it back—all except the customs treasury. Right away I turn loose my wolves again. Then I send message to the dictator—'I turn everything back to the officials, and the people now chase the officials in the hills. I have not yet turn the treasury back; shall I turn that back to the officials too?' "

"Somehow I can't believe it will work out quite so smooth as that," Cloud said.

"Now look," said El Fuerte, leaning forward again. "If you know Mexico, you know that power in this country changes hands all the time, in exactly this way. Now a little bit of power is about to change hands again. Maybe you better take my word for it, I think! This is your big chance, Mister—your own partner governor of Baja. With a governor—maybe even a cabinet general—for a partner, there is nothing that you cannot

174

do. You can build to the greatest herds in Baja—maybe later to the richest herds in all Mexico. For I tell you that I am not a man who can be stopped. You are up against a choice, Mister. Whichever way you choose, this country breaks wide open. If you have eyes you can see that—and you can see that I must win. Make your choice carefully; such a chance never comes again."

"What is it you want from me?" Cloud asked.

"You are an American," El Fuerte said. "Do not misunderstand me. I do not fear that the United States will interfere; anything that your government says will have very little effect. But there is some advantage to me if I can count on certain things. It will help me if I can say to our government, 'The Americans like me. Ask Tom Cloud, the biggest of them all.' You are very strong among the cattlemen of Baja. Maybe the time comes when you can say to your government, 'Only El Fuerte protects American cattle in Baja; only El Fuerte means safeness for us here.' For you see, Mister, our government is interested in what your government thinks because of the rate of exchange on the peso."

"Is that all you want?"

"What else have you got?"

"No money," Cloud said.

"No money," El Fuerte agreed.

"Beef?"

"We are partners in the Flying K. Nobody fools with El Fuerte's beef. A little dole, maybe; it costs us maybe a hundred head. That helps make the new governor look generous. But I already save you more head than this will cost."

Cloud tried to find a way to shrug off the claims of El Fuerte; but he could not. This was the sort of thing that happened over and over again in this strange country below the line. If El Fuerte had been a lonely dreamer building plans on paper, Cloud would not have given him a second thought. But he had seen the hundreds that had poured into La Partida, he had heard them cheer the least gesture of El Fuerte's hand. He even believed that El Fuerte was right about the attitude which the central government would take.

"We will rise together, you and me, Mister!" El Fuerte said.

There was reason for thinking, Tom Cloud believed, that he could probably count on the later friendliness of El Fuerte if he backed El Fuerte's play now. Cloud by no means underrated El Fuerte's suggestion of the strategic importance of a friend who was an American cattleman. Since Old Beard had for many years been a Mexican citizen, Cloud was the nearest and perhaps also the most important of the American cattlemen in Baja. No question but that he could help El Fuerte's political position. And it was true that the Mexican leaders stood by their friends. Cloud found himself recovering from the rapid turn of events.

"And if I don't want any part of this—what then?"

"Then I am sorry to lose you," said El Fuerte. "But I do not threaten you, Mister. When I am top dog, you go your own way, like before. Maybe I don't take any interest in your business, then; maybe you—don't gain nothing by my success. But look at this, Mister. If I fail I am finished in Baja—and you are finished with me. It is ruin, Mister. Solano is your bitter enemy. As my partner in cattle, you are in great danger of your life, if I lose; for sure, you will lose everything you own. You gain everything, lose nothing, if you help me every way

176

you can."

El Fuerte could have commanded no threat which would have swayed Cloud. What did weigh with Cloud was the suspicion that El Fuerte in truth represented the desires of the Baja people. Self government, in this country which he did not understand, seemed to take this form of expression more frequently than otherwise. He could not see El Fuerte in the role of liberator, throwing off the shackles of an oppressor. But as a political leader he certainly seemed to be the spontaneous choice of all those within his locale of influence. And Cloud could not forget the tremendous surge of power he had felt called up by the thunder in the dust.

There was nothing in Tom Cloud that was part of a timorous, or even a conservative man. He was of the breed that had taken the southwest from the horse Indians, and furnished the old filibusters, those free-lance soldiers of fortune who had raised so much hell all up and down this country in other days. One of his progenitors had been among those who had made Texas a republic. He believed now that he could not check El Fuerte; and he saw that if El Fuerte lost, Solano would certainly accomplish the ruin of the Flying K. He stood up abruptly. "I'll give you your answer tomorrow," he told El Fuerte.

CHAPTER 24

RIDING BACK UP THE LONG VALLEY OF THE WITCH, Tom Cloud swung down at the old hacienda. "Tonight is the time to see the fiesta," he told Kathleen. "What we can't see tonight, I'd sooner you didn't plan to see. Do you want to ride down to La Partida with me after supper?"

"Of course I do. But why no more after tonight? I thought tomorrow was the big day."

"Might be a little too big. I'll stop by for you pretty soon."

"But now that you're here aren't you going to have dinner with me?"

"Nope. You go ahead and eat. And don't forget to drink your milk, honey child! I've got to go get you a horse. I'll pick up something while I'm saddling."

Cloud went back to his cow camp, changed his dusty clothes, and shaved again. When he reappeared at the hacienda he was riding a fresh horse, and leading, under his best saddle, the prettiest and gentlest pony he owned.

"I'm afraid this isn't the kind of a saddle you're used to, mostly," he apologized.

"Any old saddle will do for me." He helped her mount, and they rode down the valley, her pony single-footing smoothly beside the rough jogging of Cloud's horse.

"Tom," Kathleen asked him, "will you tell me something? Why did you say that you don't want me in La Partida tomorrow?"

He considered a moment before he answered. Suddenly he knew that it was not his remark that had prompted her question. "What has El Fuerte told you?" he asked.

"He hasn't told me anything. At least not anything definite. But that man is full of revolt; he's the soul of revolt itself. He keeps hinting about the wonderful things that are going to happen, and the great things he means to do. Sooner or later there's bound to be insurrection wherever he is."

"That's true, Kathleen."

"Tom—is this the time?"

"Kathleen," Cloud said gravely, "this neck of the woods is as good as risen up right now."

"You mean—you think—"

Cloud studied her. The dusk was different tonight; there was no golden light upon the hills, but only a brooding purple, and in the west the sky at the horizon was as deeply red as clotted blood. The valley was very dark. He could not see her face very well in the poor light, but he made out that her eyes were serious and vividly alive.

"La Partida is swarming with more people than I ever expected to see in this part of the country," he told her. "Some of them are Yaqui bucks that don't belong in Baja at all. There's no question at all but what El Fuerte can raise five hundred picked fighting men in five minutes. After the picked five hundred he can probably get just as many more ordinary men as he wants."

"But, Tom, are they armed?"

"He can probably scrape together arms of some kind for two or three hundred men. But he means to strike Ensenada first. After Ensenada he ought to have enough guns to smash down on Mexicali without any fear of the outcome."

"But there's a garrison at Ensenada!"

"That's where he figures to get his guns."

"Why, I thought—" Kathleen seemed both appalled and excited—"I thought there was even an old fort at Ensenada."

179

"Have you ever seen it? I have."

They rode a little way in silence. "And then?" she asked him at last.

Briefly, in practical terms, Cloud explained to her the situation as El Fuerte saw it; sketching clearly the simple channels by which El Fuerte meant to seize the governorship of Baja. "Baja is cut into two districts, with two governors. But the southern district won't matter, if he can get the northern."

"It seems wild, utterly mad," Kathleen said. "It seems impossible that such a thing can come up so suddenly."

"That's where I was caught napping," Cloud admitted, unable to conceal his annoyance with himself. "In any ordinary situation a thing like this would take months, even years of planning. But Kathleen, I'm not at all sure that it isn't possible. These people seem like a sleepy, pretty near motionless people. But they can explode like dynamite; and when they do that, it takes all hell to stop them."

"You think he can really take Ensenada, then turn and take Mexicali?"

"I believe he can. This man has a terrible lot of say-so with these people. It looks to me like they'd follow him into anything. He has a big advantage in numbers over these little garrisons, and a foxy head for strategy. I guess he can do it, all right."

"But after that—can he really get the dictator to back him?"

"I don't know," Cloud said honestly. "But this man can persuade people into things I wouldn't have believed. It may be he can do even that."

"Tom, when he takes these towns—Ensenada, Mexicali—does that mean looting and wrecking? Will

180

this sudden army of his run wild and rob and destroy—"

"I don't know," Cloud said again. "Sometimes these rebels do that. I don't know how El Fuerte handles these things."

"I can't believe he'd let it happen," Kathleen said.

"I don't know," Cloud replied.

"Tom, if you'd foreseen this in time you could have stopped him."

"But I didn't foresee it. I can't hardly believe it now."

"Do you suppose you can stop him even yet?"

"I don't know if anything in the world can stop him. As for me—it may be that I'll back him."

She stared at him and in her face was an excitement the nature of which be could not guess. "This is like a—conquest," she breathed at last.

"More like a faro game," he grunted. "About all I know about it is we seem to be in for it."

"If you back him and he loses—"

"We won't worry about that yet. Meanwhile, I think you're safe here, for now. I'll put some fast horses where ambitious revolutionists won't be liable to get 'em; and if things get smoky, I'll see you over the border all right."

"Oh, don't worry about me."

Even from a long way off La Partida was a glow in the darkness, when the dusk had died; and from this glow was beginning to come a pulsing beat—the dull persistent thudding of the Indian drums del Pino had brought into Baja "in case of emergency." The people of Baja, gaining little but cheap perfumes, gimcracks, and taxes from the advance of civilization, but rapidly losing their own culture, had perhaps not heard for a generation the voice of such drums as these del Pino had

181

brought. And now as they drew close they saw that La Partida's broad street was alight with hundreds of torches, burning yellow and smoky under the black sky.

If the street had seemed thronged before, now it was doubly so. The lighted doors of the houses were jammed with silhouetted figures, but most of the people were in the street, a shifting, perpetually shuffling crowd, denser near the plaza. The fitfully flaring torchlight struck across the brown faces from odd changing angles. Sometimes it glinted on eyes and the flash of white teeth, sometimes it showed faces with high-lighted features and deep shadows like death's-heads; or again glared strongly on a cowled *rebozo* beneath which the face was a mystery of black shadow. Vendors went wandering through the crowd with big trays on their heads, chanting fixed phrases about roast meat or *tortillas* or *dolces*. An old woman crouched in the dust frying *enchiladas,* turning them in the boiling grease with flicks of her bare fingers. All the street was full of voices and laughter and the cries of the vendors and snatches of song, and over all other sound beat the incessant, inescapable overtone of the drums at the end of the street.

Through the perpetual broken murmur of sound the people drifted about in little groups, restive, without purpose. But there was something here that was not aimless—an underlying tension of expectancy that seemed to sustain itself upon the unremitting thudding of the drums. The drum music interlocked itself with the strange quality of the night, which was turning sharp and breezy under a heavily overcast sky, with something of the smell of a northern fall in the air. The effect was as if all the *"mañana"* spirit of that country

182

were being broken up and blown away; and the unmasking of this people's tremendous animal energy was like the unsheathing of a blade.

As the two riders pressed their way slowly through the street the throngs made way before the horses, not excitably, with the intense interest accorded El Fuerte, but respectfully nevertheless; here and there a shout went up—"*Viv' el capitan Americano!*"

Kathleen looked at Cloud questioningly. "What does that mean? Are you already one of the leaders here?"

He shook his head, making no acknowledgment of the random cheers. "They saw me ride through with El Fuerte today; that's all."

Kathleen murmured, "Even his friends are cheered at sight!"

Some peculiarly ironic angle was evading Cloud; he could not put a finger on it. "*Que hombre,*" he agreed.

Just beyond the end of the street, where the *alcalde's* house made a corner that was the end of its row, the little plaza opened before the ancient church. That plaza was only a clear space between the end of the street and the façade of the church, a little square of dust bounded by the ubiquitous pepper trees, but more people were gathered here than in any equal area in La Partida. Half a dozen bonfires blazed, filling the space with light, and from among these fires came the everlasting mellow thunder of the drums. Cloud could not see the drummers because of the shifting crowd, but he knew by the tone of the taut rawhide that the drums were being played with the flat of open hands.

As they drew up for a moment, looking into the plaza from the end of the street, del Pino came running out from the *alcalde's* house, and once more Cloud found himself astonished by this little man.

Always before he had seen del Pino indiscriminately dressed, neither a vaquero nor a townsman—not to be classified as anything in the world except—the hanger-on of El Fuerte; but now del Pino had blossomed out into a new entity. He was hatless, and his poorly trimmed hair had been combed in a way that somehow made his head look leonine, rugged upon his narrow shoulders. Cloud hardly recognized him, never having seen del Pino with his hair combed before. More surprising than this was del Pino's high-winged collar and flowing black tie and most surprising of all—wonder of wonders—was del Pino's long frock coat. He wore that coat regally; it seemed to set up the whole man, and though it could not make him look big, it did make him look more effective, more imposing in his own way than Cloud had ever seen him before.

"You are to come inside," del Pino told them. "El Fuerte, he expects you, Mrs. Boyce. There is a place fixed where you can see everything."

He led them into the *alcalde's* house now, not through the ell, but by a door which opened upon the plaza itself. Against this door Carlos was standing; afoot, as in the saddle, this man's sinuous, apparently youthful body was an anomaly to his curiously wrinkled face, giving him a singularly arresting appearance. A dozen nondescripts who lounged along the house wall were held there so compactly that it was obvious they were now under Carlos' command. Carlos stared hard at Kathleen, but moved out of their way.

Thus they came into a part of the house that Cloud had not seen before—that which faced the plaza and the church. A precipitous wooden stairway gave access to a

184

second story consisting of one long room; and up this stair del Pino led them at once.

The single upstairs room differed from anything Cloud had expected to find in La Partida. Once more, as was repeatedly happening to him nowadays, he was exasperated by the recognition that he knew little or nothing about the people among whom he had chosen to pursue his fortune.

For in their own way these quarters had been luxurious. The ceiling was very low, but the room was long and wide. A dozen candles, in big branching candelabra fit for a church, burned on either side of an enormous canopied bed with posts like tree trunks. The walls were mostly bare, but there were three or four religious pictures, old smoky, blackened oils, looted perhaps from forgotten missions; and in one corner a little shrine, full of gilded wooden figures, was heavily draped in embroidered cloth.

But what instantly stirred Tom Cloud were the guns. The other things here represented what this room had been; but it was turned into an arsenal now. All along the walls were piled long boxes of the type that filled El Fuerte's room at the Flying K camp; Cloud knew that in those boxes rifles lay in cosmoline, waiting their time to speak. Other rifles of varied types stood racked in the corners, and lay in heaps against the wall.

Del Pino walked across the room and flung wide the shutters of a six-foot window. Beyond, a narrow balcony ran, overhanging the plaza; but access to the balcony was by another way, for this window was barred with heavy spindles of oak. Below this outlook the scene in the plaza lay framed; its welter of firelight, broken by innumerable moving figures, forced upward defiantly, intensified rather than repressed by the black weight of a starless sky that seemed to have lowered until it was all but resting upon the housetops. The smoke of the fires swept away levelly upon the breeze, scudding off in flat streamers just above the heads of the people.

As Tom and Kathleen stood here the drum thunder rose to them strongly, its rhythms irresistible, unflagging. Without any unison the restless people that thronged the plaza seemed to sway to the drums, unconsciously and helplessly answering the syncopated rhythms of the beat. Their figures silhouetted blackly against the fires, or showed proudly golden in groups that formed and stood a little, to shift and break and shuffle again.

Beyond the throngs and the fires the tall façade of the little church shone dimly by the unsteady light of the flames. Its patched and scaling wall looked incredibly ancient, and its rococo clay ornaments were crumbling; but through its fifteen-foot doors the watchers behind the balcony could see a bank of candles burning before a shrine, mysterious points of yellow flame, dotted here and there with red where a taper burned low in its ruby glass. Drawn in blackness against the bank of candles showed a life-sized tortured figure of the crucified Christ.

Cloud was studying the people in the plaza. A few gay proud-headed girls were walking about here arm in arm answering with teasing sidelong glances the frank stares of the men. But once more Cloud noticed with a strong inward stir that the gathering here was chiefly male—lean-hipped men with hard-carved faces and assured swagger. How many of them had marched and

186

raided before now under this man who called himself El Fuerte?

Kathleen said in a low, unsteady voice, "This is the kind of thing you hear about, and read about, but never, never see."

Cloud was silent. He was wondering if, having seen this once, she would ever want to see it again. Presently, perhaps, she would be willing to give a good deal to forget what might be seen in Baja before this thing was done. One of her hands was upon a spindle of the barred window, and he wrapped his fingers around it. With surprise he found that she was trembling.

"Here on the table is wine," del Pino said. "When El Fuerte comes, he will be happy to know you are here." The little man went clattering down the deep-worn steps.

"Kathleen, what is it? What's the matter?"

"I—I don't know . . . Just the excitement, I guess."

CHAPTER 25

THE SHUFFLING SHIFT OF THE HUNDREDS WHO HAD never been in this town before, who had no normal business here—that would have put tension into anybody, whether they knew what it was about or not. In a great city this gathering would have been only a handful, but here in this country of desert hills it represented the rise of a people. Once they broke loose, and began to run wild over the country, anything could happen.

Cloud understood why Kathleen should be stirred, even shaken, by the thing that was happening here. Yet,

187

because this woman was woven deeply into his heart, there was a twinge of pain in his throat for a moment— the trembling of her fingers under his own rock-steady hand made the slender frailty of her body so near and real.

Cloud himself, watching the bravo swagger of certain tall men in the crowd below, was experiencing a great warlike lift of spirits. His horizons were always the broad and barren horizons of the saddle man; beyond the light of flame and fire he could sense the background of far-flung hills, mile upon long mile. In the vastness of this dark and empty country La Partida was like a glowing, beating heart, a heart heavy with passion for action, war passion presently to be unleashed at the word of Cloud's incredible partner. Under the unremitting throb of the drums was lust, age-old emotion, and urge to battle. To the crowds below revolt meant loot and glory, fire and joyous destruction, loosing of hate, patriotic hysteria, and rapine; above all the lift of an adventure in which all rules would be off, remedying at a stroke the dusty monotony of their lives.

Even Tom Cloud could not shield himself from the drunken magic of the drums. They beat down sense, and called up in its place old forgotten things. Looking down upon the swarming plaza, Cloud knew that El Fuerte would succeed. He no longer considered the possibility of checking El Fuerte; El Fuerte could neither be stopped nor beaten. He would sweep the peninsula like wildfire, rising irrepressibly to his destined fortunes at last. Del Pino had been right, Cloud wrong.

He said slowly, "I don't know but what I'd kind of like to ride with them, when they go."

"Why don't you?" Kathleen said instantly. "How can you keep from it?"

He shook his head. "No point to it. I've got work to do here. Let him do his stuff—I'll do mine."

Yet even while he heard himself say that, he knew that he was half drunk with the fever of conquest. He had no illusions as to El Fuerte's brand of patriotism, saw no choice between one government in Baja and another, so far as the good of the people went. But the spirit of the filibusters, of the hard-handed saddle adventurers of the old frontier, was rising to his head. He was not forgetting that El Fuerte would bring ruin upon the Flying K if he failed. What was beating in his mind more strongly, like the beat of the drums, was that El Fuerte's success could mean to him fortune untold. Nothing could stop a partner of El Fuerte—if El Fuerte won.

"Look," he said, turning to Kathleen. "We don't know what the end of this will be. El Fuerte will seize the towns all right. And I believe there's a good chance that he can get himself confirmed as governor, too. But, by God, the whole works stands or falls on a couple of throws of the dice. I think you ought to know that if El Fuerte is beaten, the Flying K is wiped out."

"Because you're his partner?"

Cloud nodded. "Solano sure aches to get me. If El Fuerte loses out, the Flying K is up against confiscation, no less."

"And you—what will happen to you then? Do you think they'd go so far as—"

"Oh, if El Fuerte falls down, I'd better be long gone, all right. No question of that. But either side of the border, if El Fuerte breaks, I break with him."

189

"But he won't break," Kathleen said in so curious a voice that he looked at her sharply. "I know he won't."

Cloud shrugged. "If he wins out it'll mean—considerable advantage. The Flying K will run more cattle than has been seen under one brand since the old days, before we're through. Point is, we can't know which way she'll jump; not yet."

"You can do a good deal toward his success, I should think," Kathleen said.

"I've pretty close to decided to do what I can. But I want you to know this. I never owned a calf, or a pony, or a length of rope without I made it myself. If I go down I'll come up again—faster this time than before. Up or down, they'll never stop me—can you believe that?"

"Tom, anybody that knows you would know that."

He was silent for a moment, turned full toward her, his eyes on her face. Her dark, soft hair was back-lighted by the mild candlelight; but the pulsing red-gold light from torch and flame was strong upon her face, and the light of the flames was reflected in her eyes. A little pulse was beating in the—hollow of her throat, as if in answer to the thudding of the drums. Frail as she seemed to him, he could see in her face the spirit of Spanish conquistadors, the glory of Irish kings.

He said humbly, "You believe in me, Kathleen?"

"Tom, you know that."

It was remarkable that any sound could mean as much to anyone as her voice meant to him. But his common sense was sorting out certain practical aspects of the storm that was brewing below. To a certain extent such a leader as El Fuerte could control his men, but no living leader could control all of them all the time. He distrusted the drunken restless riders that these brown saddle men would become when presently they went crazy with battle and success. He half believed that he ought to urge Kathleen to leave the country and get over the line; but he was afraid that if she obeyed him, which seemed unlikely, he might never see her again. He did not doubt his ability to win this woman and make her his own. Before the shock of John Boyce's death had so changed her, she had been as good as his already. But he was not at all sure that he could hold her imagination against distance and separation.

"Look," he said, "look here." His voice was uncertain. He could not get around the fact that lately she was more or less of an unknown quantity to him. "I don't know as I feel right about you living alone, there at the hacienda, the way this thing is boiling up around here."

She shot him a quick glance. "I've rather been expecting that," she said.

"Expecting what, Kathleen?"

"You're going to suggest that I leave for the border."

"No," he said slowly, "I don't believe I could ever ask you to go that far away from me again."

He felt her hand tighten upon the window bar, and his own fingers closed more strongly over hers. "Look here," he said; his voice was low and husky, his lips very close to her ear. "There's only one other way. I worship the ground you walk on—you know that. I can't let you go out of my life, not ever any more. If Boyce had lived I'd have taken you away from him, some day; even if it took all my life to do it. I could have done it, and I would have, Kathleen."

Kathleen Boyce did not move, and her fingers were

191

not trembling now; it seemed to him that they were cold under his hand. He took his hand from hers and stood very close to her, but not touching her. Cloud had never been so uncertain of himself in his life. This was not the way this sort of thing should be done; he knew that. He could have won her gently and easily, he thought, if he had time. But the murder of John Boyce, which had set her free, had also put her emotionally out of his reach for a time, by sheer raw impact. And now the irresistible rise of violence that had been conjured up by El Fuerte pushed Cloud into a play for which Kathleen was not ready.

He went on doggedly, feeling keenly the disadvantage of his situation, for she had given no sign that he could use for a guide. "I love you," he said; "I love you with all the heart there is in me, Kathleen. Nobody ever loved anybody any more truly than I love you."

He paused; with as great an intensity as he had ever known he was watching for the sign that still did not come. Below in the little smoke-hazed plaza the drum thunder rose and fell in a rolling, swaying beat. Tom Cloud said suddenly, "Dear God, Kathleen—don't you hear me at all?"

He saw her draw a deep, choking breath. She said almost inaudibly, "I hear you." Although no more than half an inch separated them, it seemed to him that she was a thousand miles away, utterly beyond his reach.

"Come here," he begged her. "Come here to me."

Suddenly he took her shoulders and made her face him. Her face was white and frightened, her eyes enormous and very dark; after an instant they did not meet his, but shifted right and left as if seeking escape. She averted her face toward the fire and the drums, and the light from the plaza glowed in her hair.

He took her in his arms and held her against him, and she stood unresisting. After a moment she let her head rest wearily against his chest, but without suggestion of surrender or response. It was as if she leaned against a patient horse. He pressed his mouth against her hair. "I'll split the west wide open for you, Kathleen! There's nothing in the world I can't get for you, given time. I want you to marry me, Kathleen."

A long moment passed and another, filled with the insistent drugging tempo of the drums. At last Kathleen said, "Perhaps; some day . . . *Quien sabe?*"

"Not some day—now. Tonight!"

She stirred in his arms as if she would move, away from him but did not. "I—that's impossible."

"I tell you it's the only way I can take care of you through this thing. You can have any terms you want. You can go on living as if we weren't married at all. But you'll be safe then—I can see to it that you're safe."

He could hardly hear her words. "From what?"

"Kathleen, take my word for it, this is the best way."

"Tom, I can't! I can't!"

"Kathleen, why not? If it's the ghost of that infernal Boyce—"

"I don't think it's that."

"Then what is it?"

"I don't think—I know myself what it is."

"Kathleen, Kathleen—"

She suddenly stiffened in his arms. "Look!" Her eyes were on the plaza.

For a moment he hesitated; then abruptly dropped his arms. Instantly she turned to the window. A ragged storm of cheering suddenly went up in the plaza, and

193

sardonically Cloud's eyes followed hers.

Into the plaza El Fuerte rode. The machete-faced Bravo and two other horsemen were at his flanks, but though these men were tall, El Fuerte's long-legged palomino set him head and shoulders above them, as if he were someone out of some different, mightier race than theirs. He was wearing a white blouse with a high collar of the old military type, without insignia; its gold buttons made his big figure gleam and flash. The torchlight flickered too on the intricate silver of the palomino's headstall and saddle as it pranced, so that horse and man were a primitive glory, irresistible. El Fuerte waved his big leather-embroidered hat; the crowd shouted and threw things into the air, and some of them let off their guns.

Kathleen Boyce said in a queer voice, "Did you ever see anything like that in all your life?"

They were silent as El Fuerte rode slowly across the plaza toward the *alcalde's* house, the traveling center of a wild ovation. For a moment there was a disturbance as an aged woman suddenly rushed at El Fuerte's horse, screaming curses, and shaking clawed hands above her head; but a dozen laid hold of her, suppressing her cries as they carried her away. After this unexplained incident El Fuerte pushed on toward the house from which they watched.

As he drew near, del Pino ran out, a struggling little figure in his frock coat, and El Fuerte leaned low to hear what he said; then immediately stood up in his stirrups to wave exuberantly at the window from which they watched.

Dozens were clustered about El Fuerte's stirrups. Two or three red splotches that looked like the big blossoms from the *sangre de Cristo* vine struck against his white jacket; those would be from the bold-eyed girls. But now El Fuerte pressed his horse quickly through the crowd and, swinging down, disappeared under the balcony beneath their feet. The drums which had risen to a thundering diapason while El Fuerte was in the plaza subsided again to a hollow endless growling; it was as if something which the drums had been trying to call out of the night had come there for a moment, then gone out of sight again.

El Fuerte came clattering up the stairs with a great ringing of spurs. He was always a big man, but in the white military blouse he seemed taller than ever, and his shoulders looked enormous. And at the same time he seemed more competent than before, as if he were no longer a man getting on in years and thickening in the middle, but a youngster swinging into his first prime. He saluted them flamboyantly with an upward swing of both arms, and all his good teeth flashed in his triumphant grin. He was theatrical, he was stupendous; but somehow here against his background of stacked weapons and throbbing drums he was the most real figure in the room or in the night. It was as if he were the vital essence of a nation, of two races successfully welded into one.

He came striding down the room, and struck Cloud mightily on the back with the flat of his hand; he set the whole room to vibrating merrily with the ring of his spurs and the impact of his high spirits. He picked up Kathleen bodily, with one arm about her waist, and kissed her mouth, then set her down again and whirled on one heel to the window. Kathleen pressed the back of one hand to her mouth; above it she looked at El Fuerte with astonished eyes. But before Cloud's resentment

195

rose, El Fuerte had flung an arm across the shoulders of each of them and turned them to the window.

"Look, Mister! Look, *mi señora!* What good fighting men have come here from a long way!"

Below, in the plaza, several of the crowd glimpsed his white jacket behind the bars of the window; somebody sailed a hat onto the balcony. El Fuerte hugged both Cloud and Kathleen, then released them and turned away. He was all triumphant energy tonight.

"I have two things I must do," he told them. "Then we all have a big supper here, no? With much to drink. I try not to be long—you wait here for me. Watch what you see there," he commanded with a wave at the window. "And think—this is only to begin! Tonight is not the night. Tomorrow night— then you see!"

He went clumping and ringing down the steep stairs and was gone.

For a little while Tom Cloud and Kathleen stood and stared at each other, as if left immovable in a vacuum caused by El Fuerte's withdrawal.

In Kathleen's face still showed the tense surprise implanted there by El Fuerte's exuberant kiss. Her mouth was very red, as if the blood had been pressed out of her lips and had suddenly come rushing back. Then abruptly Kathleen seemed to wilt, all over, with a sudden utter fatigue. Her eyes darkened and her mouth distorted in something very like terror. Cloud stepped toward her as he thought be saw her sway.

Kathleen cried out huskily, "Take me away from here! I want to go away from here. I want you to take me home."

CHAPTER 26

THE SUDDEN NERVOUS FATIGUE THAT HAD COME UPON Kathleen Boyce must have made the five miles from La Partida to the hacienda seem interminable to her. The wind had turned damp and cold and raw; sometimes it moaned with a sound of vast emptiness up the flat Valley of the Witch. Twice Cloud felt a spit of rain. He tried to make the ride easier for Kathleen by loping the ponies a half mile at a time, so that presently they steamed until rolls of lather appeared at the edge of the saddle blankets even in the cool of the night. Between times he tried once or twice to talk to her.

"I don't understand the man, even yet," he said once. "When you watch him, and see his people around him, it seems like he can really do everything he thinks he can do. Maybe he'll make himself one of the big guns in all Mexico, some day."

Kathleen was silent, and after a moment Cloud added, "But I wouldn't have let this happen, if I had seen it coming in time."

"Because the Flying K will be wiped out if he loses?"

"No; it isn't that. I don't think he's going to lose."

"Then why, Tom?"

"I don't get this country," Cloud said; "you know that. But I've seen a little of it in the course of a lifetime. When you turn the wolves loose in this country it isn't a pretty thing. They know how to go just as kill-crazy as wild animals."

"I've heard of that. But this—is El Fuerte."

"What difference does that make?" he said sharply.

"El Fuerte's different, There's a great strength in that

197

man. And a great—gentleness."

Cloud was startled.

"Gentleness?" he repeated incredulously.

"Only the strong can be truly gentle."

"I'll tell you what I saw once," he said, "in a little adobe Indian town. It was the Easter fiesta, and there was a war captain from the hills there, something like El Fuerte. He was running everything. In the fiesta they used to have in that town, they used to burn an effigy of Judas, and I was there when they did that. But when my pony got a smell of the smoke he turned and tried to bolt. Then I noticed how life-like the effigy looked, and saw what the pony had known in the first place. The effigy was not an effigy at all. It was the body of a man, some little *mozo* who had offended the war captain in some way. And all around the flames was dancing and celebration."

"Oh, that's terrible!"

"There's a vein of something or other in these people," Cloud told her, "that you and I won't ever be able to understand. It's more or less in them all. It's in El Fuerte."

"I can't believe that," she said; and they fell silent.

Again, he said, "I didn't mean to let El Fuerte manhandle you tonight. I didn't see what he was going to do. But it didn't seem like he meant anything. So I thought I'd let it go by without making anything of it."

"Tonight? When?"

"When he picked you up and kissed you."

"Oh, that."

"You can't always count on what these people will do," Tom Cloud warned her. "Not even El Fuerte. But if ever he bothers you—you let me know. By God, I'll

198

break him in two."

She didn't answer him. It seemed to Cloud that she had become irretrievably remote, unreachable. He wrapped his romal around his pony, forcing it to lope again, and her horse kept pace. At the hacienda he opened the gate for her, and held her pony as she dismounted.

Kathleen said, "Good night"; then turned instantly, and was gone into the house. Cloud was left standing with the reins of the two horses in his hands and a gone, empty feeling in his middle.

He shrugged his shoulders, mounted, and rode the two miles to his cow camp, profoundly disturbed. It was a new thing to him to have events rise and swirl about him, deciding his fortune, while he yet took so little part; and he was lost as he tried to understand what had come over Kathleen. He couldn't believe that she found herself swayed by a man who got himself up like a Christmas tree.

It was nearly midnight, but he had no thought of turning in. He sat before his adobe listening to the hiss of the damp wind in the lonely pines, very watchful and broad awake without having anything to watch for. When a horse came up the valley from La Partida he heard it a long way off, half an hour before the rider came into view.

The rider was del Pino. He ran his horse toward the corrals, zigzagging uncertainly; then turned, came hammering to where Cloud sat, and pulled up sliding, his horse wind-blown and foaming. Del Pino was not wearing his frock coat now, but a shapeless bundle tied behind the saddle might have contained it.

He scrambled down from the saddle, then for a

moment seemed nonplussed to find that Cloud was alone. "Where is he? Where is he?" the little man jerked out.

Cloud did not have to ask to whom del Pino referred. "How the hell should I know where he is? Last I saw him, he was in La Partida."

Del Pino raised hysterical hands to the stars. "This is always the way! I never knew it any different! This is what comes to a man who spends his life trying to raise up El Fuerte! The hour comes, and all is ready—and where is he?"

Cloud could not restrain a sudden chuckle. "Maybe he's gone to look for quail seeds," he suggested.

An inarticulate whimper burst from del Pino and, turning, he flung himself up the side of his horse.

"Just a minute." Cloud came to his feet smoothly and swiftly, and seized the rein of del Pino's horse. The hard-run animal reared, almost unseating the little rider. "Don't move so quick. You'll stampede and scare yourself, del Pino."

"Let me go!" del Pino gibbered. "Let loose, I say! *Mil diablos*! There is not a minute to lose!"

"I want to know what's up; and the quicker you let me know, the quicker you'll be gone from here."

Del Pino's efforts to jerk his horse free from Cloud's hold subsided, and words rushed out of him. "I tell you I have seen this thing before! I tell you I know how these people must be handled! These people will do anything for El Fuerte. But he must seize his chance at the right time and in the right place. When the people are ready to rise up, then you must rise them up—immediate! Tomorrow will not do, tomorrow night will not do! In this thing a man must seize his hour."

"You're all excited," Cloud told him.

"I tell you I know what I'm doing," del Pino said savagely. "Tonight I can raise him near a thousand men. Tomorrow—*quien sabe?* But it's not too late yet! I know where he is. I could have had him halfway to La Partida now, but I rode past like a fool because I saw no lights. By Dios, I'll get him out of that! *Cristo y Recristo!* Of all nights, what a night for it! But I'll get him to La Partida if I have to drag him out from between the sheets. Let me go!"

"I think," said Tom Cloud softly, "I'll go find El Fuerte for you myself."

"Then come quick. Maybe you catch me on the road. But now I must go!"

"You're staying here," Cloud told him. "It just comes to me that I want to look into this little thing alone."

Del Pino stared at him blankly. "But—are you crazy? I—"

"Get down off that horse," Cloud ordered him; and as del Pino hesitated he dragged him out of the saddle by the belt. Del Pino danced and gibbered, unloosing a torrent of Spanish. With a few motions Cloud stripped saddle and bridle from del Pino's horse, and sent it stampeding into the dark by tossing the whole saddle rigging across its hocks.

"Quick. New horses!" begged del Pino. He fumbled about his overturned saddle for his rope.

"I'll tend to the horses." In the horse corral Cloud roped the best pony that was left, and quickly saddled. Then he kicked down the bars of the gate, mounted, and routed the few remaining ponies out into the dark. He sent up a long hazing yell, and, pulling his gun, let loose four or five shots into the sky. With a rush of hoofs the

201

horse bunch scattered into the night.

"What do you do?" cried del Pino, almost weeping. "What is this thing? Sir, I tell you—"

"I told you I wanted to look into this thing alone. I meant it. You don't act to me like you'd stay put, if there was any way for you to keep from it. But you'll stay put now." Cloud knew well enough that del Pino, awkward with the rope, would have no luck at catching any one of the ponies in the dark. "Now just you sit tight and cool off. By and by maybe somebody'll send you a pony. I don't know yet." His voice was drawling, very hard and cool; so changed that the horrified del Pino must have felt he was listening to another man. Certainly all the frantic steam suddenly went out of del Pino. He stood limp and silent, his face tragic, as he watched Tom Cloud drift off down-valley at a swinging lope.

CHAPTER 27

WHEN KATHLEEN HAD CLOSED THE DOOR UPON TOM Cloud, she stood where she was, and leaned her forehead wearily against the heavy panel. Now that the door was shut between them she no longer wanted him to go away, but realized immediately that above all things she dreaded to be alone. Almost she opened the door again and called out to him; but as she hesitated she heard him mount and turn his horses. And she let him go, though the sound of retreating hoofs gave her a progressive sinking of the heart, much like the feeling of a little child when adult footsteps recede down the long stairway, leaving him alone in the dark.

For just lately, for the first time in her life, Kathleen was afraid of the dark. The aged peon people who took care of the house for her lived in a couple of two-room adobes, several hundred yards away. They would hear her if she called out, of course—only nothing was going to happen that would make her call out. Sometimes she wished that something would, so tight did her nerves get, alone in that old house that became cavernous with the night.

She could not forget that this room in which she stood was the room in which John Boyce had died, and with the darkness in front of her eyes she could see again his lifeless, unnaturally sprawled body in the corner, half behind his chair, with the blue steel of the rifle barrel beneath. Not that she was afraid of death, or ghosts, or John Boyce, living or dead; she wasn't even afraid of the violence that had killed him. It was only that shock and horror could live again in the dark. And in this house at night she was so utterly, terribly alone. It made the Valley of the Witch—even the whole country— seem strange and hostile. The peons could not even talk to her in her own language; and Tom Cloud, the nearest person she cared about, was two miles away.

She turned away from the cold surface of the door and walked through the house to her own room steadily, with her chin up. It was a little more friendly here, because the room was smaller, and the light from the shaded lamp was nice. It helped too when she touched a match to the kindling that was laid in the adobe fireplace in the corner of her room. Without saying anything to her, Cloud had ordered one of her *mozos* to lay that fire every day. He did it better than Pepe, the little grinning muleteer whom the rurales had killed.

Kathleen undressed, and resolutely blew out the lamp. Instantly the darkness came closer again. The little fire, already dying, filled the room with wavering shadows without seeming to give any light. She unlatched a window, which Tom had asked her not to do, crept between the cold sheets of her immense bed, and for a little while lay curled up, shivering. Even when she wasn't cold any more she lay curiously rigid, unready for sleep.

The big unsquared timbers of the roof were beginning to talk now, complaining of the change in the weather, but it was not the unsilence of the old house that kept her awake tonight. It was the drums, the everlasting, insistent, untiring drums of La Partida that would not be still and let her rest. The distant lowing of cattle, down by the fence where Tom Cloud weaned calves, was silent now in the midnight quiet that always came upon the valley; and, straining her ears, Kathleen thought that she could hear the drums at La Partida beating still, carried across five miles of hills and valley by the raw wind. Or maybe it was only that they were beating in her head—even beating somewhere in her body, under her heart.

Under the hammering of those drums Kathleen had found herself strangely racked; their pulsing rhythms had not repelled her, but drawn her with an hypnotic fascination, as if some strange primitive part of her that had never wakened before was stirring in its sleep, trying to rouse and, answer their urgent, unintelligible pleading.

Looking in her mirror as she undressed she had noticed how slanting her eyes seemed; they always drew upward at the corners when she was in need of sleep

204

and could not sleep. The shadows about her eyes made her face look thinner, so that her cheekbones seemed very prominent. She had wondered if by any chance there could be any of the blood of the ancient Aztecs in her veins, a heritage from the Spanish part of her ancestry. Certainly she had been at a loss to know herself as she had stood half-hypnotized behind the La Partida balcony, watching the light of fires twitch upon dark-faced figures; as if the drum-madness could reach out and touch something within her, as it visibly worked upon the Spanish-Indian people.

Kathleen pressed her eyes with the palms of both hands. The black emptiness of the house was unbearable, and she hated the lifeless, impersonal pressure of the mattress against her body. She kept remembering that if she had surrendered herself to Tom Cloud tonight, as he had urged, he would be here now, with the great steady strength of his arms about her, shutting out forever the loneliness and the dark, and the nagging of little-understood drums. She could not understand why it had been impossible for her to let Tom Cloud into her heart, and herself into his arms. In the few months that she had known him Tom Cloud had become very dear to her, and more than dear. He was never out of her thoughts for very long. Her need for him had mounted almost by the hour, since the first time she had ever seen him; until she no longer concealed from herself that she wished to be possessed by him, completely and forever, more than she had ever wanted anything in her life. Yet she had come once more into this dark house alone, and closed the door.

She only knew that she had felt incomplete, unready—and that above all she was a stranger to

205

herself.

Certainly she was not in love with El Fuerte. Very strongly she sensed the great, vital strength of the man, a vitality of the soil, of horses, of the brown mountains and desert winds; but in many ways the extraordinary hill-captain actively repelled her. His way, upon occasion, of walking about barefoot in the dust—with splayed toes that suggested his having worn sandals once for a long time—was inexplicable to her, and made him seem like a horse, or a wolf, and not of a civilized human breed.

Yet, even while it frightened her, that sense of the earthy vitality in El Fuerte did something else; it fascinated and disturbed her with a faint sense of the hypnotic, like the muffled thunder of the ancient drums. She knew now that before she had ever heard those drums, she had sensed them through El Fuerte. It was as if they were an expression of El Fuerte—or perhaps it was simply that she sensed the same quality of the elemental in both.

When she had stood in their pulsing beat at La Partida, and El Fuerte had caught her up in one arm and kissed her mouth, all those primitive unknown things within herself that the drums called up had surged to her head, making her utterly unknown to herself.

Behind that was the reason that she had stood aloof from Tom Cloud these last weeks—loving him, sometimes, as if her heart would cry out loud, yet uncertain of herself because of the strange primitive stir that had come into the depths of her. For even before she had heard the drums, the same effect had been in the serenading of El Fuerte.

Sometimes during those weeks, Cloud could have had

her for the asking. If he had taken her in his arms, if he had grinned and commanded her, she would have clung to him and begged him never to let her go. And she knew he would have done it, if she had given him a sign, by so much as looking him in the eyes. But she had given no sign, held frozen by something she could not have named.

So now she lay unmoving, very terribly alone; and the timbers of the roof spoke in imitation of footsteps that seemed to come and go in the ancient house, and the drums of La Partida throbbed silently, unceasingly, as if they were beating in her soul.

Then presently she knew that she was not going to be alone, all this long night. A loping horse was coming up the valley trail. It could have been someone sent with a message to Tom Cloud; but somehow she knew that it was not, and that the pony would not go hammering past the hacienda, but would stop. And before the first tentative tuning chord whispered, out by the garden wall, she knew who had ridden the five miles from La Partida.

Her heart beat heavily, but her taut body relaxed as, ten yards away from her open window, rose up lustily the swinging, swaggering song with which El Fuerte always began his serenades.

> "Alla-a-a—
> En mi rancho grande,
> Adonde yo viviá—woopee!—"

It was good not to be alone for a little while, in this long night; to know that close by someone was thinking only of her. El Fuerte was not a singer, except insofar as

207

he was all things. But when El Fuerte had been singing for a while this listener forgot that he could not sing. The roughness of his voice presently seemed a huskiness such as certain emotions can produce, and the faint inaccuracy of his notes became a half-hidden suggestion of the wildness of the brown hills. Behind the voice was an effect of the lazy power never actually roused or released.

The raiding, riding song of carousing rancheros rose to noisy crescendos, subsided again, and trailed away. El Fuerte, evidently satisfied that if Kathleen was not awake by this time she ought to be, began singing songs of a different kind, to a modulated accompaniment of the guitar.

"Porque no quieres mirar—

"Why do you not want to see
Moonlight nights beside me?
Why do you not like it that in the well,
Clean and clear, I see myself beside you?"

El Fuerte's way of singing a love song was like no one's else on earth. True that his voice was not especially good. But lazily, easily, without any effort, he could make live again old timeworn words that had been sung for a hundred years; almost as if all the desire of all the people who had ever sung those songs lived again in the night to which he sang. Just casually, he could open his throat and let all those forgotten people speak through him, sing through him all their longing and sorrow.

"To you I come to say good-bye . . .
Because I go, tomorrow . . ."

The singing alone could not have got all that effect,
perhaps, without the gentle mourning whisper of the
guitar. The guitar that was scarred by the brush, that had
laid hidden so often in so many distantly separated
thickets of chaparral, was singing tonight as Kathleen
had never heard it sing before. Ordinarily El Fuerte was
greatly given to a slashing, robustious type of
musicianship, ignoring more subtle effects in favor of
an occasional great ringing stroke on one of the
elementary chords. But there was no breaking of strings
tonight. The instrument wept and wailed through minors
and soft slurring runs, doing things that a guitar can
hardly be made to do. Enchanted by the sheer genius of
the fingering, Kathleen imagined the lazy, adept
flourishes of El Fuerte's big hands as he played.

Her imagination, as it happened, was mistaken. El
Fuerte, in actuality, was lying on his back on the low
wall, one ankle on his propped-up knee, his head
bolstered up on a sack of corn someone had left there.
His poncho was wrapped about him against the
increasing raw cold of the wind, and a black cigarette
trailed from the corner of his lips; its coal cast a faint
glow about his mouth when he favored it with an
occasional drag. But though the rhythmic lament of the
guitar wooed the night unceasingly, El Fuerte's hands
were locked behind his head. It was a man with a black
face and dirty white pajamas, and no shoes, who
squatted on his heels beyond the wall, playing with the
caressing gentle stroke of a genius.

209

"Let me see you for the last time;
        Let me see myself in your eyes—"

The liquid run of the Spanish words, enunciated slurringly, but beautiful still, took possession of all of the night. El Fuerte was taking longer at it than usual, for this time his singing was not that of a capricious serenader who had all the time in the world to get where he was going. This was the singing of a man who had only tonight, whose tomorrow belonged to horses and marching hill cavalry, mud and commissariat problems and guns.

"... for perhaps in the depths of your eyes ...
        I may see that you cannot forget me ..."

Kathleen supposed that she was listening to the serenading of El Fuerte for the last time. He could not afford to be here now—she knew that. In preparation for the blow he had planned to strike there would be a hundred minor leaders to bargain with, a hundred plans to lay, a thousand details that no one could take care of but himself. The materials of war were white hot in the fire, needing his hammer—and he was here singing to her. It seemed to her almost as if he had been drawn by her terrible loneliness across the miles.

She could not, of course, know that del Pino, whose life was harassed by pursuits of quail seeds, could have explained this thing to her most snappily. What she was thinking was that she would probably never see this extraordinary figure again. Perhaps she would see him ride off on the gorgeous palomino mare, at the head of all that ragtag and bobtail of mounted men that could

210

become so dangerous in his hands. But after that, never any more. It was hard to remember that he was no better than a bandit, that he was not of her people, never could be of her people. Easy to remember that few of the great company of adventurers to which El Fuerte belonged ever lived for long. You couldn't seek the smoke of gunpowder forever without some day feeling your horse swing from under you and the ground strike up.

Or perhaps stand with your back to a pitted adobe wall, with the steel-rimmed empty eyes of a firing squad's guns looking at you from five paces in front. Not strange if this was forever the last of singing in the night.

> "Let me speak to you for the last time—
> Let me say that I adore you . . .
> That locked within you is something
> I can never find again . . .

Some of that song was timeworn, and some of it was new; perhaps even a little of it had been made by El Fuerte himself, to take the place of parts he had forgotten. But behind the words was something that came partly from the brush-scarred guitar and partly from the voice, and this was brokenly urgent and pleading, and more specific than the words. It was as old as the first wolf call, yet new and young as spring rain. It was arrogant in the lusty command of strength, yet humble too, and supplicating. It was all things that has kept life self-perpetuating, since first life began.

> "Let me kiss you for the last time—
> Let me, for the love of *Dios*—"

211

The drums of La Partida were throbbing and pulsing in the song, so that it was like a song from the heart of the earth itself, as if the deep latent forces of the earth were singing through an instrument and a man.

Kathleen Boyce never knew what happened to her as she listened to that song. A primitive hypnosis was upon her, so that she was unaware of where she was, or who was singing. Then suddenly she remembered that El Fuerte had sung for a long time, and that this must surely be the last of his singing; in a moment the last whimpering of the guitar would die away, and she would sense the moving off of the singer, leaving her alone. For a moment the unbearable black loneliness of the house chilled her heart.

She lay quiet a moment more, and her heart was beating like the drums behind the song. Then she got out of bed as if she were drawing away from something that might seize her in the cold dark, slipped into her sandals, and caught a serape about her. To go out of the house on the side where El Fuerte waited, she had to go along a little hall, to a door which opened upon a little gallery, which in turn opened upon the yard. Down this hall Kathleen walked unsteadily and mechanically, as if she walked in her sleep, and slowly unlatched the door.

As the door opened a draft of icy air rushed about Kathleen's ankles, and her breath caught in her throat as if she had been suddenly awakened from an hypnotic sleep. Out where the wall ran through shadow the guitar still murmured, improvising for the moment; but against a post of the gallery, facing her, a figure was silhouetted against the faint luminosity of the low sky. It was a tall, lean-shouldered figure with a broad Stetson hat, and it

212

lounged against the post very casually, and quite relaxed—the figure of Tom Cloud.

For a moment neither of them moved. Then Kathleen gave a little gasp, and took two quick steps toward him before she swayed and he caught her in his arms.

He picked her up and carried her in, and put her into her bed. Then for a while he knelt beside the bed with his arms about her, and brushed her soft hair away from her face with his big fingers. She clung to him, incoherently repeating his name, completely unstrung.

Presently, when she seemed relaxed and steady in his arms he kissed her once, gently, as he might have kissed a child; and disengaged himself.

She said, "Don't go away from me any more."

"Just for a little while. You try to go to sleep."

Outside, only ten yards from the window, El Fuerte still sang, very softly now.

> "*Las almas que se aman*—
>
> "Souls that love each other
> Have no good-byes—"

"What are you going to do?"

"I don't know yet," he whispered. "Rest easy, child. I'll come back when I can." Moving silently, he stepped out through the window, and walked across the dampened ground toward the shadows where El Fuerte was.

CHAPTER 28

EL FUERTE HAD COME TO THE END OF A SONG AND WAS disputing with his accompanist in undertones, out of the side of his mouth.

"Then play the beginning of *Chihuahua de mis Amores*," he ordered.

"*Mi General*, I don't know that one either. You sing—I will follow."

"How the devil can I sing when I don't remember it myself? Aren't you good for anything? *Sangre de*—"

Suddenly he snapped bolt upright and his heels thudded on the ground. "*Quien es*?"

Tom Cloud stood two strides away, his thumbs hooked in his belt, regarding El Fuerte ironically. "Who does it look like?"

El Fuerte stared at him. "Oh," he grunted without noticeable delight. "It's you, is it? Now where the hell did you come from?"

"From the house," Cloud said shortly. "Where did you suppose?"

They stared at each other, unable to see much in the heavy dark; and gave a long moment to silence. "Kind of enjoyed the serenade," Cloud told El Fuerte. "Much obliged to you. Getting kind of tired of it now, though. Don't you ever expect folks to sleep?"

El Fuerte's big bulk seemed impassive, but an ugly edge came into his voice. "Mister, I don't understand much how it is you are here."

"You don't, huh? Maybe I don't understand much how come you're here, either."

They were silent again. By a faint crackle of paper El Fuerte knew that Cloud was making a cigarette. Cloud thrust the tobacco sack into El Fuerte's hands, and mechanically El Fuerte took it and made a cigarette of his own. It was curious how their hands went through accustomed, unhostile motions, while they stood here eyeing each other; two men neither of whom knew anything about giving an inch to anyone, facing each other in a situation from which there would be no retreat.

Tom Cloud waited El Fuerte out, while the raw wind moaned in the pepper trees; a handful of cold drops spattered the back of his neck. The other spoke at last "This is no time for us to quarrel, Mister," El Fuerte said. His voice was hardly more than a whisper. "We have other things to think, besides making love to women. Within two days I strike Ensenada; and that is for us both, for we are still partners in cattle. When that thing is done, and my *insurrectos* return to their *milpas*—than maybe you and I take this thing up again, here. Until then—it is very foolish if we quarrel, Mister."

"Suits me," Cloud grunted. "Any time you want to take anything up with me you know where to find me."

"But," El Fuerte said, "I do not expect to find you here."

"How was that, again?" Cloud let a mocking incredulity come into his low tones.

"Mister, I do not want to quarrel with you, as I say. Only I must tell you this one necessary thing. You must not come to this place any more. You must not see this woman any more. You are getting off very easy, Mister; I advise you not to push me too far. Remember that

215

things are different now than when I first come. There is not any man in Baja who can live to reach the border if I choose to turn loose my wolves."

"Sounds right unfriendly," Cloud said without expression.

"I still want to be your frand. I even want certain help from you; I have already tell you what it is. But be careful what you do. *Nombre de Dios*! Do you think I kill a man to make room for you?"

Slowly Tom Cloud blew out a lungful of smoke in a thin slender stream; it took what seemed to be a long time. "So you killed John Boyce," he said at last.

"Of course. Who do you think kill him? That peon the rurales catch? I chase that peon out of here myself!"

"You chased Pepe out," Cloud said thoughtfully, "and set the rurales on him—and he's dead . . ."

"Very good thing for you to think about, maybe," said El Fuerte.

"I kind of thought you did that," Tom Cloud said slowly, "when it first come up. But somehow I got steered off, later on."

"You are easy to steer off, Mister," El Fuerte said, almost contemptuously. "But now you know the truth. Maybe that is one more reason we are frands, no? I think maybe I save you the trouble of killing that man yourself, some day."

Tom Cloud said, "Perhaps." He knew that it was true that he might some day have killed John Boyce. But El Fuerte's killing of Boyce, and what Cloud's killing of Boyce would have been, had he ever come to it, were two vastly different things. Conceivably, Cloud might have found himself so driven by the tormenting of Kathleen that nothing would have been possible to him

216

except to try to destroy the man in an even shootout. But to shoot down Boyce as a casual gesture, because he was in the way—that was something else. Cloud was thinking now of a time long ago when he had seen an effigy burned that was not an effigy; he was thinking of Pepe, terror-stricken and bewildered, somewhere, in the hands of the rurales; and of other things. And suddenly he knew that he understood El Fuerte more clearly than he had ever understood him before. An immense weight seemed to lift from him; he drew a deep breath, and grinned.

It was not true, as El Fuerte had always supposed, that Cloud was a man who thought slowly, and could only with difficulty muddle his way to a decision. He had seemed so to El Fuerte only because he reserved his judgments.

"Since this thing happens," El Fuerte was saying, "naturally I cannot leave you here. You can see that. Our cows will take care of themselves for a little while, I think. You now ride with me to La Partida. After that you ride with me as we strike Ensenada, then Mexicali. You will stay with me until this thing is through."

As they were silent again El Fuerte peered at Cloud through the dark; and when he had done this he chuckled, not unpleasantly. "You think," he diagnosed; "always it takes you a long time to think. But this time I think you know what you are going to do. Is true?"

"I know what I'm going to do, all right," Cloud said.

There was something peculiar about Cloud's voice as he said that; and now the smile dropped from El Fuerte's face and his eyes narrowed again. "What is it you are going to do?" he demanded sharply.

217

"How many men can you raise in La Partida?" Cloud asked drily.

"Maybe a thousand men. What you think of that? Now answer me, and be quick!"

"I'm going to kick your revolution to flinders," Cloud said.

El Fuerte could not believe what he had heard. "You—*what*?"

"I'm going to bust up your fool revolt," Cloud repeated, "and run you out of Baja."

El Fuerte was too surprised to anger. They stood there a long moment more; and now as they stood, the rain came at last, a long hissing whisper that raced up the valley, rattled across the roofs of the hacienda, then suddenly enclosed them in a world of cold downpour. Neither of them paid any attention to it.

"You are only one man," El Fuerte said at last, his voice raised against the rain. "All alone in a country strange to you. I am a thousand men—and you talk so to me?"

"Sure I'm only one man. There's only one revolution, isn't there?"

El Fuerte made an abrupt gesture. "*Cristo*! You've had your chance, *por Dios*! I—"

Cloud swayed a little closer to El Fuerte. "My gun's in my hand," he told him through the falling water. "Even if you draw and fire, I can kill you as I fall."

CHAPTER 29

"I do not know why you come here," Solano told Cloud.

"I told you I came here to talk to you," Cloud said.

"We have nothing to talk about, I think."

"We have plenty to talk about," Cloud contradicted him. "You damn well better bring yourself to listen to what I have to say." Cloud's eyes flicked to the face of Old Beard, then fastened themselves again upon Solano's steady gaze. "Boot your thugs out of here," he told Solano. "I'm damned if I'll talk to any man with guns in my back."

The three vaqueros who stood behind Cloud did not exactly have their guns in his back, but it amounted to that. The approaches to Solano's hacienda, he had found, were being carefully watched. Riding casually into a knot of Solano's own private guard, he had been held up, well prodded in the ribs with rifle muzzles, and taken promptly to Solano himself for further orders. Inasmuch as Solano was the man whom he had come to see anyway, Cloud had submitted with what little grace he could command.

Now Solano looked Cloud over, without seeming at all well-accustomed to the sort of thing he saw. Cloud was so thoroughly drenched that he already stood in an increasing puddle. He was always lean-hipped and lightly poised on his feet, but now, with his shirt plastered to him so that the muscle ridges showed below his ribs, he looked incredibly slim-waisted and broad-shouldered. Wet as he was, he seemed neither cold nor discommoded; and his light eyes lay on Solano with an all but arrogant composure. Solano looked at Beard, hesitated; then gave an order in Spanish. The three dark-faced vaqueros behind Cloud withdrew.

The room in which Cloud stood was big and square, with a tremendously high plastered ceiling; for though Solano's hacienda was not large, what there was of it was well built and spacious. The room was cluttered

219

with neither the guns and saddles with which the lesser rancheros filled their rooms, nor with the elaborations a woman would have placed here. The few decorations were of a religious nature, and very old, as if they had not been moved since Solano's wife had died, long ago. The whole place had a barren, cleanly swept look, as if this man lived rigorously, rather than with comfort.

"I don't think you misread what goes on at La Partida," Cloud said. "Well, I've come here to make a deal with you."

Beard was still silent; he sucked upon his cold pipe. After a moment Solano said, "There is no deal you can make with me."

"I think there is," Cloud contradicted him again.

"I advise you," said Solano, his words heavily accented, meticulously chosen, "not to weigh too heavily the fact that you are an American citizen. Of your own will, you have placed yourself in a very critical position."

"I see well enough where you have a kick coming," Cloud admitted. "I've been a stranger here; it's been heavy going for me to get onto how things are run in this country."

"You have taken a great deal on yourself for a stranger!"

"If I had had any neighbors fit to call themselves such," Cloud told him, "none of this stuff would have come up. As it is, I've had to handle things whatever way I could. I've made mistakes, and plenty; but I'm willing to play my cards out as they lie. Now I'm ready to tell you what I can do for you, and what it will cost."

A hard, angry glint came into Solano's eye. "Do I understand that you are threatening me?"

"Yes," Cloud told him.

"You're not talking to a peon, Cloud!"

Cloud shrugged. "El Fuerte can raise a thousand men in La Partida; at least four hundred of them will be well armed. Those men will have to be fed. If you want a thousand men turned loose in your beef herds, say the word. You're not any too well liked, Solano. Once that rabble turns loose on you, do you think they'll leave anything behind?"

"What you speak of I cannot stop," Solano said. "I will resist as I can, of course, and I recognize the cost. But I warrant that nobody connected with this thing will escape punishment. There will be two regiments in Baja within two weeks; if necessary they will be followed by a brigade, a division—whatever is needed. It is not going to go easy with people such as you."

"You expect to be here to see that?" Cloud asked; and Solano shrugged contemptuously.

"As it happens," Cloud said, "I didn't come here to threaten you. I came here to tell you that none of this is going to happen. Maybe I've been slow in getting hold of this thing. But I know now what I'm going to do. As it happens, I'm through with this El Fuerte."

Solano almost smiled. "This is a fine time for that," he answered.

"A little late," Cloud admitted. "But it'll serve the purpose."

"You harbored this man," Solano pointed out. "You, and you only of the cattlemen—of the true cattlemen— were in a position to know exactly what he was doing. I have never seen a man so clever at working under cover as El Fuerte. By the time his intention was plain the whole country was ready to burst into flame, and we

221

had such a concentration of fighting men at La Partida as Baja has not seen in two decades. All this he does—and you give him what help you can. Now when it is too late, you guess you are through! *Por Dios*, no! You cannot crawl out like that! You are in it as deep as the rest!"

"That may be and it may not," Cloud said. "Nevertheless, I figure to stop this revolt."

Solano and Old Beard exchanged a long glance.

Cloud angered. "I'll tell you exactly what I'm going to do, and how I'm going to do it. For the second time, I advise you to listen to me!"

A little flush was beginning to show over Solano's cheekbones. "I'm getting just a little tired of this," he said. "You may as well know at once, sir, that you are a prisoner here! To my country I have certain duties that you would not understand. As you have said yourself, you do not understand this country or its people. If you did—but it is useless to discuss."

"I think you don't understand your own people," Cloud said disgustedly. "Go look at the faces of the rabble in La Partida. Then maybe you'll know what I already know: that they have no leaders there—only men ready to follow and fight and loot."

"Such men as El Fuerte naturally would choose, and gather," Old Beard said mildly. It was the first time he had spoken.

"There's your cue," Cloud told them coolly. "This El Fuerte is something like a fever tick. He can fasten himself onto a piece of country and inflame the whole works. But take him out of this and what's left?"

"And who's going to take him out of it?" Solano demanded hotly. "Even when I talked to him at your

222

camp, did he unguard himself to an open break? At least two rifles could have picked me off that day, if I had touched my gun! How much more so now, surrounded with the fighting men of his other outbreaks—wary every moment, now that what he has afoot is plain!"

"You don't think you can take him? " Cloud said.

"You speak like a fool! Nobody can take him! Until the regiments come, and then only after—"

"Then," said Cloud, "I'll take him myself."

Solano jerked to his feet, exasperated, his patience at an end. "I've listened to enough of this infernal—" He was striding to—the door. Cloud knew that in another moment the vaqueros would be in the room.

"I've taken him already," Cloud told them with contempt.

The old ranchero stopped; and for a long moment the two others in that room stared at Tom Cloud. "You mean to say that by treachery—"

"Treachery, hell! He told me that I was virtually his prisoner. I put a gun in his ribs and showed him where he was virtually mine."

"I can't believe this!"

"But I have him, just the same," Cloud said; and waited.

"Where is he?" Solano demanded at last.

"Within a half mile of here."

Suddenly Solano raised clawed, shaking hands in front of Cloud. "By God, sir, if you lie to me—"

"Why the devil should I lie to you?" Cloud asked.

"If this is true— What is it you want from me?"

"I want you to hold them here for three days. I want your word of honor to give them back to me after that,

223

unharmed."

"Them? How many are there?"

"Three. El Fuerte and del Pino; and a guitar-playing nigger with a split scalp. He tried to put a knife into me when I took El Fuerte's gun; I had to slug him down. I had to take him too, or he'd have spread the alarm in La Partida. Later there will be two more that must be taken out of it—the men called Bravo and Carlos. Bravo is the worst; the Yaqui riders from the mainland will follow behind him like a drift of wildfire. But Carlos can bring them all down on us too, if he's free."

Solano tossed his hands in a tense, despairing gesture. "Better than nothing, if it's true that you have El Fuerte. *Nombre*! I would have sworn that it could not be done! But we'll never hold him against the horde!"

"I can tell you exactly how we're going to hold him, and keep on holding him, until we're ready to put him out of the country."

"You don't know what you're talking about," said Beard's matter-of-fact voice.

"You've never seen this thing," Solano said with a bitter savagery. "Me, I have seen it many times—four times at least. You say you have counted a thousand men in La Partida—four hundred under arms. Now I can tell you what type of men those are. They are fighting men of a reckless and irresponsible kind; the most troublous class in Mexico. Not fifty of them will be able to read. They know nothing of politics nor economics nor government, nor anything whatever but horses, guns, and what leaders like El Fuerte tell them. That isn't Mexico rising! That's rabble and scum, always ready to follow anyone who promises battle and loot and rapine. Without inciters they would still have

224

been contented and at peace. But now they are gathered and roused with promises—and it's too late! Twenty little squabbling leaders will try to jump into El Fuerte's shoes and seize the government of the state. They will go raiding over this country like a scourge. Nothing and nobody will be safe, not a cattle herd, nor a little store, nor a home, nor a barefoot girl. Here and there honest peaceable men will bravely try to defend their own, and then there will be smoke in the sky, and corpses bloating unburied in the streets. The garrisons of Ensenada and Mexicali will be overpowered and martyred. In the end the disciplined Federal troops will come and blow the rebels apart, and hunt them down in the hills. But by that time there will be such shameful ruin in Baja that three generations will not cover up the scars."

"I tell you—" Tom Cloud began.

Solano flamed at him furiously. "Now that the thing is already out of all control, you tell me that you have fixed everything—you have seized El Fuerte," he said with savage contempt. "Captive or free—what difference is it now?"

"Let's try to look at this thing a little more quiet," Cloud said calmly. "I know we're in a jam, all right. And I'm willing to take my share of the blame. But I can still tell you how this is to be stopped."

Solano turned away from him, his face grey, his hands still quivering with the nervous force of his outburst.

"How many men have you that you can count on?" Cloud asked Beard.

"Seven or eight. Against—"

"These men of yours must ambush Bravo and Carlos

225

at my camp. We'll get Bravo and Carlos to come there alone—at once—by message from El Fuerte himself. He won't write it, but we'll send something that Bravo and Carlos will recognize as belonging to El Fuerte. When they ride into my camp, you have got to nail onto them. It's part of my orders that they're to be taken alive."

"Your orders?" said Old Beard, startled.

"By God, it's time someone gave orders here!"

"And then?"

"You must pack out of my camp everything that belongs to El Fuerte. Hide your prisoners, and hide the loot from my camp, and keep it hid."

"And what's that for?" Beard said sarcastically.

"I'm going to bluff the rebels out of La Partida. I'll have a better chance if they can check up and find out that El Fuerte appears to have gone over the hill."

Silence fell in the bare, bright-lighted room. It lasted a long time. "How do you figure," Beard said, "that one man can bluff a town-full?"

"Maybe," Cloud said, "it can be done by letting them bluff themselves."

"I'm tired of this empty talk," Solano said, his voice ugly. "There is nothing about it that is not beyond all possibility."

"One thing, and one thing only, makes it barely possible," Cloud said. "The rebel mob in La Partida is badly sheltered. Morning will find them cold and wet, and full of hangovers. There won't be any music or drunken speeches or drums to go against."

Again that long, electric silence. "There's this," Old Beard said at last. "This boy don't understand this people. But neither do these people understand him.

226

He's a plumb mystery to 'em, whatever he does." Another long pause. "And it's true that these revolts sure damp down in the rain and the cold."

"The man who tries to disband that horde will be destroyed," Solano said disgustedly. "There are too many men there who care nothing about human life. There are men there who would dress out this Americano like a steer, in no more than a moment of ill-nature."

"What the hell is that to you?" Cloud asked. "If that happens you're no worse off than before."

"There's a chance it might work, Miguel," Old Beard said doubtfully. "Might do worse than let him try it, seems to me."

"How can we trust this man?" Solano demanded.

"No great need to trust him. He gives us El Fuerte, and his main hangers-on; we're glad to get them, I guess. About the only catch I see to letting him go to La Partida is he might get loose from you. But if that's what he's driving at, he had no call to come here to begin with. Can't say I see any stickers to it."

Solano growled inarticulately, and was silent.

"You act funny," Beard said to him. "What's the point you set there and grunt? Here's a boy offers to go out and die."

Solano turned slowly, and studied Cloud with curiosity, as he might have studied a madman.

"About the slimmest chance ever I see; but a chance," Beard added.

"To go there and die," Solano repeated speculatively. "I can't imagine what his motive is."

"Motive, huh? He's got everything he has in the world tied up here in Baja, same as you and me."

For two minutes more Solano considered. He got to his feet, nervously inpatient at last. "Let's have a look at this Contreras they call El Fuerte."

When he said that, Tom Cloud began to believe, to his own astonishment, that they were going to help him in what he meant to do. For Solano to reconcile himself to working with Tom Cloud would take a little time; wrangling here would not help them toward that. Never in his life had Solano had any liking for Americans; and a lifelong experience had confirmed his attitude. But against his will Solano was beginning to see that there was a chance.

Nothing but urgent necessity could ever have brought the two of them to work side by side. It was not until his three prisoners were in the hands of Solano, and there had been a message sent to Bravo and Carlos at La Partida, that Cloud could be sure of his ground. There was much argument, and more words than Cloud had used in a year before at last Cloud knew that he had prevailed.

Yet, in the end, Solano gave Cloud his confidence in a way Cloud would not have expected or believed possible.

They were at Cloud's Flying K camp, by then. El Fuerte and del Pino were prisoners at Solano's hacienda, in the charge of Old Beard; and Miguel Solano had himself come to the Flying K camp to manage the capture of Bravo and Carlos—if they came, as Cloud believed they must.

Cloud was ready to ride. "There's one more thing," he said to Solano. It was the last moment before he mounted. "I have to get down-valley now; what's going on has to be explained to Mrs. Boyce. Because the one more thing is this: I realize I may talk myself into trouble in La Partida. And I want you to promise me this. If anything goes wrong, or I don't come back—you see to her safe conduct out of the country. I wanted to leave that to the last, until everything else was straightened out. But unless you can give me your word of honor on that, the works is off. Without that I don't dare take the chance."

"I promise," Solano said.

"*Bueno.* There isn't any more to be said." Cloud stepped into the saddle. Many as were the things he didn't like about Miguel Solano, he believed in the man's good faith, once he had pledged his word.

But as he turned his horse Solano stopped him. "One moment, *señor.*"

He extended his hand. A little surprised, Cloud gripped it. Solano's face was very somber. Beyond any doubt, Solano was deeply impressed with the fact that Cloud was pushing himself forward into what, as Solano saw it, was plainly destruction.

"If I never see you again," Solano said, "I want you to know I admire this thing that you do. You are a brave man. I am sorry now that we have never understood each other; and I want you to know that I blame myself."

"That's all right," Cloud said awkwardly. He drew away his hand, and would have ridden on.

"One thing more. I want you to know this one thing more. For as you know, I no longer doubt that you will do what you say; and it is my belief that you are going to die. I am sorry that I have seemed a bad neighbor. But it is not true that I did nothing to stop the rustling of your cattle. I could not bring myself to work hand in

229

hand with an American, then. But I went against your enemies in my own way. And it cost me the life of my son."

"*What?*" Cloud could not believe that he had understood.

"He had the reputation for being reckless, and wild," Solano said, his voice monotoned. "I sent him to ride with the thieves, to get evidence so that they could be cleaned out. Luck was against me. His first raid fell in with El Fuerte and his men, and the rustlers lost their horses. They turned upon my son, believing that he had given them away. That is how my son was lost to me, *señor*."

"Do you know—who—"

"He died without giving any name. What I have told you, I have found out; not anything more."

They were silent a moment. "You did this thing for me?" Cloud said at last.

"No, *señor*. It would not be true if I said that. It was for the people themselves, more than for you. It is not good for our people to learn to live by thievery. They are desperately poor, now, here in Baja; but they must find other ways."

"I'm sorry," Cloud said slowly, at last. It was all he could think of to say.

"I wanted you to know that one thing," Solano said, "in case you do not come back. For a time I blamed you, in part, merely because you were here. I do not blame you now. But I promise you this. If you come back, you and I will work together in all things; and we will clean out the Valley of the Witch!"

This time it was Cloud who extended his hand, and once more they shook hands gravely. Without another word Cloud raised his romal in salute, and started off down the dark valley.

CHAPTER 30

It was nearly eight o'clock in the morning as Cloud rode into La Partida in the grey rain. Yet there was little light, as if the dawn had come on reluctantly and with pain, unable to bring itself to turn into day. All over the broad valley and the hills the rain fell steadily now, a soaking, drenching rain from an overcast sky as thick and unbroken as a sheathing of lead. The rain hid the hills behind whispering curtains many miles deep, so that the village seemed peculiarly isolated in a wet, and dark, and faintly ghostly world.

Because of the cold soak of the weather Cloud would not have been surprised to find La Partida less crowded today; he had thought that at least the makeshift shelters outside of the town might be deserted. But they were not. Under the ineffectively thrown together thatches of palm leaves and grass and brush the many men and few women of the outposts squatted on their heels about little smudgy fires, the serapes under which they huddled steaming dismally. No cheering now as Cloud rode into La Partida alone, no singing, no games, no exuberant harangues; even the smell of cooking had turned stale and watery, with a peculiar odor to it as if dishrags were being stewed with the *frijoles*.

Cloud pushed his sulky horse into the village, squishing cannon-deep in mud. The street was almost deserted now; the tables and benches where so many

231

had been fed in the open air the day before were abandoned skeletons, streaming rainwater. But—here and there under an improvised lean-to little knots of people were camped desolately in the wet; and sometimes against an adobe house-front a row of four or five blanket-wrapped men squatted on their heels, tight against the wall to gather what shelter they could from the eaves—stoic, unmoving men, their dark faces beaded with the rain whipped into them by the fitful wind. They would not have been crouched here in the raw cold and the wet had they not been crowded out of the houses in which they must have slept. They sat impassive, their eyes as dull and heavy as the lead in their guns, and waited for better things.

Perceiving by these evidences that the town was still crowded, Cloud experienced a queer stir of emotion, almost of regret. The cold rain would have emptied this overcrowded town, had this been any ordinary *grito*; by this time the last of the strangers would have been prodding their drenched burros ahead of them, straggling home over the long muddy trails. Not ten men in Mexico could have raised a revolt in the teeth of such dismal weather. But now Cloud knew that El Fuerte would have been able to raise them; the very fact that El Fuerte could hold them here, just by not telling them they could leave, told Cloud that these people would have followed El Fuerte through rain and cold, and hellfire too, perhaps. Now they waited doggedly in the cold and the rain for a command that was not going to come.

Halfway up the length of the street a little knot of three men walked out, more than ankle deep in mud, to speak to Cloud. After a moment or two of hesitancy, two more came out from under the eaves on the opposite side of the street and joined them.

"*Dias*," they grunted.

"*Buenos dias*," Cloud acknowledged.

Four shifted in the mud uncertainly, but the fifth spoke up. "Where is *el General?*"

Cloud looked them over slowly. The speaker was tall, the color of yellow leather, and blind in one eye. The living eye was direct and hard, the eye of some minor predatory animal quicker in action than in understanding. The blunt dark faces of the uncertain ones told Cloud nothing; only that the speaker was of interest, a potential leader hero, among these others who were perhaps his kin.

Cloud said, very solemnly and slowly, "You don't know where El Fuerte is?"

"Why the devil do you think I ask you?" The one-eyed man let his voice raise a little. "Are we to set here in the rain—"

With a gesture Cloud cautioned him to silence. "You had better come and talk to me," he told the one-eyed man. "Come to the *alcalde's* house." He regarded the other mournfully for a minute more; then set his eyes into the mists ahead of him, and pushed his horse forward. The one-eyed man had to step back sharply to keep from getting a foot stepped on; yet there had been no arrogance in Cloud's move. It was simply as if the peons who clustered about him had dropped out of his mind altogether.

He moved on down the street through the rain and the mud, neither glancing back nor listening to see if they followed. He knew that after a few minutes they would come, drawn irresistibly.

233

A harsh reek of drowned charcoal and ashes hung over the end of the street nearest the plaza; it hung suspended peculiarly in the downpour, as if the ghosts of last night's dead fires were here—intangible presences that the rain could not bear down. About the door of the *alcalde's* house lay a sodden litter of the emptied corn-husks from tamales, and the butts of cigarettes. Cloud tied his horse to an iron ring beside the door, and went without knocking into the ell he had first entered with El Fuerte.

Instantly the dense, atmosphere of the room pushed against his face, almost as palpably as the shove of a sweaty hand. Men were packed into the house of the *alcalde* like brown beans in a pot. They lay sleeping in windows, wrapped in their serapes upon the packed adobe of the floor; they squatted everywhere on their heels, they stood in groups that had no room to sit down, they roosted all along yesterday's improvised bar. Beyond the inner door, which was wide open to the flooded patio, more men could be seen close-packed under the shelter where yesterday Cloud and El Fuerte had drunk together, discussing El Fuerte's campaign to glory. Still more were huddled in the stable shelter beyond the rain, so that the burros, and even the fighting cocks, had been crowded into the open downpour.

Sometimes a whiff of clean-washed air would slip into the room, a little gust of unbelievable freshness in all that dense reek; but mostly the atmosphere was a seemingly impermeable compact of tobacco smoke, sweat, steam of leather, and the characteristic, unforgettable odor of dark skin long scorched by the sun.

The little *alcalde* came pushing through the press to Cloud. His bushy grey mustache was in spiked straggles, giving a curiously wild, edgy look to his pudgy face. His earnest, mildly stupid eyes were hard and bright with a question which he obviously did not wish to voice.

Tom Cloud stood with his back against the door. Always, except when he was with Bravo or El Fuerte, Cloud's height towered over these people; and now, though his head was thrust forward and down like a stubborn steer, he dominated everyone in that packed room by a head.

"Clear the room," he told the *alcalde*.

"You come from—you are sent by—" the little man began.

"Clear the place, I say! I want everyone out of here. At once!"

The head man of La Partida hesitated a moment more, meeting Cloud's eve with a distraught stare. Then he turned abruptly, almost in a panic, and began shouting and pushing the packed throng toward the patio. "Out, now, out—pronto! In the name of the general! *Borrachos! Ladrones.* We must have this room!"

They moved out slowly, eyeing Cloud, stumbling over each other; for the most part sullenly silent with the torpor the cold and the wet had put upon them. In the typical dry weather of Baja these men would have slept by their little fires in the brush, heads hidden in their tight-wrapped blankets, as at home on the ground as coyotes. It was the raw drench of the rain that had brought them in from all their little scattered fires, and packed them into shelter like swarmed bees.

235

"See that these men stay near," Cloud ordered the *alcalde*, and the little man shouted appropriate warnings. Cloud already knew—and a hurried check-over of the pack confirmed this—that these were the key men of all the fighting men in La Partida. Many as they were, Cloud knew that no one of them had had the nerve to seek shelter in the very headquarters of El Fuerte without believing himself of importance. These were the squad leaders—men who had brought with them three or four or twenty relatives whom they dominated, men who had brought horse bunches, or little stores of cherished and long-hidden arms.

When the last of them was out the *alcalde* closed the patio door, by main strength and with difficulty, against the press of men. Instantly he whirled and extended nervous questioning hands toward Cloud.

"Where is El Fuerte?" he demanded in a rasping whisper. He spoke only Spanish.

"Where is El Fuerte?" Cloud repeated aloud. "That's what I've come here to find out."

Panicky excitement made the little *alcalde's* draggled mustache twitch and curl away from his bad teeth. "You don't know where he is? You haven't seen him? He did not come to your rancho? He left no word? Ay! What is happening here?"

"When did you see El Fuerte last?" Cloud demanded. He appeared serious and angry.

"Not since last night! He is here, he is everywhere, in a white uniform on his great horse. Then he is no place. Then comes del Pino, and he is furious, he is hunting for El Fuerte, very worried and upset. Then del Pino disappears, too. Many ask for El Fuerte. I send them to Bravo. Bravo is of cold blood, he treats them with contempt—that keeps

236

them happy. But now—ay, *señor,* I tell you—"

"Where's Bravo now?"

"He is gone. Also his great palomino."

"You mean to tell me El Fuerte has run away?" Cloud almost shouted.

The little *alcalde's* panic broke in sputters. "Sh! *Cuidado*! Ay, be careful! They will all hear, and then— Ay, *Dios,* why should he run away? That's ridiculous!"

"Is it?" Cloud said darkly.

"What would he flee from?"

"You don't know?" Cloud said with pity.

"*Dio,* what's happened?" the *alcalde* jittered.

There was great reason, Cloud thought, for this little man, long since disarmed against emergency by his sheltered officialship in this quiet village, to worry about being left with the sack. The house was fairly bristling with arms—as good as an arsenal, as Cloud already knew.

Cloud shrugged. "Bring in that old man, the man with the serape that is like a *tarjeta.*"

CHAPTER 31

THE *ALCALDE* UNBARRED THE PATIO DOOR, STEMMED the press that almost fell into the room; and presently secured for Cloud an ancient man with the face of an Indian, tight-wrapped in a blanket of red and black. "Is this the man?"

"He'll do. *Jefe*," Cloud directed, "be seated"; and himself sat down. "You are called Teotac," Cloud went on, eyeing the old man steadily. "You are ranked as a chief of Yaqui scouts. You must have brought with you

237

many good men."

The face of the old man was blackened by perhaps more decades of sun than he himself could have named; it was as if his face were deep carved out of fire-hardened wood. Out of this face peered little red-rimmed eyes, as evil as any Cloud had ever seen. But for all his age, his movements as he had walked in and taken himself a chair were as light and smooth as a coon-cat's.

"Good men," the old man agreed.

"Such men as keep their eyes and ears open—know what happens in the night?"

"Maybe." His voice was dry and harsh; and he did not trust this gringo.

"Then tell me this." Cloud's grey eyes bored in hard, and his face was grim as the rocky crags in the cold rain. "When last night did a rider come here on a spent horse, looking for El Fuerte?"

A hostile spark came into the old man's eyes, and though he had sat quietly before, he now turned as completely immobile as if he had ceased to breathe. He did not give an answer.

"So," Cloud said slowly, "you are hiding this thing from the rest of us."

"*Cuida'o!*" the oldster snarled at him viciously. "Be careful how you speak! I hide nothing."

At this point the door to the street was tried, so that its oak bar boomed in its slot. Someone began pounding impatiently. A quick gleam of hope appeared in the *alcalde's* face, and he sprang to unbar the door, but the gleam disappeared as the one-eyed man, who had accosted Cloud in the street, tried to force his way into the room.

The *alcalde* tried to close the door again, crying, "Stay out! You cannot come in here."

The one-eyed man cursed the *alcalde*, and the *alcalde* cursed him in return; the voices rose in crescendo. Behind the intruder Cloud could see a dozen other poncho-tented figures in the rain.

"Let this one come in," Cloud ordered, "and no others." The one-eyed man, admitted, leered insolently at the *alcalde,* and leaned against the bar, waiting.

An angry rumble of voices from those who had been shut out subsided.

Cloud turned back to the ancient. As his eyes clashed against those of the old man he had the curious feeling that the other's eyes had not left his face for an instant during the interruption.

"You know nothing," Cloud prompted sharply, "about a stranger on a worn-out Circle Bar horse, seeking El Fuerte here after midnight?"

"Circle Bar? The Circle Bar is halfway between here and—" The *alcalde* checked himself and gulped, as if trying to swallow his words back. His face was congested, his eyes popping.

"Halfway between here and Ensenada," the old Indian finished for him, with a glance of venomous contempt. He spoke bad Spanish; Cloud had great difficulty in understanding him. "Yah! You think we're afraid of the Ensenada garrison? Let them bring us their guns. It'll save us the march!"

The lank yellow-faced man with the one eye put in two sentences in a low, flat voice that yet seemed to conceal a savage vehemence.

"Ensenada is a port. How do we know how many

239

troops are landing in Ensenada this morning?"

The old Indian snarled like an animal. "If troops land in Ensenada within the month it's because this country is full of spies, and other snakes," he lashed out at the one-eyed man.

"There's only one way for snakes to be used!"

"What do you mean by that?" the one-eyed man blazed up.

The old Indian met the single-barreled glare with little eyes that had turned unspeakably vicious. "Not everyone that has come here is known to the old *compadres*," he said.

The yellow-faced man impatiently turned away his single eye; it was like the turning away of an angry dog who has been outfaced.

The old *jefe* turned on Cloud. "What's this coyote doing here?" he demanded.

"I've got questions for him, too," Cloud said shortly. He turned to the one-eyed man. "You know the man called Carlos? I thought I saw you drinking with him yesterday?"

The questioned man grunted.

"Where is Carlos now?" Cloud thundered at him.

"I haven't seen him since last night."

"What is this? What has happened to us?" the *alcalde* stammered. "A stranger—a messenger or a scout—rides hard from Ensenada. The general disappears, and his horse later, and Bravo and del Pino and Carlos—all those closest to El Fuerte! What—"

"Hold your tongue!" the old chief of scouts snarled. He leaned toward Cloud, his little ugly eyes like coals. "Gringo," he said in a grating voice, "I think you lie."

"Lie?" Cloud growled back. "How the hell can I have

lied when I haven't told you anything? By God, I have a right to know where El Fuerte is! For all I know, La Partida may be empty of fighting men by nightfall; already it seems to be empty of captains. I can't take to the hills; I have my herds to look out for. And I cannot have lied, because I have told you nothing."

"I think," said the old man, "you had better tell us something now."

The menace in that was undisguised. There would be no question of escape if the old *jefe* sang out for his Yaqui scouts. No question either of there being any responsibility or mercy in any of these people if they once decided to wring from him the information he possessed. These were people who could turn savage as wolves.

"Then I'll tell you this," Cloud answered harshly. "Last night while I was not at my camp, everything belonging to El Fuerte was moved from there. If you think you can learn anything more from me, try it! But it will get you nothing."

A silence came upon that airless room, and in the quiet they could hear the whip of the rain against the panes. The crowd in the street had increased in the last few moments to half a hundred. Already it must be all over the village that some unforeseen crisis was at hand; but there were no voices from the many packed outside.

The old chief of scouts stared at him piercingly while a man might count fifteen. Then, turning, he sprang to the patio door, flung it open, and shouted a jerky series of commands in his own unintelligible tongue. Instantly five slim young men with brown, smooth-skinned faces and obsidian eyes came shouldering through the outer

241

crush and went half running through the room to the street door. They dove out into the downpour. After them the old chief of scouts went striding, his back suddenly as straight as a gun-barrel.

The one-eyed man hesitated, moved uncertainly; then edged out, and went splashing and shoving through the crowd that had gathered in the street.

Against one wall a bench stood, and now Tom Cloud moved a table close to it by kicking its legs. "Give me something to eat—and drink," he ordered the *alcalde*.

"Ay, I have little left! I am being drunk out of house and home! Beef there is plenty, and they are killing more; but the tequila has run away like water. I—"

"Bring me some anyway," Cloud snapped at him.

"Si, señor."

Cloud edged behind the table and sat down, weary with the strain of his night's work. He could hear yet, behind the steady run and whisper of the rain, the fragmentary choruses of wild, exuberant marching songs—now as effectively stilled by the rain as the throbbing pulse of the drums. Even had del Pino been here those drums could not have spoken now, for the weather would relax the rawhide heads, so that a drummer might as well beat upon a wet pillow. If El Fuerte should ride down the street today, with his captains at his back, there would be no thunder in the dust, but only a great splattering, squishing sound. There can be no such thing as thunder in the mud.

Yet Cloud knew that if El Fuerte were here the weather would not matter to these people; the great smashing vitality of that man would be able to lift and sway them as before. He was greater than the elements,

242

greater than a cold, wet dawn full of hangovers; he was greater than a storm. Not the break of the weather, but Tom Cloud, and Tom Cloud alone, had put himself between Baja and the guns of revolt.

For a moment Cloud experienced a bitter regret that circumstances had chosen him to play the part which he now so hazardously attempted.

But he could see that his part had been inevitable. El Fuerte as a cattle partner was a different thing from El Fuerte as the murderer of Boyce. Just as El Fuerte, the adventurer, the soldier of fortune, was a different thing from El Fuerte as the self-proposed lover of Kathleen. El Fuerte could inspire those brown hill people to lay down their lives for him; but he was not one who could do anyhing for them when the fighting was done. Just as El Fuerte could ride a horse to death, gaily, without any thought for the animal, so could he ride a people into deeper misery, leading them to pay all the cost of fortune.

Cloud believed now that there was a cog missing in all El Fuertes.

The little *alcalde* came scurrying distraughtly, bringing Cloud meat and *tortillas,* and a tall bottle.

"Look," he begged Cloud, "look! If you know where El Fuerte is, if you know what has happened, in God's name tell me! I am a man of position here. In my time of life I cannot scatter myself into the hills, like these common men. If you know—"

"I have nothing to tell you," Cloud answered.

"I'll be left holding the bag," the *alcalde* whimpered. "If the Federals come and find this house full of guns, where am I? I'm ruined! Ruined!"

"You'll be in front of a firing squad, most likely,"

243

Cloud suggested.

"Ay! I know that. What am I to do?"

"Get the guns moved some place else."

"Where? Who—"

"How should I know? You're in a tough spot, if you ask me."

The *alcalde* stood for a moment or two, pulling at his fingers and whimpering faintly. Suddenly he turned and ran out, hatless and unponchoed, into the rain and mud of the street. Through the water-blurred window Cloud could see him pushing and splashing through the crowd like a frightened animal.

The cow man turned his attention to his food.

CHAPTER 32

AN HOUR PASSED; AND A SECOND HOUR. AFTER A LONG time the *alcalde* came back, draggled and frightened. He rushed through the ell into the other part of the house, and Cloud heard him scrambling up the stair. The crowd in the rain diminished, then dwindled away to a few stoic figures which squatted against the wall, just within the drip of the eaves.

Then into the street from the up-valley trail rode six horsemen, loping heavily in the muck. In front was the ancient chief of scouts, and the five others—they may have been his sons, Cloud thought—fanned out behind him in a loose V, trying to escape the throw of the mud. Their splattered blankets were wrapped about them to the eyes.

They pulled up in the mud, and gathered to their number other dark-faced men from various houses;

then came on, moving quickly, to the house of the *alcalde*. Immediately, at the advent of the riders, the street had filled with men, and now, with his hand on the latch of the door the old chief of Yaqui scouts was stopped by voices in the crowd. He paused to parley; and swiftly he and his young men became the focus of a seething knot.

There now followed a lengthy conference, during which Teotac twice turned to the door, but turned back to the crowd again, the second time pulled around to face them by reaching hands. At last he left the door altogether and went out of sight down the street, still the center of a dense knot of men. Some of the remainder of the crowd trailed off after them, and all of that mob that stood in the rain shifted restlessly, and drifted about in the mud.

Cloud waited, and drank; he called for a deck of cards, and laid out solitaire, and the third hour passed.

Then at last a new stir came into all that soggy mob, and as if by general consent the whole straggling mass of them seemed to converge upon the door of the *alcalde's* house. Someone ran stumbling down the stairs in another part of the house, and the *alcalde* burst into the room, his face grey as the mists.

"What's the matter now?" Cloud asked with disinterest.

"They're coming!" the little man stammered, half beside himself.

"Well—let 'em come. What you scared of?" Cloud played the three of clubs, then laid down the deck to roll a cigarette.

Through the thickened crowd without, a little group of dark-faced men came shouldering their way roughly

245

to the door. The door rattled against its bar, then vibrated to a savage pounding. "Open! Open up!" shouted several voices.

The *alcalde's* cheeks were shaking. "What—shall I do?"

"Open, you fool," Cloud ordered. Then he called out *"Pasen, Ustedes!"* as the *alcalde* rattled back the bar.

Into the room burst four men—the four who had shouldered through the crowd; but entrance did not stop with these four. Behind them, crowding upon their heels into the room, surged an unchecked rabble, jostling each other, stumbling against the leaders who had been first to enter. One of the four turned furiously. "Shut the door! I want no more—"

Those already within turned at the command, hastily forcing the door shut against the others before they should be evicted themselves.

Cloud, finishing the rolling of his cigarette, surveyed the four who confronted him sardonically. He noticed how all the others stayed a little behind, as if they faced here something which might bite. *"Que pase, compadres?"* His voice was flat, dry, bitter—but unfearful.

Of these four he noticed first of all Teotac; the old chief of scouts stood a little to one side, as if here the other three took the lead. But Cloud knew the others, also; they were minor leaders, pointed out to him by El Fuerte himself—ragged men, unkempt and unprepossessing, but with the virtue of a certain leadership in their obscure villages, or in the clannish groups of their distant relations.

Glancing past them to the men who stood at their backs, it suddenly came to Cloud that the men El Fuerte

246

had called about him were far from the pick of the country. These were fighting men perhaps—wild, reckless, and irresponsible men certainly, but far from the best of their breed. Their faces, irregular and very dark, showed hard surface-lighted eyes, behind which passion would flame easily while thought processes lagged far behind. Their noses were thick and stubborn, more often than not flat in the bridge; their lips were thick, loose and raffish, with the exception of a few that were thin and cruel, out of the more fine-drawn of the Indian breeds.

And these leaders who stood in front—the truculence in their faces made Cloud think of the belligerence of roused-up steers. La Partida was low in leadership indeed, with El Fuerte, Bravo, and Carlos gone. This, then, was a sample of El Fuerte's army of liberation—the patriotic rabble that was to have made the fortunes of them all. Unconsciously Cloud turned his head sidewise and spat.

"What's all this?" one of the leaders demanded. This was the man known to Cloud as Moreño; his bland, coffee-colored face showed a greater infusion of Spanish blood than did the others. He had brought here thirty or more very indifferent men, but more than seventy head of ponies. His eyes were narrow, his voice soft, almost sleepy.

"What's all what?" Cloud asked, looking at him hard.

Moreño's eyes did not waver before Cloud's stare. "The town is full of rumors. They say that El Fuerte is missing."

"You know damned well he's missing," said Cloud.

"They say more than that. They say that he is hiding,

that he has run away, that he is dead. They say that troops have landed in Ensenada, that they are on the march, that they will be here within twenty-four hours, within twelve, within six. They say a messenger from Ensenada came in last night on a ridden-out horse, bringing word of this to you and El Fuerte."

"No word was brought to me. The rumor, I know. But as to a messenger, or what goes on in Ensenada—I knew nothing of that."

"Now," said Moreño, still speaking drowsily in his smooth Spanish, "we want to know what you do know."

"I have nothing to add," Cloud told him shortly. "I've already told your chief of scouts that El Fuerte's stuff was moved away from my cow camp during the night. I was not there when this was done. Let your scouts go and see, if you doubt."

"We have been to see," old Teotac rasped. "Without this rain we would soon have found out where he went!"

"Then you know as much as can be learned from me."

Torreon, the sandaled, almost negroid man who had brought more than forty from the maguey patches of his far rift in the hills, now broke in angrily. In contrast to his thick neck and massive shoulders he had a high grating voice, strangely suggestive of the squeal of a boar. "We will not waste time with you," he volleyed at Cloud. "This man Contreras was your partner. For him, you are responsible to us. Come out with it, now— where is this Fuerte?"

Cloud eyed him ironically, but did not reply; and all the room waited.

"He is right," Moreño said, so softly that he was almost inaudible. "We will know the truth from you now."

"It's plain that El Fuerte is gone," Cloud said. "There's nothing that can be done about that now. Begin asking yourselves instead what you are going to do next. If I—"

Here the aged chief of scouts burst into a snarling flow of the language unknown to Cloud. All three of the others listened to him, and Torreon nodded.

"It seems," Moreño said, "you do not want to talk to us, *señor*. *Bueno*!" His voice suddenly sharpened and hardened. "Very well! Perhaps neither have we anything to say to you. But neither are we to be altogether cheated, *señor*. Gringo, stand up! You are going with us!"

Tom Cloud stuck the cigarette he had finished into the corner of his mouth, and struck a match. The flame did not tremble as he lighted the cigarette. Across it as he drew the first few, slow puffs he looked at the four, one after another, meeting the malevolence, the truculence of their eyes. Then slowly he got up and walked around the table.

Until he stood up, he had not been conscious of the many eyes fixed so steadily upon himself; he had known that they were there, but they had had no place in his thoughts. Strangely, he was feeling now for the first time the true danger of his position; the danger which, foreseen by Solano, had made the old ranchero look upon Cloud as a man already dead.

He had known from the first that he must come to this moment; the moment when anger and disappointment and frustration, suspicion, hatred—all the strength of frustrated lust for battle and loot—should seek a scapegoat, and turn to him. No good to him now to point out that he was El Fuerte's friend—or that he was not. They knew El Fuerte had either met with violence or had run away. If the latter, then Cloud, as El Fuerte's partner, must face the blame; if the former, it must be to Cloud that suspicion turned.

Glancing over the many faces, whose eyes neither wavered nor blinked before his own, he was thinking that he was beginning to understand these people at last. He had seen them happy and light-hearted and lazy, asking only to loaf in the sun and strum ballads until they were hungry again; he had seen them toil endlessly, with the uncomplaining patience of burros—and in both those things was a great strength. But in his mind now was a memory of flames rising about an effigy that was not an effigy; he was thinking of Boyce shot down as casually as a man might shoot a lizard, and of the bleeding flanks of horses ridden by vaqueros who sang of love. And he knew that in all his life, death had never edged so close to him before. He recalled Solano's somber voice as he had said, "They will dress out this Americano like a beef—"

He walked around the table, and half sat on its front edge. "*Compadres*," he said gravely, facing these irresponsible ones from whom he had snatched their dream of glory, "we are heavy losers here. Whether something has happened to El Fuerte, or whether he has left for reasons of his own—that makes no difference here. The thing is that he's gone. If he had led this revolt—I was his partner. I would some day have been one of the greatest rancheros of all Mexico. That is gone. *Compadres*, you are brave men. With you El Fuerte would have taken Baja."

He raised his arms, and rested one hand on the shoulder of Torreon, the other on the shoulder of Alcazar, the hawk-faced man whose lean cheeks bore the blue, stippling scars of gunpowder. Astonished, they did not for the moment move. "You are lucky that you have places to go to, other things to return to, at your homes. I cannot go; I must stand my ground. When you want me, you will find me here. This year, next year, the year after—when you want me you will find me in the Valley of the Witch. But this revolt is done."

Torreon jerked his shoulder clear with an oath like the explosive snarl of a tiger. "This revolt is only begun! I can take this army and throw it into the face of half the troops in Mexico, by God! And I will, if I need to. I'll drive them in front of me like rabbits. And you—as for you—*sangre!*" He whirled. "Here you—Felipe, Luis! Take out this man! Loupe! Call the rifles up!"

"Wait," Cloud ordered. He knew that the last supreme moment of balance had come. In another minute he would know whether or not he would ever again see the sunlight come fresh and clean upon new grass. As Torreon whirled upon Cloud he found Cloud staring past him, beyond the crowd, beyond the window's streaming panes. His face was weary, and the stamp of utter finality was upon it now. He lifted his arm, and pointed; and against his will Torreon's eyes followed the pointing hand.

Strangely, the mob outside had thinned again; and now down the middle of the river of mud that had been the La Partida street moved a little procession of three burros, prodded along by an old woman and a stripling girl. Four men straggled behind at a little distance,

251

heads bent low, trying to look inconspicuous; two of them had rifles slung on their backs.

"There goes your army!" Cloud said slowly. "By sundown you'll not have enough men left to guard a *frijole* kitchen. Not many will pass before your eyes in this street. But they're leaking out of the town by fifteen different ways—taking to the hills and the brush like quail!"

"You lie!" Torreon squealed.

"Ask the *alcalde,* then!"

"It's true! Ay, it's true," the little *alcalde* wailed. "I've been watching from above. Already the town is half empty! What will become of us? By tonight—"

Alcazar struck the *alcalde* savagely across the mouth, and he went staggering backwards, instantly still.

"Done, finished, through," Cloud said. "Perhaps I'm the heaviest loser of all; but I alone stand my ground."

A moment of deep silence fell, while the four leaders stared out of the window like hypnotized men, and all those others behind them craned their necks for a look outside.

Suddenly Moreño said sharply, "Torreon, those are your riflemen! I told you those damned corn farmers couldn't—"

Torreon bawled a terrific oath as he saw that the accusation was true. He went storming through the throng to the door. Moreño followed behind in the path Torreon opened. "So you thought you'd take the regiment, yes? You and your deserting—"

"Look to your own!" Torreon snarled over his shoulder.

Moreño turned back to the others; the raw damp blew into the room as a dozen trooped out behind Torreon, keeping the door open. "By God," Moreño said, "if he

252

thinks, he's going to—"

Alcazar, who had stood motionless, snapped, "Fool!" and suddenly went out, half running. Moreño hesitated a moment more, then followed, with those who were left in the room trailing at his heels. Only Teotac remained, staring at Cloud with red malevolent eyes.

"Take your horses and your Yaqui scouts and go," Cloud ordered him. "The first thing the Federals will do will be to cut off the few ways out of the peninsula. By God, you'll die without ever seeing your home hills again, you hear me? Whistle up your men and get gone!"

The old Indian stared at Cloud a long time, so long that it seemed as if he had turned to an idol of smoke-blackened stone with garnet eyes. Then he drew a deep breath, wheeled, and went, walking silently in his clumsy broken shoes.

Cloud turned to the *alcalde* wearily; the little man was still nursing his bleeding lips. "Your leader is gone," he told the *alcalde* ironically, "but you've still got a man who gives orders—and I'm that man, by God! Tonight you pack the guns in this house, and you send them to me, by your own villagers. And if but one cartridge is missing, the dictator will know from me where it was last seen—you hear!"

"*Bueno! Bueno! Y mil gracias!* God knows I want no guns in this house. And you—*que hombre, señor! Ay, que hombre!* You are like one of our own Mexican people!"

Wearily Tom Cloud went out and stepped aboard his cold horse. Slowly, so that anyone who wished to stop him might know of his going, Cloud rode down the street. Out beyond the houses he heard shouting, a

253

brisk exchange of shots. People of this stamp fell over each other, once they took out for cover, and fought viciously among themselves. The street itself was empty now; it was the back ways and the trails leading off over the hills that were dotted with packed burros and groups of head-down men, as far as the eye could see into the rain.

In all the long street only a single figure was to be seen—a limp form face down in the mud a hundred yards from the *alcalde's* house. One of the brawls that had come among these people, once fear was on them, had left its victim here. Solemnly Cloud regarded the prone form as he passed. Then suddenly he reined up his horse. The face was turned to the side, and Cloud thought he recognized it now.

His memory flashed back to the night when El Fuerte had sung the Yaqui song of hunger, to the throb of illusory drum beats coaxed from a guitar; and he heard again a far voice in the hills that took up the refrain, thin and quavering, answering like an echo. "When you sing to the heart of the hills, the heart of the hills answers!" By El Fuerte's own word, it was the voice of the Indian charcoal burner, answering his song from far off, that had put the war-heart in him in this new country, and made him believe he was great.

And now, sitting in the wet desolation of the place where El Fuerte's war sparks had flamed and died again, Cloud looked down at the dead face of an old Indian charcoal burner; and knew that the voice from the hills was still.

CHAPTER 33

IT WAS BY CLOUD'S INTERVENTION THAT EL FUERTE was permitted to say good-bye to Kathleen Boyce. Miguel Solano and Old Beard were not in favor of either this or any other courtesy to El Fuerte; but Cloud felt that some concessions were due a foeman who was unhorsed. Thus, at eleven o'clock in the morning, three days after Cloud had engineered the evacuation of La Partida, Miguel Solano and Tom Cloud rode to the Boyce hacienda, El Fuerte between them.

El Fuerte rode his dazzling palomino; the float of its silver mane shone like satiny metal in the clear sunlight that had followed seventy hours of rain. It set him up higher in the world than the others, and made homely plugs of Solano's lean black pony and Cloud's compact buckskin. Yet in some impalpable way the relationship of the three had changed. El Fuerte sat his horse with composure, his face expressionless, almost sleepy; but he no longer looked to be the master here. He seemed inert and lumpish in his saddle, so that it became apparent that he was a man on the threshold of middle age, becoming a little heavy in the jowls, a little thick about the waist.

Beside him the lean, lounging figure of Cloud in some way looked immeasurably the more competent. It was as if, now that the chanting and the drums were still, Cloud was the one who remained a relaxed but intensely living figure, while El Fuerte faded in the fresh sunlight, losing most of the great vibrance of color which had so nearly raised a people into war.

255

Kathleen came out to meet the three at the gate, but Solano declined her invitation to come in. Only Cloud stepped down and loosened the cinch of his pony; it was not necessary for him to ride back to Solano's hacienda where the vaqueros of Beard and Solano waited to escort El Fuerte and his three adherents, Bravo, Carlos, and del Pino, out of Baja. The plan was to put the four aboard a lugger at Bahia Coyote, and El Fuerte had given his word that they would not come back. Cloud suspected Solano of an urgent hope that El Fuerte would break his word. The old ranchero did not conceal that only his own pledge to Cloud persuaded him to free El Fuerte on any conditions whatever. If ever El Fuerte fell into Solano's hands again he could expect no such a break; and Solano most vehemently prayed for the day.

Now Solano sat waiting with disapproval for El Fuerte to take his leave of Kathleen, so that they could be gone.

"I will speak to the *señora* alone," El Fuerte said coolly.

Solano almost smiled. "Ridiculous."

El Fuerte accepted the veto with a shrug. He took off his big hat and sat looking at Kathleen with composure. "It has been a great pleasure to know you, *señora*," he said slowly, after a moment. "You have been a great inspiration in all things. It has been my single hope that we should know each other better."

At this presumption an angry flush appeared across Solano's cheekbones, and his long fingers twitched in the butt-loop of his quirt; but Cloud lounged poker-faced against the wall, rolling a cigarette, and Solano

256

withheld.

"We come to evil days now," El Fuerte said. "Some make great mistakes; mistakes maybe they will some day regret. But there is no help for that now. If we are alone, maybe I say other things. But I can only say this: maybe some day I sing to you again. No?"

Kathleen hesitated, and her eyes drifted down the valley; but she remained perfectly collected. It was an awkward moment for them all, and Cloud was beginning to blame himself for allowing El Fuerte this farewell.

He was able now to recognize the purpose that had led him to bring El Fuerte here. He had seen the effect of El Fuerte's drums upon Kathleen; and instinctively he had wished Kathleen to see El Fuerte once more as he was in the cool morning sunlight, without the background of firelight and ovation—a middle-aged man with thinning hair and thickening waist, who sat captive because, in the ultimate pinch, he had not wished to exchange shots at close range in the dark.

Here in the awkward quiet it seemed to Cloud that his reasons had been bad and weak. He had stubbornly opposed Solano's desire that El Fuerte be delivered up for trial on a charge of murder. El Fuerte's statement that he had shot Boyce in self-defense was supported by the evidence; a conviction, perhaps obtainable by reason of political expediency, would have borne no relationship to justice. And at all costs Cloud wished to spare Kathleen a rehash of a horror that was finished. That was why he had not yet told her the truth about that killing, as some day he would. What he had not seen until this moment was the unfairness to Kathleen in a situation in which the killer of John Boyce was permitted to address her, while she remained unaware.

"I always liked your songs," Kathleen said. Her tone was easy, conversational. "I liked your fiesta, too, and your drums."

El Fuerte's voice was deep and vibrant. "Some day, perhaps, again—"

"But all this parading is for children, Señor Contreras," Kathleen said astonishingly, meeting El Fuerte's eyes. "It's a bad thing among an excitable people like yours, and a bad thing for you. Why don't you settle down and get a job some place?"

The man who had averred that he was a thousand years old when Cloud was born now started as if he had been struck. His face turned grey-green, and his mouth fell open, and eyes bulged with a scandalized disbelief.

"Get a—what?" he shouted.

Suddenly Cloud began to laugh, deep inside of himself, so that although his face hardly changed he struggled with inner convulsions. He managed to get out, "Better take him away, Miguel"; then he turned and walked a little way off along the wall, to hide his discomposure. He was no longer sorry that he had let El Fuerte come.

Solano pushed his horse between the palomino and the gate. "This is enough foolishness," he said gruffly to El Fuerte. "I am tired." He bent deferentially to Kathleen. "You will excuse me if I remove him now, My vaqueros will have a long ride."

"Surely," Kathleen smiled at him.

An answering twinkle appeared in the old ranchero's stern eyes. It disappeared as he leaned down, as if on an

258

impulse, to speak to her in low tones, gravely.

"This is a good man," Solano told Kathleen, flicking An eyebrow in Cloud's direction. "This is the kind of man we need in Mexico. Mexico—the future of Mexico—has rich rewards in store for such men, who come to build, and not to loot. You will do a great injustice to him, and to us all, if you take him away from here now."

"I?" said Kathleen wonderingly; "I take him away?"

"It is for you to make him see sense," Solano told her. "After all, life here for you would not be so bad. Now that the three of us—Beard, Cloud, and myself—now that we understand each other, things will be different here. I will get new, fine vaqueros for the Flying K. With Beard and me to watch a little, it will be easy for the Flying K owners to spend the quiet months of the year in San Francisco, or where they like."

Cloud came toward them again, uneasily. He had caught some of Solano's low words.

Solano smiled faintly. "Such things are much in the hands of women," he said to Kathleen. "Remember what I have said, *señora*." He shook hands with Cloud. "It is time for us to go; my vaqueros are anxious to be on the Bahia Coyote trail with their little—ah— procession. And now—" he tossed an unpleasant glance at El Fuerte—"if the lord of all creation can bring himself to ride with me—"

Cloud walked to El Fuerte's stirrup. "So long, partner. I'm sorry it had to work out this way." He extended his hand.

El Fuerte looked at him for a very long moment, while he appeared not to see Cloud's hand; and it would have been impossible to name the meaning of the gleam

259

under his heavy lids. But at last a slow grin spread itself over his face, a rueful grin, far from effortless, but game and defiant, with a touch of braggadocio still. He shook Cloud's hand. "*Adios, compadre.* Me—I am sorry too!"

He saluted Kathleen with a flourish of his romal, and wheeled his palomino; and though he seemed somehow heavy in the saddle now, his shoulders were square, and he made the palomino prance as it turned.

"Ride a little to the front," Solano ordered curtly. "*Adios, amigos!* I will see you soon."

Solano and El Fuerte took the trail, El Fuerte riding in advance, and not too fast, as Solano had commanded. Neither the captive nor his guard looked back at the hacienda again.

Thus rode out of the Valley of the Witch El Fuerte, *jefe de insurrectos, capitan de rebeldes,* and free ranchero—the man who was like a marching storm, the man for whom whole *distritos* rose at a word; yet who had collapsed to human size very promptly before the harsh reality of one American cowman and a good rain.

When Solano and El Fuerte were gone, Tom and Kathleen still stood leaning on the wall, looking at the long valley. A cast of fresh, pale green already showed all over the broad graze of the valley floor, the green of tender new grass instantly answering the gift of rain. The clean-washed air had some of the cool tang of a northern October; but it carried also the lush, sweet growing-odors of spring, for in Baja life is continuous— sometimes latent in the dry heat, but never winter-locked under earth turned to iron by the cold.

The valley and the hills looked fresh and new, and somehow Kathleen looked fresh and new too, as if the clean rain had washed away all the ugly, hated things that had shadowed her life; and she now found herself gently eager, and a little tremulous, in the sunshine of a new spring.

Tom Cloud, though, looked tired; there had been a lot of riding to do, a lot of arrangements to make, even after the back of the revolt was broken, before they had been sure that peace was secure once more.

"I've fixed everything," he told her now.

"Isn't that nice," Kathleen said. There was an intimate mocking in her voice.

"I mean—I can take these Cayuga mineral lands off your hands, if you want."

"You have a buyer?"

"I'm the buyer."

"You've certainly been fooling me. I thought you were broke."

"I was; but I've worked a proposition out of Old Beard and Solano together, to take the Flying K. There won't be any loss, to amount to anything, So now I'm going to buy your Cayugas."

"Who said you are?"

"This'll work out the best for us both. I'll be able to turn the Cayuga mineral lands very nicely, by taking a little time. I'll be able to start a new layout, pretty soon, some place. And this way you'll be set free, don't you see? I'm glad I bought in down here; if I hadn't, perhaps I'd never known you, at all. But except for that, I see now that I never should have come down into Baja."

"You mean the rustling? But I thought that now that you're hand-in-glove with Solano and Beard—"

"Oh, that part's licked, all right."

"Then what in the world has got into you? Don't you believe in Baja any more?"

"There's a greater opportunity here," he admitted honestly, "than any I've ever known."

"Then—?"

"I'll tell you the truth," he said slowly, without looking at her. "It's got so that nothing means anything to me any more but you, Kathleen. Ten million beeves would be useless to me, if you weren't there. And you see—it's just come to me that this is a hell of a dump to strand a woman in. I can't ask you to stay here—and I couldn't go it with you gone. Only chance for me is to make a new stake, some better, different place—"

He heard her breath catch in her throat; and turned quickly to find her trying to repress a spontaneous upwelling of laughter.

"Let me see if I have this straight," she said unevenly. "You don't think you ought to marry me until we can move into an apartment hotel—is that it? Well, all I can suggest is, you go down and move your stuff out of that cow shed you inhabit, and come live up here; and we'll just worry along here as best we can until you feel equal to—"

"Kathleen, Kathleen—"

"Pull yourself together and try to make sense," she recommended. "You can't fool me. You love me pretty nearly as much as I love you, and you know it. And what we're going to do is to stick right around here and build this country into something pretty impressive! Sometimes when we get tired of that we'll have a honeymoon in the States for a while, and I'll show you a lot of things you never saw before. Or don't you believe in honeymoons until after people are married?"

Cloud tried to say something, but because he had never seen anyone with such a clear, bright face, such

262

mistily dancing eyes, he couldn't find his words. "Here—wait a minute—"

"Well, you said—"

He stooped to sweep an arm under her knees, and picked her up as if she were as light as the air; and there were tears in the eyes of them both. He said shakily, "Sure seems like it's coming on spring."

"Great stuff for the caows," she mocked him; and stopped the quivering of her lips against his throat.

We hope that you enjoyed reading this Sagebrush Large Print Western. If you would like to read more Sagebrush titles, ask your librarian or contact the Publishers:

United States and Canada

Thomas T. Beeler, *Publisher*
Post Office Box 659
Hampton Falls, New Hampshire 03844-0659
(800) 818-7574

United Kingdom, Eire, and the Republic of South Africa

Isis Publishing Ltd
7 Centremead
Osney Mead
Oxford OX2 0ES England
(01865) 250333

Australia and New Zealand

Bolinda Publishing Pty. Ltd.
17 Mohr Street
Tullamarine, 3043, Victoria, Australia
(016103) 9338 0666